Carly had one cold lucid sensation of panic
before everything inside her stopped dead. All the years
of loneliness and confusion welded together and
became a great weight in the center of her chest. As her
senses slowly came back, they were totally saturated
with memory. "Shane." The hoarse whisper coming
from her throat sounded like someone else's voice.
Stunned by seeing him again, she could not find the
words to say anything more.

"Hello, Carly." A muscle twitched along his
jawline. "How are you?"

"I'm fine." Her heartbeat quickened. She struggled
to stay composed but could not stop her body from
reacting. To disguise her trembling she took a small
step backward.

Shane reached out to steady her.

She waved him off.

"It's been a long time. Too long a time," he said.

Drawing a shaky breath, she shook off a building
tremor that began when their gazes locked. She had
nearly forgotten how quickly he could encourage every
nerve in her body to tune into him. The sensation
stretched her tight like a rubber band waiting for
release. She wanted to stop looking at him, but she
couldn't. She wanted him to go away until she could
pull herself together and face him as she had planned,
but she knew he wouldn't leave.

She was staring like one of his adoring fans—
wide-eyed, open-mouthed, and speechless—but she
couldn't help herself. Like in one of her dreams, Shane
stood barely a breath away, looking incredible. No, he
was beyond that. He was exquisite.

Kudos for Kathye Quick

"*BACHELOR.COM* is one of the sweetest love stories. If you are a romantic, take time to read this one."

~*Donna P*

~*~

"I really enjoyed this quirky book."

~*Stacy S.*

~*~

"Snappy dialogue won me over immediately. The unlikely attraction ranked second as to why I couldn't stop turning the pages, wanting more and more and MORE!!! *BACHELOR.COM* is a winner in my book..."

~*Award-winning author Kat Henry Doran*

~*~

"If you've never read a Kathryn Quick book before, you're in for a treat. Once you do, it won't be the last of her books that you choose with great anticipation."

~*Christine Bush, author of Montlake Romance titles*

~*~

Kathye Quick is:
National Readers Choice Finalist
Winner of two Reviewers Choice Awards
Internationally Selling Author
Library Journal Holiday Choice Author

Solid Gold Bachelor

by

Kathye Quick

Bachelors Three Series

Solid Gold Bachelor

Cover Art by *Rae Monet, Inc. Design*

The Wild Rose Press, Inc.
PO Box 708
Adams Basin, NY 14410-0708
Visit us at www.thewildrosepress.com

Publishing History
First Crimson Rose Edition, 2017
Print ISBN 978-1-5092-1843-1
Digital ISBN 978-1-5092-1844-8

Bachelors Three Series
Published in the United States of America

Dedication

For Mom

Prologue

Philadelphia, Pennsylvania

From a veiled corner just to the left of a small stage in a club called Wildflowers, a young man with wind-tossed blond hair just grazing his shoulders looked out over the sea of faces. His square jaw supported an almost too-perfect face accented by transfixing blue eyes and finely detailed lips. He shifted his gaze from one person to another until he found the only face that mattered.

Carly Mitchell sat at a table near the front of the room stirring her coffee and waiting, with the rest of the patrons, for Shane Fox and the Rangers to perform their final show at Wildflowers. The sight of Carly in the muted light caused Shane to inhale sharply, and then exhale slowly with something that felt like relief. Despite her family's protests, she had come.

Even in the dreary lighting, Shane could see the sweetness surrounding Carly. She was eighteen and beautiful. A few tendrils escaped from the hairclip fastened on her auburn hair and fell casually around her face accenting her emerald green eyes. He watched the loose curls dance around her forehead and cheeks when she dismissed a visitor to her table with a firm shake of her head and a polite, but warning, smile on her lips.

Someone like Carly did not belong in this

waterfront club in Philadelphia, lost in the crowded room tinged to silver with drifting cigarette smoke. The daughter of a high-powered investment banker, she belonged in a million other places. If he closed his eyes, he could see her at Carnegie Hall, poised on the arm of a tuxedo-clad diplomat, listening to the rich tones of the symphony. With another blink, he imagined her dressed in fine ebony silk, sitting front row in one of New York's great theaters, applauding the cast of a ballet.

The difference in their backgrounds did not concern him. Not totally, anyway. True, he was leather and she was satin. Also true, he could barely pay the rent and ate from cans, while Carly lived in a big house in Princeton and ate off fine bone china. She repeatedly told him she didn't care about their differences and never once gave him any reason to think otherwise. She was here, and she was his.

Now, when the hard work the band devoted to their music over the last few years appeared to be paying off, he felt trapped with the commitment made, and he had a decision to make. Tonight. No matter what path he chose, he knew pain waited.

Just a week before, Carly's father, Noel Mitchell—not known as a man of compromise or generosity—had offered both when he sent a rather large check, along with a note, stating keeping the money required a quick dismissal of Carly. Shane had not wavered. The check went back as fast as it came, with never a word to Carly. His answer to the insult must have been loud and clear, however, because Mitchell backed off almost immediately. The wide berth allowed Carly and Shane the freedom to explore where their hearts would lead.

However, he always thought she deserved better

than he did. Much better. He met Carly when the band booked a local shopping center opening.

After the show, she came up to him and asked for an autograph on the home-cut CD handed out during the set. He looked into her eyes as he signed—and lost his heart. They had been inseparable for the past year, and he couldn't picture life without her. Until now.

For three years, the band had been playing everywhere and anywhere—small clubs, school dances, weddings, birthdays—waiting for that one big break. Then, at their last gig, a front man for an upcoming rock band got thirsty late one night and stopped at the club where the Rangers were playing. Before the night was over, the Rangers were offered a once-in-a-lifetime opportunity, and Shane grabbed that golden ring—the opening act for the headlining group.

But at what price?

For the next year, he wouldn't be living but rather trying to subsist. On tour, doing one-nighters, traveling all day, up all night, and sleeping, when he could, in vans or second-rate motels, or worse. He knew didn't have the right to ask Carly to live like that while he and the band took this shot at a dream. Unexpectedly, Noel Mitchell might have been right in principle, if not in method.

"Big night tonight, bro." Bobby Fox, twenty-three and younger by four years, hooked an arm around Shane's neck, glancing over one shoulder to see what captured his big brother's attention. "Car-leen." He dragged out the name in a voice tinged with disdain. "Should have known. You are gonna tell her tonight, right?"

Shane swiveled his head to Bobby and said

nothing, struggling with how very different they were.

Friends and family, and now fans in a growing audience, described Shane as dynamic, appealing, with a personality that could melt ice, and a restless energy about his movements that had women aching for more. But those who knew Bobby considered him sullen, inflexible, with unreadable eyes, and a cold urbanity that concealed a quick-temper from a rocky childhood and a defiant stint at a tough Catholic boarding school. The only thing the two brothers shared seemed to be bloodline and a desire to make it big.

Shane pushed away his brother's arm and walked to the rear of the darkened stage. "The band's leaving right after the show. What choice do I have?"

"Is that hesitation I hear?" Bobby snapped. "Don't go soft on me. You can't be dragging Carly all over the country. There's no room for distractions or dead weight when you're in search of stardom."

Shane thinned his lips, his eyes flashing with a distinct warning. "She's not a distraction, Bobby. This is hard for me."

"Hey, no problem," Bobby said. "I'll tell her while the band is on stage. By the time the first set's over, Carly will be on Route One heading back to New Jersey and Daddy's money."

Shane shut his eyes, pain closing his throat. "No. She deserves to hear any decision made from me."

Bobby's eyes narrowed. "Any decision? I thought we agreed on what the band was going to do."

Shane stared at his brother. "The band, yes."

"Don't you dare back down," Bobby warned, jamming his forefinger into Shane's chest.

"I'll do what's right for Carly."

"I'll tell you what's right...."

With a swipe of his hand, Shane cut off his brother. "No. Some things are both private and sensitive. But you wouldn't know anything about that, would you?"

"What's that supposed to mean?"

Shane heard the controlled anger in Bobby's voice. "It doesn't mean anything." His shoulders heaved, and he ran his hand through his long hair. "I don't understand you anymore. Talk to me, Bobby. What's wrong?"

Bobby squared his shoulders. "Nothing."

Not wanting another one of their already all-too-frequent arguments to begin, Shane controlled his voice. "Whatever I decide to do, I'll tell Carly." He wiped his hands up and down the sides of his faded blue jeans, the chains on his belt playing a tinny tune of regret with the movement. A muscle clenched along his jawline. He had planned to do this right, carefully, lovingly, but he had run out of time.

Bobby tossed his head. "Just don't change your mind. I worked hard getting this gig, ya know."

"I know, Bobby, and I appreciate all the work you did." Shane patted Bobby's shoulder to keep the fragile peace intact. Then, in spite of all he was feeling, he chuckled. "But I hadn't planned on falling in love, getting the big break, and possibly walking out on the woman I want to spend my life with all in the same week."

Bobby threw up his hands. "Breaks of the game, bro. Breaks of the game." His mouth tightened. Then, flashing a disarming smile, he pointed to his watch. "Fifteen minutes and you're on."

Pain pounded a throbbing rhythm in Shane's

temples. "I don't think I can go through with it, Bobby."

"You'd better. We all got problems."

Bobby's words had bite. His voice rose. "Carly's not a problem. She's a solution."

"To what?"

"To all the empty hours, to all the disappointments, to the setbacks, to feeling alive after ten record producers tell you that you haven't got what it takes."

Bobby laughed and pointed to a group of women standing at the bar. "Ha! Any one of those fine examples of womanhood could make you feel a whole lot better if you gave her the chance."

Shane battled the urge to walk away. "Not in a million years." When Bobby's face showed no measure of understanding, Shane gave up the verbal duel. "Better check the keyboard," he said, moving away from his brother before another scuffle broke out. "Peter complained of a loose wire at rehearsal." As he watched Bobby tug at the connections, Shane wondered why his brother was so bitter. Like a wounded animal, the slightest erroneous word or inquisitorial look caused Bobby to lash out or go on the defensive.

Suddenly, Bobby made a quick about-face and raised his chin at a defiant angle. "The Rangers are gonna be big someday. Don't jeopardize the band's future by thinking with any part of your body other than your head."

Bobby's words sounded too much like a warning, but somehow Shane retained his composure. He bit off any reply with a hard swallow and turned his back.

As he walked away, he shivered and zipped up his worn, black leather jacket against the sudden feeling of an icy hand closing itself tightly around his heart. He knew the chill had nothing to do with the dampness backstage or the bitter January wind whipping across the Delaware River and finding its way inside the building through the broken window near the back door. The feeling came from being battered by the anxiety of his decision.

He loved Carly and, as difficult as Bobby could be, he loved his brother. He also had a good idea of what the next year would be like, and he could not take care of them both. He had no choice. He had to follow through with what he thought would be best for everyone—a decision he knew would hurt terribly and for a very long time.

Even now, as the moment grew closer, he knew only time would determine if his decision was the right one. He moved to the edge of the stage and looked out again. The house lights had just gone down in preparation for the band's entrance. The room was so dark. So dark and so forever. "I have to leave you, Carly. Please forgive me," he whispered, knowing she could not possibly hear him and glad she couldn't. He couldn't tell her goodbye. If he faced her, looked into her eyes, and held her in his arms, he could never go through with what had to be done. "Someday, our paths will cross again," he continued, feeling utterly miserable with his own cowardice. "I swear it. Someday, you'll look back on this day and realize my letting you go was just another way of telling you how much I love you."

His anguish was abruptly cut by the scream of an electric guitar, and the bright beacon of the spotlight piercing the ebony air as the Rangers moved into their introduction number. Shane took a deep breath, held it for a second, and then exploded onto the tiny stage.

Their gazes locked for the last time. He would have to take the look of love he saw in Carly's eyes and make it last until that faraway "someday" finally came.

Chapter One

Ten years later

The meeting was set for 5:00 p.m. Carly Mitchell opened the door to the Victims of Abuse Center at about twenty after five and was still one of the first to arrive. She had hoped everything would be well underway, and she could slip in without much fanfare, but now she would have to wait. The delay would give her time to think. Again.

The circle was about to close, and she could do absolutely nothing to stop it. He was coming back. After ten years, Shane Fox was returning to his hometown of Hillsborough, New Jersey, and maybe back into her life in the process.

Carly walked to a rear office, controlling her apprehension by sheer force of will. Just inside the door, she could see an eight-by-ten glossy promo picture lying on the desk. In the center of the photo was Shane, his face taunting her with private memories. Although only printed on photo paper, his eyes looked right into her soul as though he stood in front of her.

Over the years, she learned to suppress lingering feelings for Shane by looking at his pictures and pretending he wasn't real. She slammed her hand onto his face and closed her eyes. How in the world could she deny her feelings when he stood in front of her, living, breathing, and forcing her to recall every detail of what they had once shared?

The noise brought Ann Tyler into the office. She gave Carly a long, level look. "I know I'm about to tread on dangerous ground, and you can tell me to mind my own business if you'd like, but what's with you and this guy?" She tapped a painted red fingernail on Shane's black-and-white face. "Can't be an old lover, can he?"

Carly looked up and let out a slow breath. "'Fraid so."

Ann's eyes widened. "You're kidding? So, what's the story?"

Carly waved away the question. "No story worth repeating. We weren't right for each other."

Ann shook her head, her short, brown hair dancing around her face with the movement. "Nope. Don't buy that. You've done a decent job of pretending to be happy when Rangers agreed to the fundraiser, but it's becoming more and more obvious you're not as thrilled as the rest of us are."

"And you know that for sure?" Carly could not even begin to count the number of times Ann had seen through a lie. As roommates, she and Ann had a tendency to tune into each other's vibes. Ann was particularly adept at honing in to times when Carly was troubled.

Ann picked up Shane's picture. "You've had your moments over the past few days when you let down your guard, and your real feelings came out."

Carly's head snapped up. "I don't have moments."

"Oh, yes you do. Especially if someone mentions his name or..." Ann turned the picture toward Carly.

"When you see his face."

Hesitating, Carly blinked back an instant's squeezing hurt. Even if she tried to lie, her face would expose the truth. "Okay, for a while, I had this crazy fantasy that the only reason Shane accepted the request to do the benefit was because he wanted to see me again." She took the photo from Ann and put it on the desk. "But that's ridiculous. I've been over Shane Fox for a long time."

"Is that so? Seems to me things still need to be settled."

"No. None," Carly said, her response a little too quick to be convincing even to herself. "There's nothing left." She felt everything inside her go silent with the lie.

Ann spun the picture to face her. "Exactly when was the last time that you saw him anyway?"

Carly clamped her jaw tight and stared straight ahead, focusing not on the peeling paint of the opposite wall, but on the last time she looked into the one pair of eyes that could make her burst into flame. "Seems like a lifetime ago," she finally said. "Shane was loading a battered van in back alley behind a little nightspot in Philadelphia called Wildflowers. The Rangers had to leave right after the show."

She stood and walked over to the bronze donation plaque hanging on the wall, and then ran her fingers over the raised lettering. "The Rangers had just gotten their first big break. The band would be opening for some big star back then. I can't even remember who it was, but I do remember the concert tour would go coast-to-coast, hitting fifty cities." She turned back to face Ann. "Shane figured the band would be gone about eight months or so."

"Long time to be away," Ann said, meeting her gaze.

"Forever to an impressionable, naïve, woman hopelessly in love with the tall, handsome lead singer of a struggling rock band."

"What happened?"

"Shane promised he would call me from every city he played, and for the first few weeks, he did. Then the Rangers started catching on, getting more popular. Before long, the band was signed to a recording contract by Starburst Records, and the rest is music history." Sadness tore at her chest. She looked down at the floor and dug the toe of her right shoe into the wooden floorboards. After a long moment, she looked up. "I never heard from him again."

"Maybe he had a reason he couldn't get in touch with you."

"Like what?"

Ann pressed her lips together and glanced away. She looked back and shrugged. "Maybe he got busy."

A nervous, sarcastic little snicker escaped Carly's throat before she replied. "Yes, busy." She felt her expression tighten. "Not long after, the pop magazines began detailing his escapades with fans." She waved a hand in the air. "And they haven't stopped since."

Ann rolled her eyes. "Like I said, the man got busy."

"Anyway," Carly continued, "after a few months I realized Shane wanted a clean break, so I gave him one."

"This media blitz for the benefit doesn't help, does it?"

"It only fuels things." Memories of her time with Shane filled Carly's mind as she fiddled with a few envelopes in the desk. "No matter where I turn, there he is, looking at me from posters or benefit announcements. Everywhere, from smartphones clutched by adoring fans, or outside speakers at the malls and discount stores, Shane's voice floats through the air, overpowering the sounds of life. His music cuts into me, reaching back into all those secret places only he could possibly know, and pulling up things I thought were fought and conquered years before." Her breath caught in her throat. She waited until the images in her mind blurred before going on. "I guess what I thought was a relationship turned out to be only the fantasy of a starry-eyed young girl. I never had a real chance with Shane." She tried hard to extinguish the last few cinders of her feelings for him with cold words.

"What do you mean?"

"We were from totally different worlds. Dad harped on the fact all the time. Society hill and back alley clubs don't mix, he used to say. Never did, never will."

"Didn't you tell him a lot of people from the wrong side of the tracks make good with a little luck?"

A sudden sense of humiliation from the past assaulted Carly. When she closed her eyes, she could still see the check she found by sheer accident in the bottom drawer of her father's cherrywood desk in his study. Shane's signature was boldly displayed on the back of the six-figured bribe."Not luck at all in this case," Carly said. "It was…" Her voice trailed away as a fist-like pressure settled into her chest when she thought about the way she was bought and sold like an accounting transaction, by the two most important men in her life back then. She squared her shoulders. "Shane's leaving was all business."

"What do you mean?"

The memory had raked itself through her like a sword, and she was weary of its pain. "The story is long and complicated, Ann."

"And you don't care to tell me now, right?"

"Right."

Ann raised an eyebrow. "But the fact remains, Mr. Heartthrob is coming home."

"This isn't his home any longer, Ann. He leads a totally different life on the West Coast, a life he always wanted."

"So what will you do?"

"Probably nothing. I'm not the type of person to be star struck, and I'm smart enough to know people don't really ever change."

"You're saying Dad was right?"

"Appears so. Things usually work out the way they're supposed to. I have a career I enjoy. You and I share a great home in a nice little town, and I'm happy. I don't need any complications right now."

"A good life on the surface, but it could also be a lonely one if you're not careful."

"I have no intentions of living the rest of my life alone." Carly's crisp voice belied her outward calm. "You found yourself a local policeman to keep you warm at night. I'll find someone, too."

"In the next day or two, I'll bet," Ann agreed, tapping her finger on Shane's picture before she noticed the sharp look Carly was giving her. "What I mean is you never know who might walk through the door to your life once you open it again."

"I have no intention of opening that door to Shane," Carly said making sure she captured Ann's gaze.

"You never know," Ann replied.

"Yes, I do know." Footsteps echoed in the hall, and Carly glanced at her watch. "But I have no time to debate you. My meeting is about to begin." She turned to the doorway, expecting to greet members of the committee, but she saw her father instead. "Dad, I thought you were on your way out of the country."

"I thought I'd find you here," he said.

Carly reached down and slid some letters over Shane's photograph, feeling much like a little girl caught with her hand in the cookie jar. "What time is your flight?"

But Noel Mitchell walked to the desk and swept away the papers. "I fail to understand how you can still be thinking about working with that man after what he did."

Knowing her father had a part in what happened, she felt her face burn with the heat of memory and lowered her chin to hide any emotion her father might read in her eyes. In spite of knowing what he did, she loved him. At times, when she remembered his part in the break-up too vividly, she thought she could also hate him. But she knew he had his own needs, possibly his own regrets, although he never showed any.

Once the feeling passed, she looked up and was caught off guard by how pale and thin her father appeared. His stooped shoulders made him look small, nothing like the powerful man she knew him to be. Funny she hadn't noticed that before. But since her mother died a year ago, many things were changing. "We were kids back then," she said very quietly. "Kids make mistakes."

"Sounds to me like you're defending the man."

"I'm not."

"Really?" Noel stiffened his shoulders.

"Yes, really." Carly scooped up a handful of envelopes and ran them through the postage meter. "If necessary, I'm sure we can work together in a calm adult manner." She hoped her explanation sounded plausible, and she thought she could get herself to believe what she just said. And maybe, just maybe, she could even find a way to handle seeing Shane again.

If she could.

She turned to her father. "When do you leave for Hong Kong?"

"Now, actually. The car is waiting for me outside. I'll be gone about five weeks." He handed her an envelope. "Here. To get the fund drive off to a good start."

Carly wrapped her father in a hug. "Thanks."

Noel pulled back and reached for her hand. For a moment, he looked at their entwined hands with lips pressed into a tight line. "I hate to leave you with that man coming here. I can cancel the trip."

Carly knew her father would leave no matter what she said. Business had always been his mistress. "You knock them dead in Asia, and don't worry about me. By the time you get home, everything will be back to normal."

"I hope so," Noel said. He released Carly's hand and prowled the room, careful to avoid her gaze. "You're all I have left now, Carly." His gaze swept the photo. His lips pressed together in a tight grimace when he looked back at Carly. "When I get back, we need to talk." His shoulders lifted in a sigh. "I did promise your mother that we would someday."

****

The young blonde shifted in the passenger seat of a dark blue sedan. "I don't think I can do this."

"You have to," a male voice grated.

"But…"

"No buts," the man snapped. "Get out, and do your job. I'll be back in a couple of days."

His sharp tone silencing any protests. The woman felt a sudden wave of panic and grabbed onto the sleeve of her companion's shirt, not daring to actually come in contact with his arm. "Don't leave me here. Please."

Jerking his arm upward and across his body, he freed himself. "Don't be stupid. You need to get things started."

The woman nodded woodenly, eased open the door, and stepped out of the car. She pulled a large, leather suitcase from the trunk and took only a few steps away before turning and running back to the car. She tapped on the front passenger side window.

The man inside threw up his hands and pressed a finger to the electric window control panel.

The whine sounded like a growl as she waited for the window to open.

When it did, he leaned over, grabbed onto her wrist, and squeezed it hard. "Now what?"

"Nothing." She winced in pain. In a voice as shaky as her insides, she said, "I'll do it. But are you really sure this is the only way?" She watched the knuckles of his left hand turn white as his fingers tightened around

17

the steering wheel.

"You can't cave on me," the man said. "Not after all the preparation and planning I put into this for you." He released her wrist and took a deep breath. When he spoke again, his voice was calmer. "Listen. She'll be out soon. You have to play this just like we rehearsed. I'll be back in a few days, and then, in a few days after that, we'll be home free." He leaned toward her and looked into her frightened blue eyes. "Didn't I promise you that everything would work out?"

The woman nodded. She bit down on her lip and turned away her head from his piercing stare.

"Go on. Do it!"

Before she could react, the sedan sped away from the curb.

Clutching the suitcase with both hands, she watched the car turn the corner and vanish. Alone in a strange town with nothing but a set of instructions and a shaky promise, she could do no more than what she was told and pray she did the right thing.

****

The meeting was finally over."Note to self," Carly said, holding the voice-activated recorder in front of her mouth. "Set up the new bank account for the concert by noon tomorrow."

Ann shook her head. "I don't see why you still use that thing. Your smartphone has apps for that."

"I prefer this way." Carly tossed the recorder into her purse. "Phones are for calling people, not holding your entire life. Do you know how often I lose my cell phone?"

"Unfortunately, yes." Ann put out her hand. "Let me see that thing for a minute."

Carly shrugged and handed over the voice recorder. "Why?"

Ann made sure the device was on. "Remind Carly to ask Shane why he came back," she said in a raised voice with a smile on her face. "That's why." She handed back the recorder.

"These things also do this," Carly replied, hitting first the rewind and then the erase before dropping the recorder back into her purse.

"You'll ask him," Ann said. She crossed her arms in front of her chest. "I know you will."

"I don't plan on running into Shane." Carly juggled a huge stack of envelopes in her arms and a larger stack of emotions in her heart. "I'll be in the back room during the show, getting the door receipts ready for deposit."

"You're not watching the concert?"

"No. I'll be too busy with door receipts."

"I wondered why you volunteered so eagerly to do that."

"My reason for helping is not what you're thinking. Being in banking, I'm the logical choice to handle the money end of this benefit."

"I suppose you're right." Ann nodded. "You haven't seen Shane in a while, and time has a way of changing things."

"I know I'm right," Carly said, forcing her legs not to tremble. She didn't know how to react to Shane's homecoming. She felt giddy, sick, trapped—everything except right. "I'll just handle his coming back logically. No romantic illusions, no fantasies. He'll come to town, do the concert, and leave." Her voice dropped. "He's very good at leaving."

"I read too many romance novels," Ann said. "I'm probably making too much of this."

Carly nodded. "Probably." She grabbed some outgoing mail. "Now, let's get out of here before the phone rings."

"How about some dinner?" Ann suggested, watching Carly lock the front door. They walked toward the parking lot. "I'm dying to try the new bistro on Beekman Lane."

Carly dropped the key into her purse. "I am, too. The early reviews are good. I'm surprised a trendy place like that opened here. Hillsborough isn't Manhattan. Hillsborough's more—"

"Laid back," Ann finished for her. "New York never sleeps. Hillsborough has a curfew."

They laughed.

"The smile looks good on you," Ann said."Felt good, too."

"Drop your tote and the mail in your car. I'll drive."

"Sounds good," were the only words Carly got out before turning the corner and running smack dab into a small woman.

On contact, the woman went one way, her suitcase the other.

Carly reached down and stood the satchel upright. "I'm sorry. Let me help you with that."

The blonde straightened her blouse and moved the strap of her handbag back onto her shoulder. "That's all right." She glanced over her shoulder, and then back at Carly. "I'm new in town. Can you tell me where I might get a room for a few days?"

"Visiting or here for the concert?" Ann asked.

The woman hesitated. "Both."

Carly shifted the mail to one hip and extended her hand. "Carleen Mitchell. But most people call me Carly, and this is Ann."

"I'm Danielle Baker. Danni."

"Welcome to Hillsborough, Danni, but I'm afraid you might have a tough time staying," Carly said. "All the motels are over near the highway, and most are already sold out because of the concert."

"There's nowhere else?" Danni looked left and right. "I really need to find a place today."

"Maybe," Carly replied. "Two blocks straight back is Charlotte's rooming house for women. The rooms are clean, comfortable, and not too expensive. I called there yesterday for a client, and a few rooms are still not rented."

"Thanks, I appreciate the suggestion."

Danni took a few steps away before stopping.

Carly waited for another question. She seemed as she might walk back to Ann and Carly but then only smiled and went on her way.

"Strange girl," Ann said.

"A little, I suppose."

"But no stranger than a super group coming home to do a free concert for only about two thousand people." Ann narrowed her eyes. "And you know this town. It's gonna rock with talk when word gets out that you know Shane Fox."

"Knew," Carly corrected. She felt her heart hitch as she realized he would never be just a forgotten memory. "I knew Shane Fox. I don't know anything about him now. Besides, a lot more is happening here than just the benefit."

"But not much more is going on in the music world than Shane Fox and the Rangers."

Carly rolled her eyes, weary of the battle—both with Ann and with herself. "Okay, you win. I give up. He'll ride into my life, sweep me off my feet, and carry me away to live happily ever after." As she finished speaking, she almost wished he would.

Ann raised her fine, arched eyebrows. "Sounds good to me. Does he have a brother?"

Bobby Fox's face materialized in Carly's mind. "Not one you would want to get to know. Let's just get this mail to the post office so we can call it a day."

****

Danni Baker looked around the room that would be her home for the next few days. It was small, with one window that looked out over Main Street. She ran her hand over the out-of-date furniture as she toured the space. The place was old, but it was spotless. The landlady took pride in her rooms. Unfortunately, she also took pride in finding out everything she could about her tenants. She had asked a ton of questions, some of which needed quick creative answers. Danni instantly decided the landlady could become a definite problem if she got too curious.

She sat on the bed and counted her remaining money. After taking the room until the end of the month, she had only two hundred dollars left. Hardly enough to last very long. But if everything went precisely according to plan, this would be the last time she would ever worry about money again.

Getting up, she walked to the yellowed nylon curtain and swept it aside with one hand. Across the street, a few women gathered near the concrete bench in front of the local bank, probably exchanging the latest gossip.

"If you only knew what you will be talking about in a few days," she whispered, quickly dismissing the guilt as fast as it came. One woman glanced up, and Danni moved her hand, letting the curtain flutter back into place.

She thought about what lay ahead, and a cold chill ran up her spine. She shivered as though the temperature in the room was well below freezing, instead of the pleasant seventy-two degrees the thermometer near the window reported.

Step one completed. She made sure Carly Mitchell had seen her.

Step two also completed. She found a place to stay.

But the easy part was over. What frightened her most was what she still had to do over the next few days.

Chapter Two

The front section of the tour bus rocked with an impromptu jam session as it sped down the highway. Troy Stone rapped a pair of drumsticks on the metal table, keeping the beat to the strumming of an acoustic guitar.

"That's good," Peter, the organist, exclaimed, jumping in with a little rhythm on a portable keyboard. "Now all we need are some lyrics, and I think we could have another hit."

As the RV transported the Rangers through the New Jersey countryside, the last thing on Shane Fox's mind was penning the words to another song. He sat on the bench seat at the back table, his right elbow leaning on the tabletop with his chin resting in the palm of his hand, staring out the camper's side window. In the lightly tinted glass, he could see the reflection of his face.

The years had been more than kind. Only faint lines swept outward from his eyes. Neatly trimmed, his blond hair layered and combed away from his face brushed his shoulders. In his left earlobe, a diamond stud earring glittered in the sunlight. But, etched in the lines of his face, he also saw a sadness that deepened with each mile the RV logged toward home.

"Hey, lighten up, brother dear. We're going home."

Shane looked up as Bobby made his way to the

back before blowing out a breath of air to calm his jumbled nerves and again looked out the window.

Bobby knocked Shane's outstretched leg from the bench seat and sat across from him. "If you didn't want to take this gig, then why did you agree? We had a big thing in Dallas I had to put off because of this charity business."

Without moving, Shane just shifted his gaze from the road to Bobby and back to the road again. "You know I have to do this." His voice was thick and unsteady, his admission drudged up from a place beyond logic and reason.

"I don't like it," Bobby said, waving to the carload of adoring fans driving next to the RV.

With the driver leaning on the horn and keeping pace with the RV, the girls with her shouted and waved.

Bobby opened the window and waved back. "And I suppose you're hoping Carly shows up."

Shane waited before answering. "Do you really care what I hope?"

"I know you. The B-movie in your head goes something like this." He spoke with exaggerated hand movements. "She rushes to your arms. You kiss her. She kisses you. Gently, you lift her onto the back of your white horse and ride off into the sunset to live happily ever after in your castle on the hill." Bobby's acerbic laugher filled the back of the camper.

Through the window, Shane waved to a young brunette throwing kisses from a passing Buick. "That will never happen," he said, though his heart skidded with hope.

"How do you know for sure?"

"I know, and so do you," Shane said, pulling down

the window shade.

"Well, I also happen to know that she may have more than just a passing interest in your homecoming."

Shane saw a grin settle onto Bobby's face, and a cold feeling settled in his gut thinking Bobby may have spoken to Carly before he could. "Did you see her?"

"No."

"You know I don't want you talking to her before I can."

Bobby held up his hands. "Easy, man. While I was in Clinton renting the estate, I found out she's spearheading the benefit thing we're doing. That's all." He sputtered with a suppressed snicker. "And I also heard she kicked over one of your life-size promo posters outside a local store." He laughed. "I guess she's still upset."

Shane knew Carly was co-chairperson of the charity concert committee. Her involvement was partly the reason he agreed to do the benefit. From time to time over the years they were apart, he made a point of finding out what he could about her. Each little detail would sustain him, like a thirsty traveler drinking cool water in the lush oasis refuge of a hot, dry desert, until the next bit of information came his way. Between those times, his pain only released when he set it free through notes and lyrics that gave birth to another soulful hit song.

But now, faced with the prospect of seeing Carly again, the pain circled his mind like a hungry vulture waiting to pick at the remnants of his heart. He leaned his head on the back of the big bench and stared at the ceiling, convincing himself for the millionth time he'd done the right thing then by letting her go, and was doing the right thing again by agreeing to this concert hoping to see her. "She's been better off not being part of the three-ring circus we deal with," he finally said with a sigh.

"Hey, you love the life!" Bobby corrected, drumming his hands on his knee. "We're rich, successful, and the band is definitely hotter ever since the release of the new album. And the latest single shot right to the top of the pop charts and hasn't moved for weeks." He stood and whacked the back of his hand on Shane's chest. "We got it made, man. We got it made!"

Shane watched his brother walk to the front of the RV. Nothing about the music business ever fazed Bobby. Not the cutthroat contract negotiations, not the long concert tours to press the flesh to sell the songs, not even the endless hours in recording sessions working on the next hit.

However, he could not disagree with Bobby. At thirty-five, Shane was more successful than he ever dreamed could be possible, and he was rich enough to leave everything behind if he chose to do just that. But nothing in his life felt right. He needed to pay his karmic debts by giving something back to everyone who had helped him get to the top. That was the second reason this benefit was so important.

The first had always been Carly. Time was long overdue to explain what happened all those years ago, and face the consequences when he did. The debt he owed her was larger than any.

"What's up?" Niles Lane, lead guitarist and the only British member of the band, asked. "I can tell you're thinkin' about her again, mate."

"Yeah, I just can't get Carly out of my mind. I

never really could. But now that I'm nearly home, I feel like I should pass the exit and keep going."

"Still time to back out."

Shane shook his head, curls dancing around his neck. "No. I may be a coward for leaving without so much as an explanation, but I have to face what I did to her."

"But what about you?" Niles reached over and patted Shane's chest. "What about what's goin' on in here? It's tearin' you up. Any fool can see that. Why put yourself through something to explain a past that can't be changed?"

Shane pulled his brows together in a frown. "Niles, I have to see her. I have to explain why I left and ask her to understand and forgive me. I need to do this. For her"—he patted his chest with his left hand—"and for me."

"Will she listen? Been a long time to have somethin' like this hurt the lady."

Shane turned his head toward the shaded window and wondered if Niles was right. "I don't know if I would listen if I were her. But I do know I have to try to explain. The only time I don't feel the regret and the pain is when I sing." He swung his head back, his voice fading and losing its steel-toned edge. "And I can't sing forever."

****

Carly went to the rural high school five miles out of town right after work ended. Hillsborough Regional sat in the center of a sprawling fifty-acre campus dotted with practice athletic fields and parking lots. She drove to the rear entrance to the auditorium and parked in the teachers' lot.

Inside the school, a flurry of activity was already under way in preparation for the concert. As she removed her beige linen suit jacket and opened the top two buttons on her white silk blouse, a loud screeching sound made her turn her head in time to see a pushcart filled with gear race toward her. She barely sidestepped out of the way as the cart roared by and bounced to a halt.

A volunteer peeked out from behind one of the six-foot speakers. "Sorry, didn't see you. The equipment's been arriving all morning, and if we expect to set up before rehearsal tonight, we've gotta hustle."

Carly instantly knew. Shane was coming. Here. Tonight. A sudden emotional clash of anticipation and anxiety held her immobile.

A petite, white-haired woman carrying a metal clipboard stopped only briefly near the curtains to shout a series of orders to a few technical people before walking to Carly. "Is everything set with the bank?"

Carly was about to answer when a loud crash stage left got everyone's attention.

"Wait here," the woman said. "I need a favor."

Carly glanced toward the sound and nodded. She watched Emily McKennan, co-chairperson of the event, sort through the confusion. Mrs. McKennan was the driving force and brain thrust behind the highly successful Center for Abuse Prevention for which Carly volunteered her spare time. The wife of a local judge, Emily looked more like someone's grandmother rather than the dedicated dynamo she was.

Emily's husband, Judge Edmond McKennan, talked Carly into helping with the concert one day while he was doing his banking.

But that was long before Carly had any idea the job would become so complicated.

Emily brushed dust from her skirt as she walked back to center stage. "I do wish those men would be more careful." She tapped her pencil onto her chin. "Now, where was I? Oh yes. Is everything ready at the bank, Carly?"

Carly nodded. "I have the account opened, and the night drop bag ready. All I need is the money."

"Edmond said I could count on you."

"Judge McKennan is a very persuasive man."

"Edmond certainly is, dear," Emily said. "And wasn't it nice of the school to allow us to use the auditorium for the concert?"

Carly could hear the pride of forty years of marriage fill Emily's voice. She smiled, suspecting no one would have dared to turn down Emily's request. The Center for Abuse Prevention was Judge McKennan's favorite charity. "I want to get a look at the music room," Carly said. "I'm using it to count the ticket take." She turned toward the back of the stage.

Emily stopped her with a hand to her arm. "The favor I mentioned. Would you mind staying on stage for a few minutes? The lighting director would like to do a set check." She scratched a few notes onto a yellow pad before signaling her okay to the control booth. "The lighting technician promised the set-up wouldn't take very long."

Another loud crash made Emily turn. She pointed a pencil at a stagehand standing nearby. "Young man, do see what that was?" She shook her head. "I do hope the band doesn't drop things, too." She wrote a few notes on her clipboard paper on before looking up. "And

Carly, you will help us, won't you?"

"I'll stay as long as I'm needed," Carly said with a smile.

Emily waved toward the control booth, and a bright spotlight came on, bathing Carly in brilliant white. With her suit jacket tossed over one arm, the other tensed at her side, she stood perfectly still. Her thoughts raced as she mentally planned everything just right so she would not be anywhere near the school when the band arrived for practice. With a little luck, she might not have any direct contact with Shane and the Rangers at all.

****

"Good old high school," Bobby said, hitting a locker door with the palm of his hand so hard the metallic rattle echoed down the hallway. "Remember the times we had in this place?"

"Sure do," Shane replied.

Bobby pointed to the left. "There's the auditorium. I'm going backstage to check on the set-up. You comin'?"

Shane shook his head, sending a few stray locks into his eyes. Raking them back with one hand, he turned and walked to a set of doors. "No, I want to take a look at the place from the back."

"Suit yourself," Bobby said.

Shane waited until Bobby was out of sight before opening the double doors leading inside the large assembly hall. As soon as he stepped inside, he saw Carly.

A tinny voice from the control booth in the balcony directed her to various locations on the stage where she instantly became bathed in lights of various colors. Shane felt his heart begin to pound. He slid into a seat in the last row, daring not to move for fear she would see him. Content to just observe her from a distance for now, he watched her move around the stage.

A moment later, Bobby appeared from the left side. "Hey, Car-leen!" he shouted when he saw her.

Carly shielded her eyes with one hand, squinting in the direction from where the voice had come. "Yes?"

"C'mon, Carly. It's Bobby." He held out both arms. "Bobby Fox. Surely you haven't forgotten the handsome younger brother who hung around the all-night practice sessions back in the day?"

****

Of course, she remembered him. "Bobby, how are you?" She forced herself not to react when the spotlight snapped off, and he became a person instead of a dark form outlined in light.

Bobby walked to Carly and threw an arm around her shoulders. "Man, you look great!"

His touch sent a shiver down her spine. "Thank you." Her words had bite, and she was instantly annoyed they did. She and Bobby may not have been close, but he wasn't the one who hurt her. She looked over his shoulder. "Is Shane here?"

Bobby shrugged. "Somewhere. The Rangers are gonna do a quick rehearsal as soon as the rest of the band gets here."

"When do you think that might be?" Carly asked, forcing her voice not to quaver.

Activity near the drummer's platform caught Bobby's attention. "Hey, no. That's not how Troy likes the snare set. Let me do it." Giving Carly a quick wink, he stepped around her. "Gotta go. Stay in touch. Got a lotta years to catch."

"Sure," she said dully, relieved he didn't linger to talk. She had no intention of walking down memory lane and smack into a tangled web of the feelings she was having for Shane. Whatever was on Bobby's mind wasn't nearly as important as getting out of the school as fast as she could. She absolutely had no desire to be around when Shane made his grand entrance.

She started toward the stage stairs when a dark premonition suddenly held her still. Her body tightened. She could sense Shane's closeness. He was already here. She felt unstrung, loose at the ends, and knew if she came face to face with him now, she would crumple before his eyes. Carly sprinted for the stairs leading down the stage.

The house lights were low from the spotlight tests, so the hall was dim. While walking toward the exit, she noticed someone in the last row on the opposite side of the auditorium. Slowing her steps, she watched the figure rise from the seat and ease toward the aisle.

She didn't have to see Shane in gray shadows. She knew the man was him. One step, and he was in the aisle. Three more long strides, and he stood in front of her.

Carly had one cold lucid sensation of panic before everything inside her stopped dead. All the years of loneliness and confusion welded together and became a great weight in the center of her chest. As her senses slowly came back, they were totally saturated with memory. "Shane." The hoarse whisper coming from her throat sounded like someone else's voice. Stunned by seeing him again, she could not find the words to say anything more.

"Hello, Carly." A muscle twitched along his

jawline. "How are you?"

"I'm fine." Her heartbeat quickened. She struggled to stay composed but could not stop her body from reacting. To disguise her trembling she took a small step backward.

Shane reached out to steady her.

She waved him off.

"It's been a long time. Too long a time," he said.

Drawing a shaky breath, she shook off a building tremor that began when their gazes locked. She had nearly forgotten how quickly he could encourage every nerve in her body to tune into him. The sensation stretched her tight like a rubber band waiting for release. She wanted to stop looking at him, but she couldn't. She wanted him to go away until she could pull herself together and face him as she had planned, but she knew he wouldn't leave.

She was staring like one of his adoring fans—wide-eyed, open-mouthed, speechless—but she couldn't help herself. Like in one of her dreams, Shane stood barely a breath away, looking incredible. No, he was beyond that. He was exquisite. He had gone from a determined rebel with rough edges to a handsome man of polish and success. She dragged her gaze from his eyes and focused on the wall.

****

"You look wonderful." His smile faded when Carly did not respond. A wave of sadness passed through him, and he realized he had to be very careful. He wrestled with the urge to sweep her into his arms. She looked more beautiful than she had when he saw her for the last time in Philadelphia. The changes time had stamped onto her face only made her more appealing.

34

Her hair was shorter, but still had an auburn fire that framed her face in graceful curves and accented her deep green eyes. He resisted the almost-overpowering urge to trace the line of her cheek and discover if her skin was as soft as he remembered. "Will you be staying for the rehearsal?"

Carly moved her gaze from the wall to his face. "No. I have some work to do." She started to push past him.

By touching her arm, he blocked her way. "I'd really like you to stay and wait for me," he said, his voice low.

****

Carly tried to shrug away his hand, but he held on. She kept her gaze trained on the door. "What for? I waited for you ten years ago." She recaptured his gaze. "I don't wait for anyone now." She felt his fingertips tense and lowered her gaze to his hand on her arm. Her skin felt on fire where he touched her. Familiar feelings stirred.

Slowly, she raised her chin, uneasy with what might happen when she looked again into his eyes. When her gaze leveled, for a fraction of a second, she almost gave into the feelings churning inside her. Somehow, she managed to tighten her features and force her gaze to remain steady. She could see turmoil swirl in his eyes. When he let go of her arm, she moved away quickly.

In the bright light of the corridor, she turned back and watched the double doors slowly close, blocking out the sight of his face. Sudden tears blurred her vision as she made her way out of the building and into the parking lot. With each step she took, she felt shock yield to anger. *Why do I still care?*

She hammered her fist on the hood of her car. Repeatedly, she tried to cast out the remnants of their time together, and over and over each memory refused to leave but grew stronger now, fueled by seeing him. Carly could do nothing but accept fate had brought Shane home and hope she somehow survived the reason he returned.

****

Inside the auditorium, the rest of the band was setting the instruments for practice. The sound of chords wafting through the air caught Shane just as he was about to go after Carly. The song the band played—a version of the Hall and Oates hit "Melody for a Memory"—the first song the Rangers released went solid gold on the pop charts the year he left Philadelphia. The song was now a painful reminder of how much time had passed since he last was this close to her.

Though he wanted to run after Carly, he knew any attempt to talk would be futile. She wouldn't listen. Not today. The hurt he saw in her eyes had been too raw, too deep. She needed time, and he needed providence to be on his side for once. He looked at the auditorium doors and shook his head. Providence had never been his friend.

His emptiness grew as he walked down the aisle to join his band on stage. Once there, he picked up his charcoal gray bass guitar from the stand, looped the shoulder strap over his head, and plucked at the strings without much animation. He struggled to concentrate on the music. Carly occupied his mind now and would stay there until things were finally settled.

****

Off to the right, out of Shane's sight line, Danni Baker felt a strong hand clamp onto her arm. A second later, she felt someone pull her into the backstage shadows.

"What are you doing here?" Bobby asked with a sneer in his voice. "I told you to stay away."

Danni stared, her heart pounding. "I'm not here to see you. I'm here to see Shane." As the grip on her upper arm tightened, she flinched.

"I figured as much. What were you going to do, walk right out on the stage and interrupt the session?"

Ignoring the question, Danni shook herself free of Bobby's hold and peered around his blockade.

Shane was into the music now, moving across the stage to the upbeat tempo crackling from the huge amplifiers. Bathed in a white circle from the spotlight, his hair gleamed like spun sunlight. Like the harmonies in any of the songs he performed, his body became one with the music. He moved with an almost graceful rhythm capable of making each woman in any audience think he performed only for her. Danni could not tear away her gaze as he closed his eyes and sang the chorus to her favorite song.

Seeing Shane made her heart thud, and her cheeks flush with sudden heat. She became mesmerized. This was the only man she would ever love and the only man she wanted. In a few days, he would be hers and hers alone. She had been about to step onto the stage when she was suddenly pulled backward into the shadows once more.

A sneer curled Bobby's mouth as he spun her toward the exit. "I'm gonna ask you once more, and then I'm gonna throw you out—what are you doing here?"

Somehow, Danni found the courage to defy him. "It's none of your business why I decided to come here."

"My brother *is* my business. If you want to see him, make an appointment. Now get out!" He pushed Danni toward the stage door.

She stumbled backward into some equipment and smashed her left arm into the wall. "I'll be back," she rasped, massaging her aching forearm with her right hand. "Just tell Shane I was here." Her mouth tightened, and she stormed off.

The commotion prompted Shane to hold up one hand in a signal the rest of the band recognized. When the music stopped, he walked over to Bobby and got a fleeting glimpse of someone leaving through the side stage door. "Who was that?" He tossed his head toward the exit.

Bobby scowled. "Danni Baker."

Shane's face drained of color, and he took a step toward the door. "Did she say what she wanted?"

Bobby shook his head, his mouth taking on a unpleasant twist. "No, but I have a feeling we'll find out before very long."

Chapter Three

Carly arrived at the school the next day, and technicians were unloading video equipment. She welcomed commotion of the intense preparation for the concert and hoped Shane was too preoccupied to think about her.

As she stepped inside the building, she heard a rock song soaring down the corridor. Trying to ignore the music, she walked straight to the room behind the stage. She found the space packed with props and panels of scenery from various plays put on by the high school drama club. Most of the sets were stored against the back wall, but racks of costumes stood everywhere. If she was to count the ticket money and get the receipts ready for deposit, she would have to clear out a small section in which to work.

However, even as she cleared boxes of costumes, she could not concentrate on even the simple task of moving costume racks out of the way when Shane's voice filled the room and wrapped itself around her. Helpless to fight the pull of memory, she opened the stage door, leaned on the frame, and listened.

The Rangers were doing their version of the Whitney Houston hit song, "Where Do Broken Hearts Go."

Even from a distance, Carly could tell Shane was not just merely singing. He was living the words. His expression looked sad and wistful, like a heartbreak about to happen.

When he turned to cue the lead guitarist, his gaze locked with hers.

The waver in his voice would have only been noticeable to a trained ear, but anyone close could have seen the intensity deepen on his face. Now, pinning her to the spot with his gaze like a doe trapped in headlights, he sang the rest of the song to just her.

A sudden sensation of physical intimacy engulfed her. Troubled, she took a step backward, more uncertain than ever about her feelings. The message in Shane's eyes loomed vividly. His gaze caressed softly as it traveled her face before moving slowly over her body. He radiated a vitality that drew her like a magnet, and she felt herself flowing to him, helpless to stop it. All too quickly, she was back at Wildflowers, and they were still in love.

Bittersweet memories assailed her, filling her with a dizzying current, giving her both pleasure and pain, and making her ache for his touch. She shut her eyes against building tears. She would not let Shane see her cry. She would not let him know how much he still affected her. Somehow, she broke free and retreated into the prop room. After slamming the door, she sank into a seat and cradled her head with trembling hands. In that instant, she realized the music had stopped.

****

With every step Shane took toward the prop room, his muscles became tighter, his face more tense, his heart more eager. The feeling was almost like a hunger close to being satisfied. But now, with his hand gripping the doorknob, anxiety knotted and writhed inside his stomach. He waited for what seemed like an eternity before opening the door.

As soon as he did, he saw Carly. She sat on a cast-off throne from a medieval play. His world suddenly shifted, and she belonged in that throne. She was Guinevere, and he was Lancelot, and today they finally would admit their feelings.

The clicking of his boot heels on the bare wood floor gave away his presence, but Carly did not look up. "I'm glad you came back today." His voice sounded clear and steady, but inside he felt as erratic as a sudden summer storm.

Carly raised her head. "I believe in the cause this concert is benefitting." She looked fully into his eyes. "Volunteering to help is the only reason I'm here."

The muscle along Shane's jaw clenched when he spoke. "We have to talk."

In one fluid motion, Carly was on her feet. "You haven't wanted to talk for ten years. Why now?"

"I need to explain." He shifted his weight from one foot to the other, uneasy with the moment.

Carly shook her head. "Explain so you can wipe your conscience clean?"

She threw the words at him like spears. "No, because when I do finally tell you the truth, we can both be free of the past."

"Free?" She laughed. "You actually think a few words can erase the years?" Taking three steps backward, she put more distance between them before turning on him her words coming rapid-fire. "I used to dream about something happening to bring you back to me. I saw your eyes every night. I felt your kiss on my lips in the dark. I traced your body in the air until my fingers were numb."

He lowered his chin but held her gaze. "You have to try and understand…" He reached out to touch her but pulled back. "…some things are done for all the right reasons at first, but…" He looked down at his hands "…then the situations get complicated, and what happens next can't be helped."

Her eyes widened. "Can't be helped?" She paused, gathering her thoughts.

Shane watched the anger dart around in her eyes before exploding, full force, on her face. "You disappeared as though I never existed in your life."

"I didn't have a choice!" Strain tinged his voice as he protested. "Leaving you was the only decision I could make. I didn't want you to give up everything for me, for a chance on something I wanted. Something so remote and unreachable for most people." He closed his eyes and sighed. "I've practiced the words for so long, but now, they sound all wrong." When he opened his eyes again, he looked fully into hers. "Despite what you think, I did it for you." Her flashing eyes clawed at him like talons.

A choked laugh escaped her throat. "For me? You decided I was an emotional liability and dumped me without missing a beat, and you say you did it for me?" Her lips tightened, and she frowned. "If you made a decision for anyone, it was for yourself."

"Don't!" Shane shouted. "You can't possibly realize what I went through after you left."

"You mean, after you left." Carly snickered. "After all, you were paid a hefty sum to leave me." He started to protest, but she held up a hand to stop him. "Damn it, Shane, I know all about the check. Don't make this worse by lying."

For a second, Shane uttered only disjointed sounds and strangled groans until a sad truth completely registered inside his brain. Bitter thoughts hit him all at once. No wonder Noel Mitchell had gotten off his back right before the tour. Mitchell had gambled that Shane would have to limit his contact with Carly while the group toured. He played right into her father's hands by keeping quiet about the check for Carly's sake. The sourness growing in the pit of his stomach spread to his throat. He held out his hands. "I never took the money, Carly. I sent the check back to your father."

Carly waved her hand. "No more lies. I found saw the endorsement. I know your signature. When I confronted Dad, he told me the whole story. He said he was testing you to see if you really loved me or loved his money. You made your decision pretty clear when you cashed the check. Dad didn't mind. He considered it money well spent."

"If someone cashed that check, that person wasn't me. I would never have—"

"Perhaps you just considered signing the back nothing more than an autograph."

Her voice sliced the air like a whip. "I didn't take the money," Shane insisted. "Maybe Dad arranged the whole thing to make it look like I cashed the check." He closed his eyes for a second and corralled his rising anger.

"Everything has changed since Philadelphia. You can't erase the past, and you can't go back and begin again."

"But the present isn't right for us like this." An edge of desperation shaded Shane's voice. He put a hand over his eyes. "Look, even if you believe the check thing, that isn't all of it. I…" He stopped, having lost the words. Dropping his hand, he looked at Carly. "The story is very long and very sad, but I need you to hear it all." He smiled. "I know you will understand."

A rasping sound escaped her throat. "Oh no. The legendary Shane Fox cannot charm away the pain with just a grin. I am not an adoring fan with a fantasy." She looked away and then back. "I had the real thing and—" She dropped her chin.

Her palpable anger intensified memories he had so carefully conserved. Their time together ruffled through his mind like wind upon water. When she glanced at him and looked away, he realized she might be trying to hide the emotion he would see in her eyes.

"I have memories, too, Carly. I also have reasons for what I did," Shane snapped, his tone clipped. "You deserve to hear those reasons, even if they are ten years late in coming." He watched emotions explode in Carly's eyes, feeling, at any moment, he would be showered by the shrapnel of her broken heart. He hated himself for what he was doing, but he had to press her now, while she was at least in the same room. If he let her leave, he would probably not get another chance.

When he spoke again, he forced his voice softer. "If you can look me in the eye and tell me you have no feelings left for me, then I will leave and never try to see you again." He knew he was taking a chance. His pulse raced. "But I think you do, Carly. I think they are as strong as the feelings I still have for you."

As soon as the words were out, Carly's sharp intake of breath echoed in the room. She felt her insides turn to ice. Yes, her father made the offer to Shane, but, over the years, she accepted his reasons for doing so and forgave him. He could not possibly have done what Shane said he did and still tell her, with comforting words, he only made the offer to see if Shane was an honorable man. The thought her father cashed his own check was much too painful to comprehend. She took a step backward and balled her hands into fists at her side. She could not deny any longer she still loved Shane, but she could not tell him. Not yet, and not now.

She closed her eyes as the room surged with Shane's charisma, sapping her strength. Like finding the missing bead from an old necklace, the truth in his words completed the circle, bringing him back to her, and making everything she still felt very real. Slowly, she recovered enough courage to look at him.

The hopeful glint washing through the deepening play of tenderness she saw in his eyes made her shudder, and sent her common sense skirting the shadows of the past. When he was just a figure on a record cover, she never had to face the way she really felt. She could hate him for leaving her, because he was just paper without emotion and warmth. But now, with him so close, she no longer felt that way. Instead, she felt the memory of his arms wrapped around her, and the heat of his lips on her skin. "I don't want to still care, but I do," she whispered, defeat in her voice.

Shane reached out and smoothed Carly's hair with his fingertips. "Want me to tell the band to wrap rehearsal?"

With all the strength she had, Carly fought back her tears and shook her head. "We can't talk here."

"Then where? When?" He took a step closer and put his hands on Carly's elbows.

"Finish your rehearsal. I live on Sunrise Lane. You can..."

Shane pulled her close and kissed her, cutting anything else she tried to say. Their mouths found the past, their tongues swirling like before, their passion rising like before. He kissed away her groans of weak protest until she surrendered and molded into the curves and hollows of his body. "Carly," he whispered into her ear as his tongue nipped at her lobe, "I've missed you so much."

****

Carly felt herself drowning. The murmurs of her past suddenly become the explorations of the present as Shane's hands moved over her body. His kisses turned from tender to hot until they felt like a fire raging out of control in a parched forest. His scent permeated her, making her feel alive for the first time in many years. Her mind spun, her body pressed against the solid wall of his chest and thigh until she felt weak.

Her senses faltered in the fight to stay unaffected until somewhere in the distance, like a beacon slicing through the thick seacoast fog, a voice began. Softly at first, but getting more insistent, the voice warned her— believe him and be lost forever.

By some means, she summoned the strength to push away Shane. "We shouldn't do this." Pressing the back of her hand to her lips, she held his gaze and let her arm fall slowly to her side. "This is wrong."

"No, it's right, Carly,"

Carly found herself caught in a fragile web of her own weaving. She should never have admitted anything. "I can't let you get inside my head. I need to think."

Shane took a step backward. "I'm sorry."

She shook her head. "So am I." She broke eye contact. "I think you better get back on stage. The band probably wonders where you are." Carly's head spun with questions both unasked and unanswered. She struggled with what to do next.

"I never stopped loving you," he said. "I know you have no reason to believe me, but I never stopped." He pulled her gently back into his arms. "Never." He stood silent.

When she pulled away, she could feel his muscles tense. Searching his face, she tried to find the meaning behind his words, but read only the regret in his eyes. "You should go."

Taking a deep, unsteady breath, Shane nodded and began to walk away.

"But remember," she called out, watching as he slowly turned back. "Hope is sometimes more pleasurable than the truth." As she saw his face tighten, she knew she hurt him, but she needed a defense, because at this moment, her feelings had nothing to do with reality.

Shane nodded. His mouth curved with tenderness before he left the room.

In another minute, the music began once more.

Leaning back against the wall, Carly bit her lip until it throbbed like her pulse. Only when Shane was gone did she dare relax. What did she want of him, and more important, what did she expect of herself?

****

"That's right, tomorrow," Bobby said to the caller. He moved his cell to his other ear and walked to the hallway outside the auditorium. He angled his body so some of the nearby workers could hear. "We've got to get this show on the road. I'm running out of time." He paused to let the person on the other end of the line finish speaking. "I've taken care of everything. No, no, you don't need to do any more than I've arranged. Trust me."

He laughed. Was it that long ago when he couldn't afford a cell phone and had to rely on borrowing one? No more. Soon, he would not have to rely on anyone for anything, not even his big brother. He had some loose ends left, but most everything was on track and going according to plan. "Well, brother dear…" he said aloud to no one in particular, pausing with his hand on the doorknob."This will be one concert no one will forget." The cutting laugh that followed caused some people inside the hall to turn and look. Touching his forehead in a mock salute, he brushed off their questioning stares and pushed open the doors.

A group of young girls ducked under his arm and bolted for the stage, screaming as they rushed down the aisle."Shane, I love you!"

"Peter, over here!"

"Shane…Shane…Shane!"

They ran up the stage stairs, reaching the Rangers at about the same time a few of the band's security guards caught up.

"Please," one of them wailed. "Can't we just have an autograph before you kick us out?"

"Not today, dearie." One of the guards put a hand on her shoulder, preparing to escort her out. "This is a closed rehearsal."

Security surrounded the girls and ushered them toward the exit."Hey, wait!" Shane unhooked his guitar strap and leaned the bass against one of the amplifiers. "If these ladies went to this much trouble to see us, then the least we can do is give them an autograph."

"Oh, wow," a petite redhead said. As soon as security's hold on her released, she ran to Shane and threw her arms around his neck.

"Thank you, honey." He leaned down and accepting her kiss on his cheek.

"I'm your biggest fan, honest!" The girl crossed her heart with her forefinger and thrust a CD cover at him. "Can you sign this, please? You're the best."

"Thank you, again," he replied with a wink. He took the black pen from her hand. "What did you say your name was?"

"Jenny. Just write, "To Jenny." When she accepted the signed CD, she pressed it to her chest and rolled her eyes. "I think I'm gonna faint!"

Shane took a few selfies with the girls and signed some promo photos. Watching the girls collect autographs from the band members, he grinned. Connecting with the fans, the very reason the band was at the top of the pop game, was the part he liked best. Without fans, the Rangers were just another club band.

He picked up his guitar and looped the strap over his head. "If the Rangers are to be sharp for the concert on Friday, we really have to practice. Would you girls mind staying?" He raised an eyebrow a fraction with the question.

Peter winked.

He and the rest of the band knew the drill. Depending on the circumstance, inviting fans crashing practice to stay for a while was something Shane liked to do when he could.

"Stay?" a dark-haired girl with eyes as wide as saucers asked in a shaky tone of voice. "You're not throwing us out? You want us to stay?"

"Of course we do," Shane replied. "How else can we tell if we sound good enough to face an audience?"

With screams of delight, the girls left the stage, breathless with the anticipation of their own private Rangers concert. They settled in the front row of seats where they compared the autographs they were given.

When Shane looked out from the stage, he could tell not everyone in the audience was happy with the decision.

"You know I don't appreciate when you let in the fans to watch practice." Bobby heard the commotion from the hallway and then watched the exchange from the back of the hall. "Doing this is like you're giving everything we worked for away for nothing. Fans gotta pay for the music, bro. It's the circle of life. Otherwise, we may as well go back to playing in a garage."

"Lighten up. What's the harm? We only have two numbers left to rehearse." Shane felt his equilibrium slipping away. For a while, he thought the brotherly rivalry was finally behind them, but lately, Bobby didn't approve of very much of anything. "I'm just being friendly."

"Yeah, like you were just being friendly to Danni Baker a few years ago. Look where that got you."

"Let it rest," Shane demanded. He began the introduction to the next song. "Nothing happened."

"Oh yeah? Not the word I hear," Bobby snapped back. He exchanged a glacial look of annoyance with his brother as he took a step closer. "I've worked hard getting you to the top…"

Shane cut him off in mid-sentence with a chaotic twanging of guitar strings that shot disjointed chords through the air.

The rest of the band stopped playing and stared as the brothers faced off.

"What you've worked hard at is playing the ponies and hoping for an inside straight!" Shane called out from between clenched teeth, feeling the muscle along his jaw tighten with tension.

Shaking his head, Bobby raised both his hands and inched backward. "That was years ago. I haven't placed a bet since. I'm clean. Besides, that has nothing to do with this."

Bobby's voice had lost its steely edge, and Shane could see apprehension building in his brother's eyes. He should not have brought up Bobby's mistakes. He looked at the fans in the audience.

Having witnessed the exchange between brothers, they were suddenly silent and staring, mouths agape.

Flashing a smile, he walked to the edge of the stage. "Sorry. My brother and I still think we're in grade school and fight sometimes." He saw the girls' faces relax.

One of them agreed. "Yeah, my little sister is a pain, too."

Shane nodded and walked to Bobby, his voice low. "Look, I'm sorry. I didn't mean to snap. I have a lot on my mind." He saw the angst in Bobby's eyes subside and extended his hand. "You're the only family I have left, and I don't want to fight. We have to stick together. Okay?" But Shane knew their relationship wasn't okay. Bobby was acting strangely again, almost the way he had when he was in deep with the loan sharks.

Bobby grasped the outstretched hand. "Okay." He agreed, and then fell silent.

For a long moment, the brothers stared at each other as though looking for a safe, common ground.

A drum roll snapped the tension in the air. "Come on, man, let's get to it!" Troy rattled the cymbal, and in another minute, the music started. The brotherly battle temporarily put on hold.

****

Once away from Shane, Bobby's insecurity kicked in. "You almost had me there for a minute, brother dear." His eyes narrowed. "But my time's coming." A tap on his shoulder interrupted any further predictions. He turned.

Emily McKennan waved a slip of paper in the air. "Robert, someone called for you," she said. "The man would not leave his name, just this number."

"The name's Bobby." He took the message from her hand. "I don't like to be called Robert."

"Of course, dear." Emily nodded and left the stage.

Bobby looked at the paper. He recognized the number, and concern instantly replaced his anger. As he dialed, he began to perspire. He pushed through two sets of doors as he counted each unanswered ring. Outside, he leaned against the brick wall and waited.

"Look behind you."

He heard the voice on the other end when the call connected. When he turned, he nearly dropped his cell as an ebony stretch limousine pulled up. The darkly tinted rear window inched down, and slowly, Bobby disconnected the call and approached the stretch.

The caller motioned for him to follow. The limo

stopped in the far corner of the parking lot, and a massive man got out of the front seat and stood next to the rear door.

"Mr. Scodari," Bobby said, walking to the car window. "You didn't have to come."

The large man brushed aside Bobby with the back of his hand, opened the car door, and moved away.

Erno Scodari stepped out. "Robert, I must protect my interests."

"Mr. Scodari, you know me. I wouldn't do anything…"

Scodari held up one hand.

Instantly, Bobby stopped talking.

From his inside coat pocket, the tall man clad in all black starkly contrasting with his pale skin and a full head of silver hair produced a silver case. He opened it and offered a cigarette to Bobby.

Bobby looked from the case to Scodari. "No, thank you."

Scodari laughed, removed a cigarette, and tapped one end on the back of the case. "Dirty habit. I wish I could stop."

With trembling hands, Bobby took a lighter from his pants pocket, thumbed the spark wheel, and blocked any breeze from the flame with his free hand.

Scodari furrowed his brows. "You do not smoke, yet you carry a lighter?" He lit his cigarette, and then he laughed. "Good boy, always prepared."

The panic Bobby hadn't felt in years rushed back, nearly choking off his breath. "Why are you here?" he asked, unable to keep caution from his tone.

"I told you, I'm here to protect my investment. You do know what I mean, don't you, Robert?"

Bobby ran a hand through his hair before giving a barely perceptible nod. The panic rioted through him, and he had to will his legs to hold him erect.

Scodari took a final puff on the cigarette before tossing it to the ground. He turned to the large man positioned near the front of the long limousine and smiled. "You see, Tino, I told you he would understand."

"Sure, boss," the stocky man replied.

"Robert is a businessman, I'm a businessman. Businessmen understand intangibles. Shane and the Rangers are important to me. An unfortunate setback happening now would be a shame."

A rare sense of kinship surfaced, and, surging forward, Bobby reacted to the subtle threat. Instead of reaching Scodari, he bumped into Tino's beefy chest and stumbled backward in surprise. He didn't remember seeing the man move.

Scodari stepped around his hired man. He patted Bobby's right cheek a few times with his open hand before pinching the flesh between his thumb and forefinger. "Don't do anything stupid. You know how upset Tino gets when I become tense."

Heart pounding, Bobby looked from Scodari to Tino and nodded.

Point made, Scodari returned to the car.

Tino quickly shut the rear door, leaving Bobby with no other option but to stand and listen to the electric window whine shut.

Once the window fully closed, Tino thrust his forefinger into Bobby's chest. "You heard the boss. Don't do anything stupid. Now, move!" He began to walk around the car when he suddenly stopped and turned back, gaze narrowed. "I don't like you, kid." His gaze bore into Bobby. "I don't like you at all." Then, flexing the fingers on his right hand a few times, he made a slow deliberate fist and punched it into his left palm. "You understand?"

Unable to speak, Bobby nodded in agreement.

Tino roared with laughter and slid into the driver's seat of the car.

In another second, the limo was gone, leaving Bobby standing in the center of a swirling cloud of dust. His body shook as he walked back into the school. Anxiety pounded inside his head, the pain distracting him, and he ran headlong into Carly when she came out of one of the school's rooms carrying a receipt box in her arms.

"Bobby, are you all right?" she asked, spinning in a small circle to keep from dropping the box. "You look worried. Does it have to do anything with the man in the stretch?"

"Stretch?" He swallowed hard.

"Yes, the car with all the chrome covering the front hood. I couldn't help but notice the way the sun flashed off all that silver as I passed by the rear office window. The glint nearly blinded me. I saw you talking to the owner. Is everything all right? Hope he didn't give you bad news."

Bobby nodded, rocking in place. To call more attention to Scodari by denying Carly's remark would be senseless. "Business stuff concerning the shows, tours, videos, and fans. The usual. Shane's got quite an adoring public, you know."

Carly lifted her chin. "Actually, no, I don't," she said before walking away.

"Yeah, yeah," Bobby replied, unconvinced, as he watched her leave. "I'll just bet you really don't." He watched Carly disappear around a corner at the end of the hallway, and a new worry skirted his mind. He had better be more careful. The last person he needed nosing around in his business was goody-goody Carly Mitchell.

Chapter Four

Carly stood in front of the mirror near the living room door, finishing her makeup when Ann came home.

After taking one look, Ann circled like a hawk eyeing its prey. "He's coming here, isn't he?" She walked to the picture window and scanned the street outside. "I'll just bet he pulls up in a car a mile long. Wait until the neighbors see that. They'll all be on the front lawn gawking."

Carly felt both her excitement and apprehension rise. "You're making too much out of this."

Ann crossed her arms and nodded. "I knew he was special. This is so romantic. Answer the question. He's coming here, isn't he?"

"Yes, he's coming, and I know what you're thinking." Carly snapped the blush case closed and struggled to remain composed. "But this is not a romance novel. I don't see a happily ever after.""So this meeting is strictly for hand-to-hand combat?"

Carly scowled. "Of course not."

"Then he wants to get back with you."

The scowl deepened. "Double of course not. What we had happened and ended a long time ago." To Carly's dismay, her voice wavered. "First and foremost, I want him to look me in the eye and answer some questions, all of them beginning with the word 'why.'

Then, I intend to look right back into those incredible eyes of his and finally say all the things I've only said to the night air over the past ten years." She tried to gather her drifting thoughts. A feeling of unwanted excitement welled again, a feeling so huge she was sure it would jump out and become a separate being. Her driving need to see Shane shocked her.

"So that's the plan, huh?" Ann crossed her arms and leaned back.

"That's the plan," Carly confirmed.

Ann's eyes narrowed. "Suppose, just suppose, things don't quite go according to the plan."

"Then I'll adapt."

Ann laughed. "Like you've adapted from hand-held voice records to smartphone apps?"

"I don't like apps."

"That's because you don't know how to use them."

"In technology, sometimes the old way is better." This old argument again.

Ann's laugh turned into a serious smile. "Sometimes in love, too."

Carly shot Ann a quick, denying glance. "I don't believe in miracles."

"I do." Ann winked. "And so far this looks like it could be one in the making."

A loud roar from the street cut any comeback Carly might have made.

Ann glanced out the window, a flicker of amusement dancing across her face. "I think you need to get out of that silk dress and throw on some leather. Your prince is here on a Harley."

Carly gasped and ran for the bedroom. "Stall him." She slammed the door shut.

Ann yanked open the front door before Shane had a chance to ring the bell. She looked him over from head to toe. "Why hello, handsome. My, my you're even better looking in person than you are on the cover of your CDs." She held out her hand. "I'm Ann, Carly's roommate and BFF." She could see a blush creep across Shane's cheeks.

He acknowledged her with a smile. "Thank you. Is Carly here?"

Ann opened the door wider and tossed her head. She waved Shane inside. "She is. Come in. She'll be ready in a minute."

Walking behind Shane, Ann rolled her eyes in admiration of the way his leather pants perfectly hugged his body. The matching black jacket grazed his hips as he moved, emphasizing the swagger in his walk. To keep herself from commenting, she stuffed a knuckle into her mouth. "Sit anywhere," she said when they reach the living room.

He pointed to the sofa. "Here?"

"Sure."

He nodded and sat. He leaned back and slid his arm across the top of the cushion, when the sound of approaching footsteps made him look toward the hallway.

Carly stood in the archway.

He got to his feet, but said nothing.

She hesitated for a moment then walked toward him. "Hello, Shane."

****

Shane held out his hands. "You look great." As he waited for Carly to respond, heaviness descended, preventing him from saying anything more. A hundred yesterdays came rushing back, bonding him to the spot as if a bolt of lightning had struck. He didn't know what to say. He just stared.

She had on stonewashed jeans with short brown leather boots. Her long-sleeved light lilac blouse revealed the tips of her collarbones and the fine gold chain holding a brushed gold heart at the hollow of her throat. The thin leather belt around her waist accented her curves.

Seeing her shift her gaze to the window, he smiled, hoping his eagerness to get her alone didn't show in his eyes. "I didn't want to bring the limo. Stretches just invite attention."

"So, you brought a motorcycle instead." A slight grin shaped her mouth. "Much more subtle."

He shrugged. "I like bikes. I hope you don't mind."

She walked to the window. "Where are we going?"

"Somewhere quiet."

Carly's eyes widened. "What?"

"Not secluded. Just quiet. Is that all right?"

"As long as you understand we are only talking."

He nodded but did not confirm nor deny her subtle warning.

****

Carly's breathing quickened with the thought of being alone with him. While her heart leapt at the notion, her mind soured. Her emotions were a yo-yo, and Shane held the string.

Ann swatted Carly playfully on her arm and ushered her to the door. "Better get going, you two. Mark is coming here after his shift is over, and you know policemen, they always get their man." She winked. "Or woman." She yanked open the front door.

"Your two-wheeled carriage waits."

Shane and Carly walked to the bike in silence. He opened the rear storage compartment and handed her the spare helmet.

As she tucked her hair underneath the thick padding, she reconsidered her vow to remain detached. Being so close to Shane made her heart turn over. She fumbled with the strap, unable to find the coordination to fasten the snap.

"Let me help you." Shane placed his hand over hers. On contact, they both reacted to an immediate and undeniable flare sparking between them. His fingers brushed a path against the side of her neck as he adjusted the chinstrap. "Better?"

Carly wondered if the question held a double meaning and instantly realized she needs to set some boundaries. She tried to vocalize a warning, but the words forming in her mind refused to come aloud. She watched as he unzipped his jacket, his movements slow and full of sensuality as he peeled the leather from his frame.

The well-built lines of his body sent Carly's mind into intimate and total recall. Her mind flashed back to the music room at the school and the memory of his arms wrapped around her waist. She closed her eyes and commanded her heart to stop pounding. "Carly."

At the mention of her name, she opened her eyes.

"Here," he said, handing her the jacket. "I'd feel better if you wore my jacket while we were riding."

"Why? Is there an ejector seat built into this thing?" she asked, a nervous smile breaking out. Humor was her only buffer against the realization that some capricious god had predestined this moment with no chance of escape.

Shane rewarded her with a smile. He straddled the seat and held the bike steady between his legs. "Get on. I promise I won't make any sudden movements."

They exchanged intense, encouraging looks. Suddenly, no more diversions existed. They were together again with no way to tell what would happen next.

The Harley rumbled into an the empty parking lot at Colonial Park, coming to a stop in front of the Rose Garden. A gentle breeze drifted through the trees surrounding the roses, causing a hundred different aromas to blend into a single, heady fragrance. The garden was nearly deserted.

After Carly got off the bike, Shane snapped down the kickstand with his foot. He set the helmets on the bike and waited.

"I haven't been here in years," Carly said, walking to a garden planted with deep red roses. She reached down and touched the velvet-like petals of one labeled Secret Desire and almost laughed at the irony.

Shane slipped the tips of his fingers into the pockets of his leather jeans and followed her in silence. After a few minutes, he touched her shoulder. "No more sightseeing."

She made the mistake of gazing into his eyes. He was looking at her as though she was the center of his universe, and nothing else mattered. Her eyes filled with tears. "Why did you come back?" she whispered.

"Can we sit?" Shane asked.

Chaos flooded Carly's mind, and she could only nod.

Shane motioned to a marble bench in front of the

gazebo.

As she sat waiting, Carly twisted her hands in her lap, and she struggled for every bit of threadbare strength she could find.

"I hardly know where to begin." Shane sat and angled his body so he was close but did not touch her.

"Why not from where you left off?" Carly suggested, unwilling to play the fool again. "Start in the alley behind Wildflowers. That's where you set your plan into motion." She saw him flinch as though she shot an arrow through his heart and almost regretted her words.

He leaned back against the gazebo and inspected the darkening sky. "At least don't begin the attack until I've said something to deserve it."

Heat rose inside her. "You deserve a lot more."

"You don't know what I went through." He ground out the words and reached for her.

She leaned away "And you don't know what you did to me." She turned her head to hide the building tears.

He nodded. "You're right. I don't. Just hear me out. Please."

Carly tossed her shoulders. "Whatever."

Shane shot to his feet. "This is difficult enough for me without having to worry about whether or not you will even listen."

Anger now joined the emotions warring inside her. "I said I'd listen, and I will. But listening doesn't automatically come with believing you." Her words had bite, but she didn't care.

Shane shifted from foot to foot. "I have my theories about the check, but I can't prove any of them.

Besides, what I've done gives you no reason to believe me over your father." He captured Carly's gaze with his. "For now."

Carly fought to keep her emotion from rising in her eyes but found herself failing. She broke contact and looked away.

Shane bowed his head. "What happened isn't exactly a matter of right and wrong." He sat next to her and took her hand. "It's complicated."

Carly pulled away and folded her hands together to avoid any more contact.

"What happened to change everything didn't begin in Philly. It began later. In Vegas." Shane's voice softened. "By the time we played there, we were making a name for ourselves. A few record companies approached us about signing with them. The guys were delirious. The years of scratching around at second-rate clubs seemed about to pay off. We all felt the band was on the verge of finally showing the world what we could do with our music."

Carly watched the lines of concentration deepen around Shane's eyes and could tell he struggled to find the right words. He said Las Vegas. About six weeks after he left Philadelphia, about the time their contact stopped. She nodded and eased her expression.

"Bobby had been acting as the go-between for the Rangers with the record company execs."He leaned forward, rested his forearms on his thighs, and looked at her. "The guys and I couldn't take time off to stroke egos and wine and dine producers. Bobby even stayed in Vegas to finalize a record deal after we left for the next stop on the tour. He put together a top-notch agreement, too. I was proud of the way he finally handled himself."

"What does Bobby have to do with what happened between you and me?"

Shane pressed his palms to his temples. "Everything." He blew out a long, slow breath of air, and a grim expression settled onto his face. "By the time Bobby joined the tour, we were in Spokane, Washington. Just as we were leaving the hotel for the concert venue, a big car with an even bigger driver pulled up. A very distinguished, very well-dressed gentleman stepped out of the back and announced he was the Rangers' new owner."

Carly pulled her brows together into a frown. The man in the parking lot outside the high school speaking to Bobby sounded a lot like the man Shane just described.

Like a robot, Shane shook his head. "He pulled out a contract with Bobby's signature." His lips thinned. "Seems my brother went a bit overboard impressing some of the record company execs to get us a deal. He ran up a rather large tab at a casino in Las Vegas and had to borrow money from a loan shark, this loan shark, to pay it off." His brows knitted together, and a frown pulled down the corners of his mouth. "I don't even know how he wrangled a credit line at a casino in the first place, but the contract said if Bobby didn't come up with nearly a quarter of a million dollars in thirty days, this man was our new owner."

Carly found the story a bit hard to believe. Frustration spread through her like poison, making her wire tight. "What is this? Some kind of grade-B movie plot?" She watched the question dart around Shane's face.

"Please," he begged, "hear me out."

She saw his expression tighten.

He rose and paced. "Bobby swore he didn't even know the guy, but I could tell he was lying. He was sweating, looking as pale as a sheet, and was tapping his foot as he always does when he's nervous. I knew right then Rangers were finished. I couldn't come up with that much money in a year, much less thirty days."

"But you must have. This mystery man doesn't own the Rangers now."

"You're right." Shane flexed his fingers. "Much to my amazement, he agreed to meet with the band to work things out."

"What was this man's name?" Carly slid to the edge of the bench and leaned forward. The mix of emotions playing in his eyes convinced her that he might be telling the truth. She tossed aside her anger and listened.

"Scodari. A Hungarian name, I think." Shane sat beside her. "After what seemed like twenty-four hours of straight talking, I came up with a plan to repay the debt. Scodari would receive ninety percent of everything I, personally, made until the bill was clear."

A full minute passed while Carly absorbed what he said. "You mean you worked for nothing to help Bobby?"

Shane's response was instantaneous. "He's my brother, Carly."

"You always did look out for him." She smiled, suddenly caught in a crossfire of feelings. "Choices. They aren't always easy, are they?"

Shane reached for her.

But she moved to the end of the bench and clasped

her hands tight.

"When the rest of the band found out what happened, they rallied around Bobby." He shifted closer. "The guys agreed to give up a portion of their wages to help bail him out."

Carly didn't notice just how close Shane had gotten until she felt the tip of his forefinger stroke her cheek. The gentle pressure was distracting, but the sad look in his eyes was even more so. She sensed he had more to say, something he was reluctant to share. She shook her head.

He moved away his hand.

"And then what happened?" she asked in a low, shaky voice.

"We worked like madmen for about a month, turning over most of what we earned to repay Bobby's debt. But then Scodari become impatient, and he demanded all the money, plus interest, within twenty-four hours."

She straightened. "What was Bobby doing to help you?" Shane's eyes flashed with predictable melancholy."He was only twenty-two. Just a kid. I couldn't throw him out. You know he had nowhere to go, with Mom and Dad both dead. He trusted me. He looked up to me since we were kids. I had to help him."

She said nothing. Shane answered the question the way she had expected—by not really answering at all. Although Shane closed his eyes to what everyone else knew, he refused to see Bobby as the talented user he was. She had witnessed Bobby play his brother all too often, pushing all the right buttons until he got what he wanted. She could never get Shane to see Bobby for what he was and knew this was not the time to try.

"Go on," she said in a voice barely above a whisper. They had come this far. She had to hear the whole story.

"I had to do a whole lot of fast talking, but finally Scodari agreed to meet to renegotiate the deal. However, he was clear the meeting would be the last one. When the dust settled, the Rangers would have to come up with three times the original amount of Bobby's loan to get Scodari to rip up the contract Bobby first signed."

Carly saw the deliberate blankness in Shane's eyes and sensed he was still holding back. She rose. "So far, nothing tells me why you vanished from my life so suddenly." She spun back to face him. Her eyes narrowed, as she paced. "You could have called and asked me for help. I would have done anything for you."

Shane got into step beside her. "And that's why I couldn't let you know I was in trouble." He touched her elbow lightly to stop her. Motioning for her to sit, he continued. "About a month later, Mike, our old drummer, had had it with the blackmail. He decided the time had come to end the threats. He met with Scodari and told him the bullying was over. He was going to the police."

Carly let her mind wander. "But Mike's plan failed."

Shane nodded. "He didn't know the type of man Scodari was. None of us did until a few days later. Sherry, Mike's girlfriend, was nearly killed by a hit-and-run driver as she crossed the street in front of the hotel. The doctors said she was lucky to survive with just a few broken bones." He leaned forwarded and rested his elbows on his knees. "The next day at the hospital, a messenger service delivered a package to Mike while he was visiting Sherry. In it were pictures of Sherry taken at various places around town. Each picture had an elaborate red "S" in the corner. When Sherry saw them, she turned as white as her hospital sheet. She told Mike she thought the driver of the car that tried to hit her was the same man who drove for Scodari. She didn't tell the police because of the Rangers' involvement."

Suspicion held Carly immobile for a few moments. "You're saying Sherry's accident was no accident."

"It was a message, Carly. One Mike and Sherry took very seriously. As soon as Sherry was out of the hospital, they took off, and I haven't heard from them since."

"Right then and there you should have known you were in over your head and asked the police for their help and protection. But you didn't. Why?" Stomach in knots, Carly turned her back and tried to make some sense of the wild story.

Shane swung her around. His eyes blazed. "Don't you understand I couldn't risk it? Scodari had gotten to Sherry, and she was on the road with us. You were thousands of miles away. Imagine what he could do to you. I couldn't risk having you hurt. I loved you."

"Loved me?" Her body tensed. "You dumped me!" His face paled, letting her know she scored a direct hit.

"I know you probably felt as though I had," his voice was neutral, "but whether you care to believe it or not, I did love you. I wanted to shield you from life on the road and the underbelly of what goes along with it."

Anger again singed the corners of her control. "If

you loved me, really loved me, you wouldn't have made a decision for me that should have been made with me. Love isn't only for the good times!" Knowing her eyes could not hide the myriad of confusing emotions she fought to keep under control, she broke from his grasp and turned away."You can't possibly know what I went through, Carly," Shane said.

"Nor what I did," she countered.

"You're right." He cleared his throat. "But things were happening I couldn't possibly control."

"So you chose to control me instead by sending me out of your life." She bit off the words, reluctant to accept his explanation.

"Damn it, Carly. I was a naïve kid back then." His voice rose. "The people I dealt with weren't actors left over from an old episode of *CSI*. They were real, dangerous, and played for keeps." He took her by both arms and forced her to look at him.

She could see fear build in Shane's eyes, and her chest constricted with dread. She winced when his hold tightened.

A muscle tensed along his jaw line as he spoke. "After what Mike tried to do, Scodari wanted to make it clear if the rest of us had ideas about going to the police, we had better just get the thought out of our minds once and for all."

Shane released her and strode away from the gazebo. He stared at the sunset as he spoke. "Scodari arranged another meeting, this time with just Bobby and me. We met him on a secluded dirt road about twenty miles off the interstate. We got there, and he pulled a file from his briefcase and threw it at me."

The edge of despondency in Shane's voice caught

Carly by surprise. She saw his expression tighten. "What was in the envelope?"

"A file on you, Carly, with pictures, dates, times, and places. The papers followed your life like a biography."

Carly shook her head until the expression on Shane's face convinced her of the truth. Her hand flew to her mouth, and a shiver rocked her body. "That's not possible. I would have known if someone was following me."

Shane pulled out his wallet and produced a snapshot. The picture was old, well worn, with peeling corners and wrinkled edges. On the bottom, faded but still obvious, was a red "S."

Carly held it with trembling hands. The implication of what she saw made her drop onto the bench. The picture had been taken at her brother's wedding. She could almost see every eyelash on her lids. Reality gripped like a hand to her throat. Someone following orders had invaded a private family gathering and had been near enough to touch without her ever knowing she was being hunted.

Shane put the photo back inside his wallet and sat. "Scodari said he could get to you whenever he wanted. Sherry's accident was a warning, but he promised, next time, he would not miss. His threat was not limited to members of the band." He swallowed hard. "He meant you, Carly."

"No, you're lying." Carly choked out the words, only more shaky and high pitched. "I don't know how you got that picture, but..." She shook her head, her eyes widening in shock. How many other times had she been followed? How many other pictures were taken?

How close had she come to ending up just like Sherry? A terrifying realization washed over her. If what Shane told her about her brother's wedding and the picture was true, then everything he said was probably true, also. A sob escaped her throat when he reached out and pulled her into his arms. She felt his body relax when she didn't move away.

She remembered what his touch could do as her body urged her to settle deeper into the his angles and curves and was stunned her body reacted so fiercely. She thought she had buffered herself against the wild hormones that raced through her irrationally. But in that first instant of contact, that first impact against his body, Shane swept past all the barriers. She realized she almost had fallen into her old pattern, and she fought to shift gears.

She pulled back as much as he allowed. "What happened next?" she whispered.

"Before I could react, one of Scodari's goons grabbed Bobby. Another thug grabbed me from behind and pinned my arms back. Another hood grabbed a handful of my hair, forcing up my head." Shane's lips twisted, frown lines forming around his mouth.

His expression tightened as if floodgates had opened inside his mind, unlocking more vivid memories, presenting each as torment and pain on his face. Carly could almost see life plunging backward through the memory in his eyes.

Shane swallowed. "A fourth man grabbed Booby's arm and stretched out over the trunk of Scodari's car." He held Carly tighter, his words coming in quick gasps. "Bobby was screaming, twisting, shaking, trying everything to get loose, and begging me to help him. I tried, I really did, but I couldn't break free." He stopped to moisten his dry lips. "I was forced to watch, totally helpless, totally immobile, as another of Scodari's men took a hammer from inside the trunk of the limo and hit Bobby's arm." His voice shattered, and he slumped. "I can still hear Bobby's screams." He shut his eyes tight and pressed the heel of one hand to his forehead.

Shane looked as though he pushed out the sights and the sounds of the past. Nausea welled inside Carly's throat. One thought barely crossed her mind before another followed. "Shane, no," she said in a strangled voice.

Minutes passed before Shane spoke again. "The bastard kept on hitting him and hitting him." He looked deep into Carly's eyes. "He hit Bobby's arm until it finally broke."

Shane's voice was a graveyard—dark, liquid, restrained. Carly was too horrified to move. Words did not seem proper. When she did speak, she gave merely a pitiful sputter. "They…they…"

"Scodari had his thugs shatter Bobby's arm just to make a point."

Fearful images built in her mind, and Carly trembled. She stared, mouth open, eyes wide as he continued.

"The doctors told me Bobby needed immediate microsurgery to save his arm, but they didn't have enough B-negative blood in stock." His expression darkened with unreadable emotion. "If I hadn't had the same blood type, then they would have amputated."

Chapter Five

Shock rippled through Carly. Shane left to protect her. She knew that now. "Shane." His name was a mere whisper. "I didn't know."

"I couldn't let you," he replied. He wound his hands in her hair and pulled her closer. "You were such a defiant thing. You would have wanted to help and put yourself in danger trying."

She looked into his eyes and reacted to the emotion she saw. Tears trailed a path down her cheeks. She suddenly realized how hard he must have struggled with the decision to walk away from her, from what they had, just to keep her safe. Bobby's actions set corrupt parameters for Shane, and he had desperately tried to fit inside them. A rush of tenderness drove through her and formed a sensual energy that vibrated deep inside. As unbridled as her desire for Shane had been in the past, this impact was nothing compared what she felt now.

A wave of panic suddenly slapped her, bringing a swell of common sense. She had let down her guard. Though she wanted to surrender, she would not. Purposely she kept her voice even. "I'm not that naïve rebel any longer."

"Neither of us will ever be that innocent again." He angled his head. "Why did you come with me tonight?"

She stared in silence and, for a moment, considered

asking him to take her home. Then something softened inside her. "Because I needed to know."

"Now you do."

She nodded and looked away. "I need to find a way to deal with everything you told me." The admission felt like an awakening that left her reeling. "If I can."

"And if you can't?"

She couldn't answer. She wasn't ready to admit she never stopped loving him. Not yet. She needed more than his sudden reappearance in her life armed with a tale of regret. She needed to believe him unconditionally. More than that, she wanted to trust him. She shook her head slowly. "I don't know."

He tucked a loose strand of hair behind her ear. "Life is short. I realize that fact all too well now. I think you feel the same way, and you got on the bike, hoping to find out what might happen if we were alone together again."

She touched a hand to her heart. "I came for the truth, nothing more." She quickly looked away to hide the lie in her eyes.

"And I told you the truth."

Nodding, she moved to pass him.

Shane mirrored her move and blocked her path. "Now that you know, what do you intend to do?"

Slowly, she looked into his eyes. "I'm not sure."

He cupped her chin. "Is there any hope for us, Carly?"

"To go back?" she whispered.

He shook his head. "To go forward."

Before she could stop herself, she imagined him holding her. She could almost feel his hand caressing her back before moving to the curve of her hip. Her gaze focused on his lips with their promise of more than just a smile. Heat rose around her as though she had walked too close to a raging fire. She should pull away, but she couldn't. His touch felt wonderful, inviting.

"Carly? Are you all right?"

"I don't know." She hoped she didn't sound as shaky as she felt.

He ran a fingertip down her cheek to her chin and then fanned his fingers down her throat and across her shoulder. "What would you do if I kissed you?"

"That would not be a very good idea," she murmured. Her gaze stayed focused on his mouth. "Paparazzi could be hiding behind the roses."

"I don't care," he whispered.

She met his gaze, and time seemed to stand still. She saw a hunger in his eyes and wondered if her eyes betrayed her as well. Could he feel her trembling? Did he know she wanted to feel his breath on her skin? Her heart raced, but she did nothing to stop him when he pulled her close.

His lips hovered just over hers. His arm tightened around her, and he nibbled ever so gently on her bottom lip before nudging her mouth apart and exploring every inch.

She shuddered and closed her eyes, allowing the sensation of his kiss to overwhelm her. Despite the very public location and the possibility of paparazzi hiding behind every tree, she felt no urge to pull away. She clutched his shirt and held on as her heart hammered inside her chest.

Just this one last time. He'll be gone again in a few days just like before.

She inhaled his scent and sank her hand in his hair,

letting the silken strands wrap around her fingers as she kissed him with everything she had. Her stomach tightened, and heat flooded her. Feeling his hand trail down her back and cup her bottom, she ignited, and her body burned out of control. God help her, she wanted him. Desire radiated through her, and she ached for more until her only thought was to lead him to a secluded area where they could take their time.

However, she knew without the answers she still needed, surrendering to her desire would be a mistake. Reluctantly, she pulled back. For several heartbeats, she closed her eyes and said nothing until the feeling of his lips on hers faded. When she opened her eyes, the desire she saw in Shane's gaze engulfed her. For a few moments, they had returned to Philadelphia, to a time they could be together, do anything, go anywhere. Back to a time devoid of fame, fans, tabloids, or prying pop scene reporters with cameras.

Cameras.

Stiffening, she pushed him away. "No, no, Shane. This could be very bad. Someone could see us."

"I don't care if someone does." His brow furrowed. "Are you afraid to be seen with me?"

She gave a half shrug."I'm sorry." Shane took a step back. "I should never have brought you here."

She put a finger across his lips. "Don't say anything. I wanted this," she admitted. "More than I realized."

Shane let out an audible breath. "I have to touch you." He pulled her back into his arms. "I can't resist you when you're this close. I never could."

"So much is working against us," she whispered. She smoothed the shoulders of his shirt before resting her hands on his arms.

"There is," he agreed.

His gaze traveled over her body—warming her, enchanting her, almost making her forget the years away. Too late, she felt one hand close across the back of her neck.

"I want you, Carly."

His voice was throaty, sounding reckless with desire. She gasped when he cupped her backside with his free hand and pressed the curve of his erection against her thigh. His mouth covered hers in a gentle exploring kiss, his tongue drawing unhurried circles across her lips. Giving into the rush of heat coursing through her veins, she parted her lips in acceptance. Their tongues met in a greeting that first tested with hesitancy and then sparked with passion. Not allowing her a moment to catch her breath, he took her face between his palms and kissed her the way she remembered.

When they drew apart, their gazes held. Shane reached out and tucked a stray strand of hair behind her ear. "I have to know. Did I make a mistake coming back?"

At the touch of his thumb grazing her lips, she suppressed the urge to flick out her tongue and taste him again. She felt on fire from his hungry look. He leaned forward, and she knew he wanted to kiss her again. In danger of recklessly yielding to her desire, she pulled back. "Don't, Shane."

He ran his fingertips down her cheek. "You used to enjoy kissing me." His gaze roamed across her face. "What are you afraid of, Carly?"

"You, the past, the future." Knowing he would see

the longing in her eyes, she looked away. "Shane, you're different. I get the distinct feeling you've done things and said these things a thousand times to a thousand other women."

"The tabloids print what the managing editor thinks will sell whether the story is factual or not," he said, his eyes darkened.

"I don't think everything in print was a lie and every picture was altered."

Shane's shoulders dropped. "You're right. If you want the man I was in Philadelphia, I can't give him to you. That man has been gone a long time."

Carly sighed and put her hands over her face. "I don't know what I want, Shane. I'm not ready for this, and I'm not ready for you." She lowered her hands and suppressed both the desire and the anxiety ragging inside her. "I'm sure there were other women," she whispered.

"And I'm sure there were other men."

Carly felt the warmth of discomfort warm her cheeks, but she refused to look away. She held his gaze for a moment before speaking. "I had friends, Shane. Nothing more. But"—she hesitated—"I knew your needs. I don't imagine you were"—she choked on the word—"celibate." She crossed her arms and looked down. "Because I thought I would never see you again, I didn't think I would ever have to actually come to terms with you being with someone else." She looked back and pressed her lips together.

His expression grew grim, and he nodded. "Yes, there were others, but none like you."

Her chest heaved. She looked into his eyes, shaking her head slowly. "None like me. Is that the standard Shane Fox line you've said to every one?"

"I don't have a standard Shane Fox line," he answered in a clipped voice.

Carly crossed her arms over her chest. "I don't believe that for a minute. Don't all rock stars have sound bites they routinely say to their groupies?"

Shane raked a hand through his hair. "I don't have a sound bite line for groupies." He turned and took two steps before facing her. "I'm not like the rest."

A nervous laugh escaped her. "You want to know what's working against us?"

He planted his hands on his hips. "I want to know what you think is."

"I'm not sure I want to adjust to the person you have become. Maybe you've forgotten the past, but I haven't."

He studied her for a moment."You think I've forgotten? Quite the contrary, I've committed every bit of what we had together to memory just to feel close to you. For instance, the day we met, your hair was long, to the middle of your back, and the sassy little red dress you had on ended just below your curvy backside. After a while, you wore your hair mostly in a ponytail with a brazen little strand that always escaped just about here." He touched her right temple with the tip of two fingers. "I brushed that wisp of hair behind your ear so many times doing so became a habit. And every time you watched the Rangers play, you'd sit on the right. You said that was my best side."

She realized she sat on his right now, studying him. His profile, dark against the fading light, looked powerful and ageless. Without her consent, her anxiety faded and desire rose, and she was helpless to stop either.

"Do you remember the time we played the Castle Rock in Trenton? Some guy got a little too friendly, and I decked him. Spent the night in jail." He laughed. "Nearly broke my hand, too." He flexed his right hand. "His tooth opened a cut on my finger. I still have the scar." He looked at his knuckles in the fading light. "It's here somewhere."

Carly placed her hand over his. "Stop. Please." In his eyes, she saw a sadness he made no effort to hide. "What do you want from me, Shane?"

"I want a chance for us to be together. I want Philadelphia."

"That isn't possible." She shook her head. "What happened has changed us." Tears gathered in her eyes and pressed her fingertips against her eyelids to stop them. She hesitated, and then captured his gaze." I'm scared, Shane."

"You didn't seem scared when you kissed me."

She dropped her gaze. "It won't happen again."

Brow furrowed, he studied her for a moment. "You're afraid I'll use you and move on again, aren't you?"

"That's part of it."

"And the rest?"

"Maybe I'll use you. Hurt you like you hurt me and move on," she admitted. "Feelings exist between us, I can't deny that, but what kind? I'm not sure if what I feel is love or revenge."

Shane looked down and then back into her eyes. "Tell me what you want, and it's yours."

She sighed. "Just because we were denied seeing where our feelings would take us so long ago, I'm not sure we should go back and find out now. I'm different. You're different. I don't want to hurt you, but it would be so easy to do."

"You aren't like that, Carly."

"Are you so sure?" She cocked her head. "It's been a long time, Shane."

"Suppose I am willing to take the risk."

Carly licked her dry lips. The longer he kept his hand over hers, the more she wanted to feel his arms around her, his lips back on hers, his touch on the rest of her body. "I know what it feels like to want something you realize may be impossible to attain. But you can't give up hoping." He cupped her cheek. "I never did."

Carly tensed and covered her eyes. "I can't do this right now."

"We don't get many second chances, Carly."

She looked at him but didn't respond.

He blew out a long breath of air. "Let's get out of here." He took her hand and steered her toward the parking lot.

She stopped walking. "Where are we going?"

"I don't know." He held out her helmet and jacket.

With a feeling she didn't understand nor wish to argue, Carly donned the gear and walked to the back of the bike.

Shane straddled the motorcycle, steadying it as she climbed on. With the engine roaring in the silence of the growing darkness, they rode out of the lot.

Tucking herself against the curves and muscles of his body, Carly rested her head on his back and cupped his taut pectorals. She could feel his muscles quiver through his thin shirt. As the air battered his unprotected body, his nipples hardened beneath her fingertips, and she wondered if the cool night air or her touch produced the sensual reaction. Sighing, she hugged him tighter, closed her eyes, and let herself dream.

****

Shane was not immune to the situation he caused. In an attempt to cool the fire raging inside him, he pushed the throttle forward and gathered speed. Even through the thick leather, he could feel Carly's breasts pressing against him. Each change in pressure as the bike followed the rise and fall of the road only caused more heat, like a match striking flint and sparking against his back as Carly adjusted her position. Suddenly, he no longer had a choice. Being with her, touching her, kissing her, only underscored what he always knew. He could not imagine continuing life without her.

Within minutes, the bike roared into the parking lot at the high school and came to a halt in front of the tour bus the band had left there.

"Why are we here?" Carly got off the bike and removed her helmet.

Shane engaged the kickstand and dismounted. He dug the RV keys out of his pants pocket. "I need some sheet music from the rear room." He took a few steps to the door.

She didn't follow him.

He turned and extended his hand. "Coming?"

She shook her head.

"I don't want to leave you alone here in the dark. Just stand inside the doorway."

She managed a weak smile. "This isn't New York

City, Shane. I'll be fine."

Shane captured her gaze and moved his hand closer. "I promise I won't touch you."

Taking his hand, she followed him inside.

He turned on the lights. "This is the heart of the beast." He pointed as he spoke. "Living area, fully equipped kitchen with a residential refrigerator, a large dining area, flat-screen TV mounted above the fireplace." He led her to a set of leather chairs across from a full-sized sofa and motioned for her to sit. "What do you think of our home away from home?

She eased her hand from his. "I guess I figured a rock band's tour bus would be more man-cave than functional." She looked around. "It's nice."

"The chairs recline." As he slid his hand between Carly and the armrest, he found much more than the controls for the chair. As the back of his hand slid between the leather chair and along the curve of her hip, heat rose on his skin. Suddenly all he could think about was high-tension wires and erupting volcanoes. When he turned his hand and rested his palm on her thigh, he caught her gaze and thought he saw something change on her face.

She gave him a sideways look. "What are you doing?"

He broke contact. "The controls for the chair are there somewhere." He hoped his voice sounded calmer than he felt. "Make yourself at home. I'll only be a minute. I left the sheet music in the bedroom."

He walked though the bunkhouse to the master bedroom and let out a long, low breath. He promised he wouldn't touch her. Granted, sliding his hand across her hip while searching for the remote was an accident, but nothing was accidental about how he reacted. He had to be more careful. He had so much more to tell her.

Sheet music in hand, Shane walked to the front of the bus. Carly stood in the center of the living area with her back to him. She was bathed in a glow from one of the recessed lights. She looked like an angel had decided to visit.

He dropped the sheet music and whispered her name.

She turned. Her hand fluttered to her lips.

"I can't do this anymore. Pretend you're an ex-girlfriend who may or may not want to hook up again." He let out a long breath as he held out his hand. "You're more. You're mine. You've always been mine."

For a long heartbeat, Carly stared. "What are you saying?"

Shane sighed and saw the last barriers fall from her eyes. "I'm saying I want you. Here. Now. Let the outside world take care of itself for an hour. I love you, Carly."

****

Outlined in light coming from the bedroom behind him, Shane looked dangerous, almost primeval. Excitement churned, and she stared into eyes alive with desire. She watched his chest heave with the effort to control his breathing. He stood motionless, hand extended, waiting.

The choice was hers. What did she want? What was right? As she stood there looking into his eyes, she realized the two questions might not have the same answer. Her stomach muscles tightened. She wanted him. He was the only man she ever wanted since the day she met him. Shane was the man whose taste lingered on her tongue since Philadelphia, the man whose scent danced through her dreams.

On the other hand, loving him now and accepting what might come later would be a leap of faith that could be disastrous. With so many obstacles still to overcome, the choice included more things than just the physical. In a few steps, she could be in his arms, the line she set gone as though set in sand in front of a crashing wave. However, if she let this moment pass, she may never know their destiny. In her dreams, she faced this moment with a thousand different endings, but the only one that mattered would be the path she chose now.

She took a step toward him, and then another, closing the distance until the heat from his body prickled across her skin. They could never have Philadelphia again, but they could have now. Trembling, she snaked her hand toward him and touched his chest. She felt the thump of his heart beneath her fingertips, and looked into his eyes. "I want this."

With a groan, he closed the scant distance between them. He dropped his forehead to hers and put his hands on her hips, caressing rather than gripping. His arms slowly encircled her. "I promised not to touch you, but I have to."

Carly didn't trust the leap of joy as everything inside her broke free. Her tears spilled onto his neck and flowed quickly by her lips. She felt a flow of rightness when she curled her arms around his neck and pressed herself against his rapidly heating body. She couldn't escape the want any longer. The feeling roared through her veins and left her dizzy. She knew everything was against them, but they could have this moment. Maybe that would be enough for a while.

Shane brushed a kiss against the side of her neck. "Can you ever forgive me for all I put you though?"

"Shh," she whispered. "This is about this moment."

He kissed her again.

Her world tilted. This moment would not be about their history or about the fear he might leave her again. This time would be hers. Shane's smell, his taste, the feel of him beneath her fingers when she slid her hands under his T-shirt and touched the ribbed planes of his torso was all that mattered. She whispered away her doubt when they molded against each other. Her hurt became his, and she felt his regret vibrate his body.

She murmured with pleasure at the touch of his hands clamped on her waist when he lifted from the floor. She wrapped her legs around him feeling his erection press against her.

Shane growled his contentment. His hands cupped her bottom as he turned and walked to the bedroom. Still kissing her, he bent low and deposited her on the bed. He straddled her before sliding a knee between her thighs and nudging open her legs.

She complied and widened the gap between her thighs until he became a willing prisoner. At first, their breaths were ragged, and they clung to each other. Soon, the kisses grew tender, and their movements settled into those of lovers exploring slowly. She relaxed, letting one leg slip down to lie flat against the mattress while the other caressed his hip. His body was hard, and he used it to encourage and invite. She lifted her hips to meet his. Lost in the moment, she let her head fall back, baring her throat to his kisses.

They broke contact only long enough to remove their clothes, and a small part of her panicked. *What the hell am I doing? This is crazy? It's a pipe dream to think we can rekindle what we had.* But she shoved aside the voice and accepted him with open arms when he entered her with a whisper.

Her name. His name. Who said the words didn't matter? What mattered was only that they were spoken, binding them together in that first moment of joining when she let him inside?

He paused, waiting.

Carly lifted her head and met his gaze. They looked at each other for a long moment until she smiled, and they met halfway on a kiss. "Is something wrong?" she whispered against his lips.

"Never." He moved within her.

Desire tightened, flooding her with a pounding need. She tangled her fingers in his hair, drinking his kisses as their bodies moved. What started as gentle love making turned into a sweat-filled scramble, moving to only one possible end. When the moment came, Carly clamped her legs around his hips and screamed his name.

Shane said her name in a groan as his climax came. He shuddered with the force of his release and collapsed against her. After a while, he moved back only far enough to look into her eyes.

A single tear fell from the corner of one eye. "What have we done?" she whispered.

"Something we both wanted," he replied before kissing her. She shifted beneath him, and he sat back on his haunches. "Time is unforgiving." He leaned forward and kissed her before standing and drawing upright. "Because I was young and made some bad decisions, I lost myself. Too many years later I realized unless I changed, my life would continue to be empty."

"Life isn't that simple, Shane."

"It could be."

She looked at her naked ring finger, her pulse racing. "Little girls dream of becoming brides. They dress up, maybe in their mother's gown, grab some silk flowers from the living room, and walk down the hallway pretending they are in a big church. When those little girls grow up, they discover reality is very different. Falling in love and becoming a bride takes a lot of work. You have to rely on people, trust them, especially those you love. Sometimes, you hit a bump in the road, and things go wrong in a relationship. But when you know love is right"—she tapped her chest— "something inside here tells you everything will be all right, and you go on."

"You don't have that feeling right now, do you?" Shane asked, his voice low.

Her chin trembled and she looked away. "For me, if you love someone, really love someone. You'd never let that person down." She lifted her chin and focused her gaze on his eyes. "You'd never leave them."

He traced the curve of her cheek. "Even if you knew life would be better for the person you loved if you weren't a part?" He held out his hand but said nothing else.

As she stood, her gaze locked with his. Deep in his eyes, she could see a combination of understanding and sadness that tore at her heart. She had hurt him. Realization struck her. Music's most famous star, the man the tabloids claimed every woman wanted, had lived a lonely existence. "With all you are and all you've done since Philadelphia, the road traveled hasn't been what you envisioned, has it?" she asked him.

"Life on the road is quite the ride." He looked away. "The band is doing great, and Bobby and I are getting along better than we ever have but—"

She touched his cheek and urged him to look at her. "It doesn't feel right." She saw the truth in her words fill his eyes. Without waiting for his answer and without thinking, she leaned forward and brushed his lips with the most gentle, chaste kiss she could ever remembering giving a man.

Yet, she never wanted anyone more.

****

As they dressed, Shane could almost see Carly rebuilding the walls around her and knew he was responsible. He took her hand and pressed a kiss onto her fingertips. "Should I apologize?"

With a one-cornered smile, she looked at him and shook her head.

"I think I need to." His arms encircled her in a loose embrace. "I'm not sorry we made love tonight, but I am sorry I put you in a situation you were not ready to confront so soon." He tucked a strand of hair behind her right ear and kissed her cheek. "Tonight was wonderful but it may have been a mistake."

She smiled. "No. I chose to—" she faltered and looked away.

He cupped her chin and urged her to look at him. "As did I." He caught a flicker in the back of her eyes. Confusion. Doubt maybe. He didn't really want to know which. He gestured to the door. "I'll take you home."

Carly crossed her arms over her chest and walked to the door.

Don't let her leave. For ten years, he dreamed about her extraordinary eyes, always twinkling when they were together. Her smile. The laughter they shared. The chance to make love again. But now that his dream had come true, he realized his dream had happened too soon. She didn't know his demons, his lies, or his sins. Once she knew everything, his lack of control tonight just may have cost any chance they had for happiness.

Chapter Six

At the rehearsal inside the school auditorium the next day, Shane greeted Carly with a broad smile. "I thought about you for the rest of the night. I wish we could have stayed together until morning."

"I was tempted." She bit her lip to keep from smiling.

"Not enough." Backing Carly against the wall, Shane put his hands on either side of her head, trapping her between his arms. He saw her look toward the stage. "The guys can't see us, but I can wait." Her smile was sad.

"I don't know if I can give you everything you need right now."

"You've already given me more than I could have ever hoped."

The look in her eyes revealed she struggled with the decision she made. He fought conflicting feelings, too. They had made love, but he had not told her everything she needed to know about the years away. He had one big mistake left to reveal, a transgression more serious than a cashed check. The weight of a thousand sinners pressed on his conscience, and time was running out. The guilt caught him and swamped him with the burden of its power. What he had to reveal would break her heart.

He released her from the prison of his arms. "I

would love to keep kissing you, but the guys are waiting."

"Go on," Carly said. "Practice makes perfect."

His smile grew. "I'd love to practice more with you."

She wrinkled her nose and rolled her eyes. "Another rock idol's sound bite? Remember, I'm not one of your idolizing fans."

He ran his forefinger across her lips. "You sure?"

"Very." She leaned away.

"I'll have to work harder then." His gaze focused on her lips. His need for more built to a fever pitch. She walked away and he sensed her reluctance to leave was as strong as his reluctance to let her go.

As guitar chords sailed in the air, he saw her pause at the auditorium door. Her hand trailed on the doorframe, and she hesitated. Her shoulders rose for a brief second before she took another step.

She looked back before disappearing into the hallway.

He walked to the door and listened to her footsteps, at first a walk and then more of a jog. He closed his eyes, wishing away her pain. Heart heavy, he walked to the stage, knowing he had no way to stop the pain that would come.

****

Carly only got as far as the school's parking lot before deciding to watch Shane perform. She made it a point of never watching any videos of Rangers' songs and avoided concerts aired on cable music stations, but today she wanted to see Shane in star mode.

Inside the hall, she slipped into a seat in the back row and watched. As she suspected, Shane's star burned brightest on the stage. She could see why his fans loved him. From teenyboppers to mature women, Shane's followers went crazy for his magnetic stage presence. He put his heart into every song the band played, singing his soul into the lyrics, and making devotees believe the message in the songs were just for them. She heard the raw emotion he poured into every word and easily imagined every other woman in America felt his soul in his music, too.

During the break, she walked onto the stage. "So, this is the man you've become."

Shane turned. His eyebrows arched. "I thought you left."

"I wanted to hear the band."

"Did you like the song?"

She nodded. "It was nice."

"Just nice?"

"Emotive," she admitted. "I can tell you put everything you have into the lyrics."

"Nothing in the world is like performing." He half-smiled and looked at her for a long moment. "Being on stage was what I thought I always wanted."

"Thought you wanted?" Her mind raced, searching for the meaning in his words.

"An appreciative audience is nice, but I've found once I get off stage and past the screaming fans, I feel nothing. It's as if I've stepped from the stage into a void." He unclipped his guitar strap and leaned the instrument against a speaker. "Once I get to my hotel room or into the tour bus, I'm in emptiness. I appreciate the fans and their loyalty, but all that is for the Shane Fox who steps into the spotlight or onto the pages of the tabloids." He patted his chest near his heart. "I'd like to know someone cares for what's in here."

She smiled and shook her head. "I suppose we all get to a point in our lives when we have to accept the choices we've made and who we have become because of them." She motioned around her. "You write songs, I play with money. We don't live in a perfect world, Shane. At some point, we realize nothing can fill all our needs."

"But every man has his needs. Even if you try to ignore them, unfilled desires claw from the inside until they get your attention. That's why I came back, Carly. I need you. I always have." He held her gaze and waited for her reaction.

Her thoughts filtered back to the first time she met him. His long hair and irreverent appearance complete with bared chest and tight jeans attracted her at first, but his persistence and the substance of his spirit were what won her heart. His wild look may be replaced with style, but she really didn't know that man now. Did the person she fell in love still remain underneath? She looked at the planes of his face and into the dark mystique of his eyes and thought back to the previous evening. She gave herself to him, and he took every bit of what she had offered. Had she made the right decision? She could not run back, but she wondered if they had a future. She was almost grateful when she saw Bobby wave from the back of the hall.

"Hey, bro. We got trouble." Bobby approached with long, loping strides and a twisted grin on his face. Once on the stage, he turned his back to Carly and gestured toward the rear of the hall. "I think you'd better handle this personally, big brother."

Shane peered around his brother and saw a woman

waiting. He placed his hands on Carly's shoulders, but his gaze staying on the figure at the rear of the hall. "Wait for me right here. This will just take a second." He waved to Bobby. "Stay with Carly."

She could see every muscle in Shane's face tense as he walked from the stage. The surge of anxiety flooding her mind worried her. "Bobby, who is she?"

"Not my story to tell," Bobby replied. He turned to leave.

Carly reached out and grabbed his arm. "Tell me anyway."

"Old business," was all he said as he shrugged off her hand and walked away.

Carly looked to the rear of the hall. Even from a distance, she could tell Shane and the woman were engaged in a very intense argument. She saw Shane place his hands on his hips and walk away before striding back to the woman. After a few more words between them, he moved his shoulders in a sign of anger and threw up his hands.

The woman jumped backward and lifted her hands to protect her face.

Carly's brow furrowed. Shane obviously knew the woman and must have or had some type of relationship with her. Carly's heart thudded inside her chest. Using the side exit on the stage, she made her way down the hallway, intent on leaving, but as she walked, the closer she got to the auditorium doors, the louder the heated exchange between Shane and his visitor became. The woman's voice floundered with uneasiness while Shane's voice thundered.

"Why here and why now?" he shouted.

Shane sounded tense and very angry. Carly

stopped. She knew if she listened, she would reduce herself to sophomoric eavesdropping. But as she turned to leave what she heard next convinced her to stay.

"I want to be with you when the results come in." The woman's voice was soft. "I asked the doctor to email me. He said he would have the results by five today. Then we'll know for sure."

"Damn it. I told you I wouldn't run," Resentment layered Shane's voice. "And I told you I would do everything I could to help you get through this. Didn't you believe me?"

Carly looked toward the row of lockers on her left, gathering her thoughts. Shane. A women. Lab tests. Agony settled heavy onto her chest as she realized there could be only one reason for the visit. Her feet felt as though they were rooted in cement.

"How do I know your story isn't a trick?" Shane asked.

"It isn't, Shane." The woman's voice cracked with emotion. "I love you!"

The choice was suddenly out of Carly's hands. This was not some starry-eyed fan professing her love. This woman was attempting to heal heartache. She pushed open the auditorium doors. Shock widened her eyes when she stepped inside. The woman with Shane was Danni Baker.

A river of tears ran down Danni's pale cheeks.

She looked fragile, defenseless, as though she might break in two at any second.

Shane loomed over her like a menacing villain.

Apparently not realizing Carly had come into the auditorium, he grabbed Danni by her upper arms and shook her.

"Love? If you cared about me at all, you wouldn't be doing this."

Danni gasped.

Shane relaxed his grip.

Tearing herself from his hold, Danni jerked to the right.

Carly ran to Danni. "What is going on?" She positioned herself between Danni and Shane. "Who is this woman to you?"

Shane paled and shifted from foot to foot. "Carly, how long have you been here?"

"Long enough." Carly walked Danni to one of the end seats and urged her to sit. "Try to relax. It'll be all right." She patted Danni's hand reassuringly.

Shane began talking as soon as Carly faced him. "Please just listen." His hand slid down her arm and tightened around her wrist. "Danni's a friend. We're having an issue at the moment. I was going to tell you."

She pulled her hand free. A feeling of uncertainty hit her full force, and trust took another step backward. "When?"

"When I knew—" He stopped and shook his head.

Carly sighed, close to defeat but unwilling to accept it. "Seems more than just a little problem, and I think Danni is more than just a friend." She walked a tightrope between belief and betrayal. "She said she loved you, Shane."

Danni bolted upright. "I do! And Shane loves me, too."

Carly felt her knees turn to rubber. The tabloids eagerly reported on all the women Shane dated, but she never expected to come face to face with one. To clear the lump from her throat, she swallowed hard then captured Shane's gaze. "Do you?"

"No. Danni is only a friend. I care about her as any friend would care, but I don't love her. I never have. I swear."

His voice sounded colored in neutral shades. Something deep inside cautioned Carly not to ask aloud what she asked herself in silence. If Danni was only a friend, why did she follow him to Hillsborough, and why was a lab test needed? A heavy tension built.

Digging inside her handbag, Danni ran toward Carly. "He does love me, and I can prove it."

Shane held up both hands. "No, Danni. For God's sake, don't." As Danni darted past, he reached for her arm but missed.

When Danni got to Carly, she held out a small photograph. "Here. This is all the proof you need."

With shaking hands and a gaze never leaving Shane's face, Carly took the picture. Slowly, she shifted her gaze to the photograph of a child with white-blond hair and shining blue eyes holding a small plastic guitar. The boy could not have been more than three or four years old. She studied the child's face feature by feature, feeling a river of ice spreading through her stomach. Her gaze darted back and forth between the angelic face in the picture and the face of the man she once loved above everyone and everything. Shane's eyes. Shane's smile. The features were nearly identical."That's Nickolas Fox. He's my son."

Over the wild pounding of her beating heart, Carly realized Danni was still speaking."My son and Shane's."

A wild flash of disbelief ripped through Carly, leaving her speechless. She looked at Shane, hoping to find protest and denial on his face. She found neither.

Hands open in a gesture of apology, Shane took a step toward her. "I can explain."

Her blood ran like cold needles through her veins. She couldn't breathe, couldn't get enough air into her lungs to drive away the pain settling in her head and her heart. Spinning on her heels, she walked out of the hall. She had to get away. She had to think.

****

Bobby turned the corner in the hallway outside the auditorium just as Carly bolted through the first set of doors. "Hey, what's the hurry?"

Blinking fast, she looked at him but didn't answer.

His gaze followed her as she yanked open the outer doors and ran toward the back parking lot. She looked frazzled. He liked that.

Not a second later, Shane burst into the hall. "Where's Carly?" He grabbed Bobby by the arms and swung him out of the way. "Which way did she go?"

Bobby tossed his head toward the exit. "Outside. What happened?"

Shane brushed his brother to one side and dashed for the doors. He jerked his head toward the auditorium. "Danni's in there. Don't let her leave."

As he watched his brother rip open the heavy double doors and sprint away in the direction Carly had taken, Bobby let his lips twist into a sardonic smile. "Sorry I missed all the fun," he quipped. "By the look of things, I think I would have enjoyed it."

****

Shane skidded around the corner of the stone parking lot just as Carly's car turned into the street. He couldn't catch her. He leaned his head against the metal camper and slammed his fist, hard, onto the door.

Everything was spiraling out of control.

Why did this have to happen now? After all his hard work, all his plans, all his self-denial? Why couldn't Danni have waited the few extra days they both needed to find out the truth?

He threw up his hands in disgust and walked toward the school. No sense blaming Danni for the mess he was in. Most of what Carly was feeling was his fault. Maybe this dream to get back Carly was unattainable after everything that happened to him, to them. He was a fool to think he could handle the emotions triggered by confession and deliverance. Once again, he tried to buffer Carly from the seedy side of the celebrity life he led, and once again, he made the wrong choice. Would he ever learn?

****

Inside the auditorium, Bobby struggled to prevent Danni from running after Shane.

"Let me go," she said from between clenched teeth. "I have to talk to Shane."

"Oh no, you don't, girlie." Bobby grabbed her upper arm and held on tight. "My brother said you were supposed to wait here, and that's exactly what you're gonna do." He dragged her over to one of the seats and shoved her into it. "Now sit here and shut up!"

Danni twisted in the seat, turning to look back at the doorway. "For how long? Shane could be leaving with Carly right this very minute. I have to stop him." She placed her hands on the armrests of the chair and leaned forward.

Bobby's grabbed her shoulder and pushed her back down. "I said SIT!"

A clear command, the words doused the fire in Danni's eyes, and she settled into the seat.

"You've been nothing but trouble since the first day I laid eyes on you. I'm not letting you ruin everything now," Bobby shouted.

"I just know Shane is still in love with her. How can I possibly even hope to compete? They might be planning a life together right now." She rocked back and forth. "What will happen to me then?"

"I'll take care of my brother. You concentrate on handling yourself once he gets back in here."

The auditorium doors opened, and Shane stood silent in the doorway for what seemed like an eternity. Outlined against the brighter light of the hall, he loomed twice his size.

Danni gasped and put a hand to her lips as he moved toward her. Her throat constricted with a brief flash of guilt she quickly banished.

"Bobby, tell the boys I have something to do," Shane said. "If they want to cancel the rehearsal, it's okay with me. I'll be back in time for the concert." His gaze never left Danni's face. "I need some time alone with Danni."

"Your call, bro," Bobby replied, shrugging. "But are you sure? I can help if she makes trouble."

Shane stood next to Danni, his gaze boring into her face, his voice thin as a whisper. "There won't be any trouble, will there, Danni?"

"N-n-no." Biting her lip, Danni looked away.

"You go on, Bobby. We'll be fine."

"You sure?"

"Yes."

"'Kay." Bobby turned and headed toward the stage.

Shane pulled her up. "We have to talk, Danni."

"Anything you want." Danni looked at her arm. Though she could see Shane's knuckles turn white, his grip was surprisingly gentle.

"I can't do this anymore."

Thinking Shane's controlled anger as surrender, Danni threw her arms around him. "We've made such a mess of things, haven't we? But everything will be all right. I just know it will."

Shane first pried her clutching fingers from around his waist and then took three strides away. "This isn't part of one of your fantasies, Danni. It's real. You're playing with people's lives. One way or another, no matter what I have to do, you will stop this delusion."

Danni gave no indication she understood but merely tilted her head and smiled.

****

As Danni stared doe-eyed, Shane felt an overwhelming feeling of building empathy. She was still the same dreamer she had been on the first day they met in what seemed like a lifetime ago. Nothing he could do or say would make her understand. She refused to acknowledge the truth. Sadness replaced anger as he thought back to the beginning.

Almost as soon as the group's first song hit the charts and went solid gold, Danielle Baker started her obsession. At first, her fixation appeared innocent. She sent small gifts and fan letters, but as time went on, the gifts became more expensive and the letters more personal.

Initially considered the attention as that of an over-zealous fan, but when the gifts arrived weekly and the accompanying notes got sexual and suggestive, he realized her delusion bordered on mania. He asked the road manager to return the gifts, but Danni refused. She made a scene at every concert venue the band played until he had no choice but to personally explain how all gifts from fans were donated to charity, and she need not go to such an extreme to let him know she enjoyed his music.

When she followed the band to every city on their tour, he became concerned but treated her fixation with kindness, thinking it would pass as quickly as the infatuation came. However, Danni's obsession grew steadily worse until he could no longer deny she was living inside a dream world. She showed up at meet-and-greets and every concert. She professed her love and undying devotion to anyone who would listen and swore only she could ever make Shane happy.

Now, as part of her fantasy world, Danni had gone too far. She'd crossed the line and involved Carly. Gentle suggestion was not the answer any longer. The time had come for Danni to understand he did not intend to play a part in her daydream.

Her features softened. "Shane, I know we will be happy. I don't care what you have done here. Our life with our son is all that matters." She ran to him, arms wide.

But Shane stopped her with a stiff arm to her shoulder. His gaze searched her face briefly before he dropped his arm and turned his back.

Danni touched his shoulder. "Nicky needs his father," she whispered.

Shane turned. He closed his eyes and exhaled slowly. "Nickolas is not my son."

Danni grabbed his arm. "But the test."

He pressed his lips into a frown and looked at her hand. "I took a paternity test to prove I'm not the father." He lifted his gaze and caught hers. "When the results prove I'm right, you'll have to accept the reality that any relationship you think we have is a figment of your imagination."

Danni shook her head. "It's real." Her voice was more a choked whisper. "Surely, you haven't forgotten that hot August night, the party, the wine, and the low, sultry music. We danced for hours and then spent the night in each other's arms." Her smile grew. "I remember."

"Stop!" Shane pulled out of her grasp. He took two steps away then clenched and unclenched his fists to channel some of the raging energy. "Okay. Yes. I found you in my bed in the morning, but we never made love, Danni. I don't even know how you got there. I told you then, and I'm telling you now, nothing happened."

"Oh no," she crooned. "Something wonderful did happen. We created Nicky, the living proof of our love."

Shane slapped a hand to the back of his neck and massaged the tightness between his shoulder blades. "You need someone to help you sort this out, Danni. Let me find you a doctor."

Danni smiled. "Yes. I think you are right. I should get a check-up. Nicky needs a brother or sister. I was an only child. I don't want that for our son." She threw her arms around Shane's waist, dropped her head into his chest, and sighed. "I want lots of brothers and sisters for Nicky."

Exhaustion swept through his body. Danni had not heard one word he said. She was back inside her fantasy, busy planning a perfect little life that simply did not exist and never, ever would. "Danni, listen to me. You're a beautiful, young woman. You have so much to offer a man."

Danni made sure she caught his gaze."And it's all yours."

"No." He stepped back and held up his hands, palms out. "I love Carly. I've always loved Carly. I've made mistakes, but one mistake I did not make was sleeping with you. Nothing ever happened between us, so I can't possibly be Nicky's father."

Danni's lower lip trembled. "Nothing?"

He shook his head and forced a sad smile. "Nothing, Danni." She was silent for a moment, but when he saw hope light her eyes, he knew she was still lost.

"Maybe if we try. Just give ourselves a chance." She walked forward.

He matched her stride with backward steps."No, Danni. I don't love you. I'll never love you. The plain truth is, I don't know how to love anyone but Carly."

Frowning, Danni swallowed hard. "But the test."

"The test will prove I am not Nicky's father."

Tears trembled on Danni's eyelashes. She dropped her face into her hands and cried.

Shane watched her small shoulders shake with emotion and felt pity building. He didn't want to hurt her, but she had to understand. For her own sake as much as for his. He reached out and touched her shoulder. When she looked up, their gazes locked. He scrubbed a hand down his face. "Listen. When the test results are in, you'll have to come to terms with everything I've telling you." He wiped a tear from her cheek with the back of his hand. "Once you understand the truth, you can get on with your life, and I can get on with mine."

"I don't want to lose you."

He could hear anguish in her voice. He shook his head. "Danni, you never had me."

Her body shook as she sobbed.

A victim to his own compassion, he reached out and pulled her close. "Don't." He stroked her hair and rocked her back and forth like a small child. "You have to be strong. If not for yourself, for Nicky."His words seemed to calm her, and the sobs stopped. After a few more minutes, he moved away.

Danni looked at him and nodded. "For Nicky."

He smiled. "I'm sorry. I have to go. I have to find Carly. Is there someone you can call? I don't think you should be alone."

As she wiped her cheeks with both hands, Danni nodded.

Damn. Why did it have to be like this? Danni looked so lost and so helpless. Despite the warnings screaming inside his head, he leaned over and gave her a light kiss on her cheek. "Be patient. You'll find someone to make you happy, Danielle. We all deserve to be happy." Then lingering only as long as the life of his smile, he touched her shoulder and left.

****

Danni's breath quickened as she recalled the undeniable and dreadful truth she saw in Shane's eyes. He was a man who would never be satisfied with only a dream. He would never belong to her. Now, she was a woman facing the harsh reality of loneliness.

Then suddenly, her breathing calmed and she

touched her cheek. Her fingertips caressed the spot Shane had kissed just moments before. "You're right, my love." She moved her hand to her mouth and kissed her fingertips as though they were Shane's lips, "I do deserve to be happy."

She took her cell phone from her purse, searched her contact list, and smiled before tapping the mobile number she wanted. "I have someone who will help me. He said he would make sure Carly did not come between us. He will know what to do. He will fix everything."

Chapter Seven

In the Rose Garden at the park, Carly sat on the same bench she shared with Shane. Her hands twisted in her lap. Surrounded by the flowers, she should feel joy, but all she felt was pain so concentrated, like a giant hole punched into her chest with no hope of repair. What she witnessed rocked her to the core. From the first moment she discovered Shane accepted the invitation to headline the benefit concert, she felt his coming home might mean trouble. Questions why he was playing such a small venue cropped up on blogs and pop culture sites on the web. A mainstream entertainment reporter was bound to shove a microphone in a band member's face sometime soon and ask why. She hoped the answer would not include her name.

Once linked to Shane she would not be immune to the press crunch, especially if the pop media found out about the baby-mama drama. Fortunately no one else witnessed the back and forth between Shane and Danni. This time. Shoulders curling, she leaned forward. Loving a man should bring a woman joy, not confusion. How could she still love Shane so completely, so desperately, as though a lapse in time had never occurred? How could she still ache for him, hunger for his touch, want to be with him forever when she still knew little about his life during the years they spent apart? Where was her pride? Her common sense? Her strength?

She knew the answers. When he left all those years ago, Shane took her heart. Only now that he was back did she again feel alive. She would not walk away nor would she let him leave her again. She stood and started toward the parking lot when she heard the roar of a motorcycle die. *Shane.* She turned and searched for another exit, but the garden was fenced. Even though the park grass muffled his footsteps, she knew exactly when he was behind her.

"I hoped I would find you here," he whispered. "We always came here to talk." When she faced him, he reached for her.

When he touched her elbow, she closed her eyes and took a deep breath. As in the past, his touch started a slow pulsation on her skin. She suppressed the building sensation as much as she could, looked at his hand, and then into his eyes. "I remember."

"Carly, I—"

With gentle pressure of her fingertips to his lips, she cut his words. "Shh, don't. I need to something before I lose my nerve."

He nodded and let his hand drop to his side.

Carly sighed and gathered her courage. "I came here to decide which would be worse—facing the pain of loving you knowing you may have fathered another woman's child or facing the pain of living without you again." She paced. "Since the day you left me, I could not commit fully to any other man. Until you came back into my life, I never really knew why." She stopped, closed her eyes, and took a deep breath before facing him. "Being with you last night made the reason suddenly clear." Throat tight, she held his gaze. "You are as much a part of me as the beat in my heart and the breath in my lungs."

Shane took a step toward her.

But she held up her hand. Tears formed as she spoke. "You may have to admit responsibility for some of your past, but I was not with you when those choices were made." Shane smiled, but she saw caution in his eyes. "I've thought long and hard about what I saw and heard in the auditorium and about how much the man I once knew may have become a total stranger. But Danni's accusations forced me to realize time changes everyone."

"Tell me what to do, Carly." Shane held out his hands. "Whatever you want, I'll do it." His voice dropped to a whisper. "Including leaving and never coming back."

She was aware of the pain she inflicted. She saw his shoulders slump with the weight of the responsibility she forced him to accept. Twice, he failed her. Would she regret giving him a third chance?

Although a woman of lesser courage might have taken the easy way out and sent Shane away, she could not. With pulse-pounding certainty, she knew they belonged together, no matter what had happened while they were apart. Their future could begin now. All she had to do was say the words.

Shane swallowed hard and opened his mouth to speak, but no sound came out. After several strangled seconds, he managed to ask, "Are you leaving me this time?"

Despite her outward calm, Carly felt a sudden apprehension grip her. A dangerous awareness flickered in her stomach. For years she had imagined this moment happening. Her emotions exploded with a force she could not control, and her tears broke free. "I don't know how to stop loving you, Shane. Since I'm forced by what's inside my heart to love only one man forever, I must love all of that man, no matter what he has done or what he has yet to do. I don't know what will happen, but I do know I need you in my life."

Shane let out a long audible breath gathered her into his arms. His eyes glazed with tears. "I swear to you, I'll never leave you again."

Carly fought to free herself from the havoc Shane's nearness created within her. They were permanently connected, and try as she might, she could never sever the link. She shook her head. "I don't know what to believe."

"Believe me," he begged.

She broke free and turned away. "Then I have to know." She turned. "Did you sleep with Danni Baker?"

Shane said nothing.

"Are you the father of her child? I need to hear the truth." Her gaze fixed on his eyes, searching for the man she knew in Philadelphia. "From you. I don't want to read it in a gossip rag or listen to an interview with a lab tech who did the test."

His gaze locked with hers but he did not react.

The resulting silence screamed as Carly felt ripples of doubt slapped at her like a building wave. Had she made a mistake when she confessed she still loved him? A dull ache settled into her chest. The look on his face told her something was seriously wrong. Her heart sank, and she inhaled a long, shaky breath. "You slept with her."

He slowly shook his head. "I don't know for sure."

To her, he sounded ridiculous. "How can you not know?" The words came out in a shrill tone, and she sounded like a scolding schoolteacher, but she didn't care. She stared at the gazebo behind him. "You don't make love in your sleep, Shane." The pain hitting her heart almost knocked her off her feet as she remembered how he used to wake her with kisses before they made love. She fought to keep her face neutral.

"I know it sounds ridiculous, but I don't know if I slept with her."

She could not stop the skeptical snicker that rose from her throat. "That explanation is ridiculous."

Shane took hold of her arm when she tried to walk away. "You rather I lied?"

She shrugged away his touch. "Of course not."

"I honestly am not sure if I slept with Danni." He rubbed the back of his neck. "I was lonely." The words came out in a sigh. "Very lonely. I missed you so much, Carly."

She laughed, partly from frustration but mostly in disbelief. "You're saying you used her to forget me?" She walked to the closest bench and dropped onto it. Crossing her arms, she challenged him. "Did you use women a lot?"

He released the breath he'd been holding. "At times, I probably did." He ran his hand through his hair and slumped. "Hell, I don't know what I did those years or why. What I do know is I never stopped loving you, Carly. I know you have no reason to believe me, and I deserve that doubt." He stood in front of her, stared off into the distance with his hands planted in the back pockets of his jeans. "You wanted the truth." He looked back. "I tried to forget you, but nothing worked because I still loved you."

A flash of irritation raced through her. Her back stiffened. "So you went to bed with women because you loved me?"

"Since I left you, my life seems cursed. In the midst of all the fortune and glory, I get terribly lonely. When I got lonely, I thought of you, of what we had, and of what I threw away. You have no reason to believe or forgive me, but you need to know the man I was. Maybe the man I still am." He sat next to her and rested his forearms on his thighs. His gaze focused on the ground as he shook his head. "Who knows why we do things when we're lonely? The things I've done"— he snickered—"worse than bad. The world thinks I have everything, when truthfully if you pick my life apart, it plays more like a badly written soap opera rather than a successful journey. Read any gossip sheet. According to them, I make Don Juan look like a beginner." He angled his head to capture her gaze. "And that might not be that far from the truth."

Sickened by what she heard, Carly stared. The urge to walk away was insanely strong, but she drove off the feeling, wanting to understand. "I have to admit, when I read those stories, I couldn't comprehend why you would cheapen yourself the way you did. I wanted to smack you and ask what you were proving." She lowered her voice to a whisper. "I guess I have my answer now."

He inhaled and let out the breath very slowly. "I really screwed up."

"You did," she murmured.

"For a while, I got caught up in the image of who I was. I let the media lead me and didn't care where I went." He pressed his lips together and shook his head. "Unfortunately, there are no do-overs and the internet is forever. My image, and the stories confirming the jerk I became, will be out there in cyberspace hanging over my head until the day I die."

She nodded and felt a pang of pity. The media never let celebrities forger their mistakes. The sins of the past made great headlines of the present especially in gossip magazines at the grocery store checkout. A rock star with a long list of solid gold hits and a reputation of almost as many relationship conquests, real or imaginary, was fair game.

Shane looked at her long and hard. "The only thing I can do is ask you to forgive me."

She pulled back and silently stared. What she saw almost tipped the scale of doubt to his favor. A single tear trailed a salty path down his cheek. She reached up and wiped the moisture from his skin with the tip of her finger. "What you told me now just leads to more questions." She dropped her hand. Her heart beat wildly, and she wondered if disappointment showed on her face as clearly as it showed on his.

"Ask them," Shane prompted.

She looked into his eyes. "I don't think the man I fell in love with in Philadelphia would give so much to help his brother with little thought to his own needs, only to later deny a son and his mother. Would this same man bare his soul to someone he claims to have never stopped loving and omit something as important a child—all the time swearing he came back to build a future?" She shook her head. "I don't think he would."

"Then you believe me?"

She saw a wave of relief ripple across Shane's face. "I want to." She rushed into speaking. "But don't think I've been totally blinded by your smile and impossible explanation. Out of the blue, you come back into my life with a tale of underworld loan sharking. I had barely time to absorb the information, when an obsessive fan announces you fathered her child." She rose and paced. "She says yes, you say no."

Shane got into step with her. "Just hold on a little longer. I've taken a paternity test."

Carly stopped, her voice fracturing. "And if the test proves otherwise?"

"It won't." He smoothed a stray lock of hair behind her ear. "It can't."

"I want to believe that, Shane, but you admitted you couldn't be sure."

He held her upper arms and looked into her eyes. "Then be with me when the results come in."

Her brow furrowed. "Are you certain you want me there?"

"Positive."

They looked at each other for one heart-stopping moment before she nodded. "Then I will." Carly found herself struggling under the intensity of Shane's gaze. She had to accept the fact she loved him and always would, but she would not tell him again until she was very sure of the truth. Even if she never again said those words, she was certain she would never love another man the way she loved Shane.

Shane caressed her cheek with the back of his hand. "Do you think we can rebuild what we once had?"

"I don't know." She stepped out of his embrace. "We have so much to work through."

"It does seem crushing," Shane's smile faded. "Maybe if we agree to be totally honest with each other, we will see where the future takes us."

She caught his gaze. "But if we have any hope of escaping this maze of feelings we have become trapped inside, we can have no more secrets."

"I promise," he agreed, his voice low and husky. "No more secrets, ever."

"Then hold me," Carly whispered, burying her face against his throat. "I remember when you held me, I felt nothing bad could ever touch us. I need to feel that way again." She looked into his eyes and saw the same tenderness she made the cornerstone of her dreams. For the first time since she learned Shane was coming back to town, she had the feeling the world was in its place. Soon, maybe their souls might finally find peace.

****

Danni's lower lip trembled as she paced back and forth in the dimly lit parking lot on the outskirts of town, waiting. He'd be here soon. He said he would help her, and she knew exactly what she needed. She looked at the ground, trying hard to convince herself the future belonged to her and Shane.

But all she could think about was Carly. Carly, with her shiny hair and green eyes. Carly, with her sweet smile, gentility, and goodness.

And Carly, with Shane.

She could not compete with someone he loved. Only one thing remained for her to do.

Get rid of Carly.

****

Carly and Shane did not realize how late had become was until one of the County Park Rangers asked them to leave because the park closed at 8:30 p.m.

Shane glanced at the night sky and then at his watch. "Guess we have been here for a while. I'll follow you home."

"That's not necessary." Carly reached out and turned up the collar on Shane's leather jacket.

He put a hand to her cheek. "I want to."

She didn't have the emotional strength to argue so walked to her car and heard Shane start his Harley as she got in. As she drove down Woods Road, she glanced in the rear view mirror.

Shane rode close behind.

Despite all the emotions warring inside, she did feel a sense of comfort with Shane following her home. Just as her gaze shifted to the road ahead, she heard what sounded like a firecracker. A second later, the windshield shattered. She slammed on the brakes and threw up her arms to protect her face. She could feel glass shards hitting her hands and pricking her skin. A trickle of warm blood ran down her skin. Her stomach lurched and panic set in. The car skidded along the shoulder of the road, and she grabbed the steering wheel to regain control. She jerked the steering wheel to the left and stomped on the brakes, narrowly missing a deep ditch before the car came to a stop in front of a line of tall trees.

Her hands trembled as she turned off the ignition. She looked at the streaks of blood running down her forearms and felt a steady stream of perspiration move between her shoulder blades. What had happened, and where was Shane?

Her answer was the thunder of his Harley pulling behind her car. He ran to her door, ripped it open, and pulled her out. "My God, Carly, are you all right?"

Carly could see his blue eyes blazing. His face, pale and hardened with the lines of tension around his lips, told her he was waging a battle to remain calm. She could only nod her answer.

"Are you hurt? In any pain?" He ran his hands down her arms. "Anything broken?"

"I'm not hurt," she whispered.

"What happened?" he asked.

"I'm not sure." Her answer infuriated her. She should know. She should have been more alert to her surroundings. She calmed a new wave of panic intent on recalling every detail just before she lost control of the car. She was surprised how little she remembered. "Maybe one of my tires kicked some loose rock when I went around the curve."

Shane pulled out the hem of his T-shirt and dabbed at the blood on her hands. "Fortunately, these cuts are little more than scratches." His voice dropped. "I want to look at the car. Will you be okay?"

Carly nodded.

He led her to the motorcycle and leaned her against the seat. He looked at her. "Don't move."

She started to shake. Not little shivers, but body-quaking shudders. "I don't think I can."

****

Shane was inside the car for about three minutes when a set of headlights came around the corner and illuminated the area. As the car got closer, he recognized Bobby's luxury sports car.

Bobby pulled next to Carly's car and opened the window. He stuck out his head. "Christ, what happened here? Anyone hurt?"

Shane walked to Carly and put his arm around her shoulders. "No, we're okay. What are you doing here?"

"Couldn't sleep, so I went for a drive." Bobby got out of his car and inspected Carly's damaged windshield. "The glass is busted like something went through it." He cocked his head. "Someone been throwin' rocks at you guys?"

"Not rocks." Shane held out his hand, palm up. "Bullets. I found this on the floor, and there's one lodged in the passenger seat headrest."

Bobby arched his eyebrows and whistled. "What the hell did you do to make someone this mad? Give them a wrong deposit slip at the bank, Carly?"

Shane bristled. "Don't get cute, Bobby, this is serious." He turned to Carly. "We've got to call the police, honey."

Carly stared at the bullet. "No. You can't call the police."

"Why not?"

"Because I'm sure this was only an accident." She wasn't sure at all, but that situation was the one she needed to believe to get through the next few minutes. "For small game hunting, some animal is always in season. Permit holders may hunt day and night with certain restrictions. Whoever did this probably unlicensed and is long gone. We'll never find him, and neither will the police."

One side of Bobby's mouth turned up. "She's got a point, bro. Bet whoever did this probably got scared shitless and ran."

"You're taking this much too lightly," Shane argued. His mouth tightened. "Carly could have been killed," he said through clenched teeth.

"But she wasn't," Bobby countered. A smirk curled across his lips. "Nothing happened."

One hand curling into a fist, Shane surged forward.

Carly stepped between the brothers. "Please, Shane, I just want to go home."

Shane's hand relaxed but his expression didn't. "We should call 9-1-1 at least."

Carly's stomach churned. Calling the police and having them investigate would take time, and all she wanted right now was to go home. She shook her head. "The newspapers have scanners, and reporters monitor police calls for late-breaking stories. Think of the publicity. Bad press could force a cancellation of the concert. I can't let that happen. Too many organizations are counting on the donations from the show to keep social service programs going. Children and families may suffer if programs are cut due to lack of funding."

"She's right about the publicity," Bobby agreed. "You know how the media loves to play with you, big brother."

"Carly's more important," Shane snapped back without hesitation.

"And so is the concert," Carly added quickly, forcing her voice to sound composed. "Besides, I'm fine. All I need is a little antiseptic for the cuts."

Shane held her at arm's length. "I don't care about press—good or bad."

"I do," Carly replied.

"Are you sure this is what you want?" Shane asked.

"Yes." Carly bit down on her lip to keep the cracks in her composure from showing. "I'll feel better once I get home."

"Then you're not going alone." He turned to Bobby. "Go to Clinton, and get one of the guys to come back here with you and pick up the bike. I'll drive Carly's car home."

"Sure. No prob." Bobby kicked a broken branch into the ditch. "Whatever you say."

Shane gave more instructions to Bobby when headlights from another car suddenly lit the area. Shane shielded his eyes as the car slowed and then rolled to a stop.

From the partially opened rear window, a card fluttered to the ground. The window closed, and the driver gunned the engine, driving off with a squeal of tires and a quick burst of speed.

Bobby picked up the paper. His eyes widened, and he angled the card to Shane. "Jesus. Get this."

A red 'S' sat in the center of an otherwise pure white page.

Carly's heartbeat rose, and she gasped. This was no hunting accident. This was a warning.

Neither Carly nor Shane spoke during the remaining two-mile drive to her home. Shane turned off the car and they got out. Halfway up her driveway, he put his arms around Carly. "How are you holding up? I can only imagine how you felt when the windshield shattered."

"I'm fine." But honestly, she didn't know how much longer she could pretend to be strong. Her world was out of control since Shane came back, and this incident only pushed her unrestrained uncertainty to an even higher level.

Shane started massaging her left shoulder. "I wouldn't think less of you if you say you're angry and upset."

"I'm both." She swallowed hard to clear the lump from her throat.

"You sure you're okay?" He wrapped his arms around her and pulled her against his chest. Then he kissed her, his embrace loose.

Carly could sense the restrained passion inside him. She tunneled her fingers through his thick hair, holding him close. His tongue thrust deep inside her mouth with long strokes she could feel all the way down to her toes. She pressed her body deeper into his, wanting to do whatever she could to make this moment never end. But suddenly everything boiled over inside her—all the confessions and admissions and a realization or two tossed in for good measure. No matter how much she tried, she couldn't keep doubt and want from waging war in her head. She knew she wanted Shane, but could she commit to a future they would write together, no matter what fate chose for them. Especially when she had questions about his past he seemed reluctant to answer. She pulled back slowly and withdrew her lips from his. He let her go, but she held his face between her hands, realizing what she saw in his eyes mirrored the longing in her soul.

"You run away every time I get close," Shane whispered.

"I'm not running." She dropped her hands. "I need to tell you something."

"Anything," Shane said.

"I've seen the car before."

Shane's brow furrowed. "The car that pulled up after the accident."

Carly nodded.

"When?"

"A few days ago. Behind the high school." Her gaze held his. "I saw Bobby with his hand on the car, talking to someone in the back seat through the open window." She watched as Shane's expression changed from concern to uneasiness.

"Are you sure? Big limos can all like alike."

"I'm sure. You don't see many customized grills like that in Hillsborough."

Shane's nostrils flared, but he said nothing. His hands balled into fists.

Carly saw anger race across Shane's face and his knuckles turn white. "What's wrong?"

"Wherever Scodari is, trouble follows." He broke eye contact and stepped away.

She grabbed his arm. "Do you think Bobby is in trouble again?"

"I hope not." Shane's words came out in a rush of air. His eyes narrowed as he scanned the area in response to a rustling sound in the bushes. "I don't want you staying here tonight. You will stay with me at the estate in Clinton." He enveloped her in an embrace and steered her to the car. "Security is there twenty-four-seven to keep out fans." Shane opened the passenger door. "I want you safe."

"I'm safe here," Carly protested. She didn't know if she actually believed it, and a low buzzing began in her ear from both the shock and the lie.

"You're safer with me."

Safer? Everything went cold inside her. "Are you

saying I'm in danger?"

"I don't know what to think. Until I can figure this out, I don't want you out of my sight."

She grabbed the front of his shirt and held on tight. "Okay, but first, promise me something."

"If I can."

"This time, we don't run."

He looked at her. "I promise," he said, tightening his hold, "I won't lose you again. No one will ever take you away again."

Chapter Eight

Bobby cursed as he tore apart his bedroom at the estate. Everything was falling apart, and he knew why. Carly. Why the hell did his brother have to play the noble knight and rescue the past?

He clenched his teeth, anger from his childhood and from the present situation eating like a cancer. What did he have to do to get control? He shoved his fist through the wall. Damn Carly. Damn his brother. Damn it all. He cocked his elbow to hammer the sheetrock again but caught sight of a band member in the doorway.

"Should I ask you why you're about to shove your fist through the wall again, or will you tell me?" Niles asked.

Bobby lowered his arm. "You're three holes late for an explanation."

Niles leaned against the door with arms crossed and glanced at the wall. "Bad day?"

As he flexed his fingers, Bobby glared. "Not your business."

"With all the noise you're making banging around in here, you should expect someone to ask."

Bobby stormed across the room and grabbed his jacket. "I have to get Shane's bike." He tossed a set of car keys at Niles. "You're driving."

Niles tossed his dark hair out of his eyes and

caught them cleanly. "Where's the bike?"

"Long story," Bobby replied, pushing past him.

"You can tell me on the way to wherever we're going."

"Or not," Bobby retorted.

Niles stopped walking. "What's going on?"

Bobby turned slowly. "Carly's car ended up in a ditch. I just happened to be driving by when the accident happened."

A snicker escaped Niles' throat, and he shook his head. "You never just happen to be anywhere."

Bobby's eyes narrowed, and a sneer curled his lips.

Hands up, Niles backed away. "If you expect me to beg you for the truth—"

"I don't expect anything," Bobby snapped. He raised his hand. "You coming or not?"

"What are you up to?" Niles asked.

"Up to getting the damn motorcycle," Bobby snarled.

"I sincerely doubt that's all you are doing." Niles followed Bobby to the driveway.

****

The highway was nearly empty on the drive to the Clinton Estate. Occasionally, headlights from a car going west on the other side of the divider flickered through the trees in the road divider, but they were far and few in between. Shane checked the rearview mirror and saw only darkness. No paparazzi following him either. Fate seemed on his side,

Carly shifted in the passenger seat and angled toward him. Her head lolled to the left. "I can't seem to keep my eyes open."

"You're probably in shock," Shane suggested.

"Close your eyes. I'll wake you when we turn into the driveway."

She nodded, leaned back into the headrest, and surrendered to sleep.

When he looked at her, Shane felt a deep sense of protection rise. Scodari tried to hurt her. He would pay for that. Shane wouldn't lose her again. He skimmed her cheek with the back of his hand.

In sleep, she turned to his touch and smiled.

Memories broke free from the prison cell they occupied in his mind and took him back him to another time and place when he held her, touched her, and taught her, and, afterward, watched her sleep in his arms. His stomach muscles knotted painfully with desire. Even after all the years, he could still remember the sound of her sweet whispers when they made love for the first time. "You were a virgin. I took that from you," he whispered.

Carly stirred and sighed what sounded like agreement.

Was she dreaming of him? Did she ever? Sadness rippled inside him as the years they spent apart moved through his mind. How could he possibly explain everything he had done? Would she understand any of it? He wanted her trust but would take her forgiveness. He often thought about returning to Philadelphia and confessing everything, but the years and the lies were too complicated and with no way out except through pain. He had walked away from a love so pure into a life that promised him everything he thought he wanted. Too late, he realized he traded his heart for a world filled with shadows and a tainted success he could not control. He spent the last ten years a prisoner of the choice he made.

But none of that mattered any longer. His homecoming put into motion a set of circumstances that had a life of their own. Decision made, he would see this journey through to the end and stop at nothing to make things right—no matter what he had to do or whom he might have to hurt.

After about twenty minutes on the interstate, he took the ramp onto a local road. Ten minutes later, the high iron gates separating the Clinton Estate from the rest of the town came into view. He slowed the car, opened the window, and entered the code into the touch pad set into stone pillars holding the gates. In a moment, a tinny voice crackled through the speaker set above security box acknowledging the code and the gates opened. With Carly still asleep, Shane turned onto the private road that wound through the property and lead to the main house.

The security lights lit the entrance to the house like spotlights, illuminating the area in a two-hundred-foot radius. Shane saw the video cameras turn toward the car as it approached the grand entrance, underscoring his decision to bring Carly to the Estate for safety. He parked, got out, and rounded the hood. After opening the passenger door, he dropped to one knee, gently stroked her cheek. "Carly, honey, we're home."

Her eyes fluttered open, and she smiled.

"Have a nice nap?" he asked.

She nodded. "I feel better."

Shane stood and extended his hand. "Here you'll feel safe, too."

****

Glancing around, she hesitated.

He took her hand. "The house has fifteen bedrooms. You can pick your own."

"The house looks deserted." She let him lead her to the front of the manor.

"Guess everyone is asleep or out for the evening," Shane replied. He opened the door and stepped aside.

Carly stood, arms crossed, in the foyer. She watched Shane walk into the first room to her right, the heels of his boots making an odd clicking sound as he walked the multi-hued slate floor. Cautiously, she followed.

He flipped on a light. "Care for a drink?"

"Maybe some water," she replied.

"How about some Asti? It's sweet and not too strong. I think I saw a bottle in the wine fridge."

She eyed him suspiciously. "You're the one who taught me to play drinking games back at the loft in Philly, I know you aren't trying to get me drunk."

"If I thought it would work, we could play right now." He lined up some shot glasses and patted his pants pockets. He shrugged. "No change. Sorry." He bent and retrieved the wine from the small refrigerator under the bar.

Carly moved to the bar. "Is there a reason for this small talk?" She didn't smile.

Neither did he. "Maybe one glass of wine won't get you drunk, but it could relax you a little."

She tilted her head. "And possibly take off your edge a little?"

He nodded.

She didn't say any more for a long moment. Then she met his gaze and nodded. "Sounds good."

He found some glasses and opened the bottle. "Sit

anywhere. I'll be there in a sec."

She chose a long sofa across from floor-to-ceiling windows revealing a panorama of meticulously decorated landscaping beautifully lit by spotlights in all the right places. Behind her, she heard the door click quietly shut, and then heard Shane' footfalls coming toward her. Wild thoughts galloped through her mind. Once she had been sure if she saw Shane again, she would feel nothing. She had convinced herself she could look him in the eye and bolster the belief what they had was over for a very long time. However, sexual attraction proved to be a powerful adversary. Staying in this house with him would definitely add to the temptation. As uneasiness raced through her, she stood before he reached the sofa and walked to a sword hanging above the fireplace. She ran her hand over the golden hilt.

"Legend says that sword has great power." Shane slid her half-full wine glass onto the hand-carved, antique trestle table positioned behind the sofa. He sat and sipped his drink.

Carly walked to the mantel and ran her hand over the dark wood before picking up her glass. "Great power. How so?" She sipped the wine and looked over the rim of her glass.

"According to myth, the sword can only to be used to vanquish evil. None but the pure of heart can remove it from the wall."

Surprised, she laughed. "Then you have no chance in hell of getting it down, do you?"

He shook his head. "'Fraid not." He smiled. "If I can't use the sword to protect you, then, maybe, you and I should share—"

"No way," she cut in. "You said this place has fifteen bedrooms. You take room number one, and I'll be in room fifteen."

Chapter Nine

Carly could not sleep. She crossed the room and drew back the curtain.

Shane stood on the stone terrace in the courtyard below.

In the moonlight, his face shadowed in silhouette, he exuded an aura of masculinity no women could resist. When she first met him in Philadelphia, she surrendered to his charm and gave herself freely and completely without thought of regret. Then he left and ripped out her heart. She tried to forget him but never could. She also tried to hate him but could not bring herself to try. Hating him would be like hating a part of herself. Still, this reunion felt fragmented, as though something was missing. Even though their connection had never really broken, a part of her felt he was holding back something. But why? As she stared at Shane's back, the wind lifted his hair like a woman's caress.

Who are you, Shane Fox? Why did you really come back?

****

Shane felt Carly watching him. He turned and moved farther into the darkness behind the manor. In days past, he wrestled with the reason he came back to claim the woman he never should have left. For ten years Carly built a life without him and, for that reason alone, he should have thought more carefully about a homecoming. But the possessive elements in his nature only fueled his need for Carly in his life. Although he thought he planned his homecoming very carefully, events he could not control were put into motion.

Even though he thought matters were settled between them and hadn't spoken to her in over a year, Danni had followed him and entangled herself in his life. The media had not yet caught up with the concert. Still, Danni had showed up. How had she known where to find him?

And Scodari. Another ghost from his jaded past had surfaced. The band's debt was paid. Why was he here?

A sharp pain pierced his skull, and he pressed his fingers to his temples to dull the feeling. His world was falling apart, and he seemed helpless to stop the destruction. He thought he had protected Carly by leaving her. He thought the threat was over when Scodari had been paid in full, but the incident with Carly's car was no accident, and shooter hadn't simply missed. Until he dealt with Scodari, he had to put his personal plans on hold. Before he could plan a future with Carly, he needed to make sure she was safe.

****

Waking suddenly, Carly sat straight up, screaming and gasping for air. She patted the surface around her. In a few deep breaths, her heartbeat returned to normal as she realized she was in bed, not running from a cowl-covered madman shooting at her. She closed her eyes. A bad dream. That's all it had been.

The door to the bedroom burst open. "Carly, are you all right?"

Shane stood in the doorway, the light from the hall highlighting his muscular body. Excitement built inside her until she could barely look at him without wanting to touch. She swallowed a heart-thump and scooted to the edge of the bed. Gathering the blanket around her, she stood. "I'm fine. I had a nightmare."

Shane started forward.

But she held up her hand, and he stopped. They shouldn't be alone together again so soon. They had too much history. Too much bottled passion still simmered. She could feel the charge in the air. She nodded toward the phone on the nightstand. "I should call Ann. She must be frantic with worry."

"No need. I called her after you fell asleep."

Carly's nervous laugh came easily. "I can only image what her brain is spinning. I should go." She glanced to her neatly folded clothes on the dresser and realized she wore a man's T-shirt and not much of anything else. She didn't remember changing and didn't want to know how she got undressed. She tugged on the thin shirt's hem. "Can you take me home?"

"I can," Shane said, his voice low, his gaze on her.

Carly swallowed. "Will you take me home?" She walked to the dresser and gathered her clothes.

"Only if you insist."

Disappointment layered his voice. With her back to him, she started to pull on her jeans, but her foot tangled near the hem. As she stumbled, she reached out and broke her fall by grabbing onto the dresser, barely staying upright.

Shane came up behind her and clasped her waist, gently trapping her between his body and the bureau.

His breath, warm on her neck, made her tremble,

and she knew he could not help but notice. "Thanks." Her voice was nothing more than a shaky whisper. "A broken ankle is something I don't need."

He didn't move.

She didn't ask him to. Instead, she turned and locked her gaze with his. "You were my first."

Emotion flickered in his eyes. "I know," he whispered. He slid his hands slowly up her back. "Don't go." His gaze roamed her face. "Please."

She smiled. "I shouldn't be here. I'm sure the word is out, and the tabloid reporters have started to dig into your reason for doing the benefit. Even a hint about a past relationship with someone—a word from a volunteer, an employee of the school, or anyone and the media will make things sounds like a celebrity cheating scandal, only times a thousand."

"I don't care," he said quickly.

She could hear the conviction in his voice. Her shoulders dropped, and she lowered her chin, sighing. "Don't make me battle you."

"I don't want to fight." With the tip of his finger, he lifted her chin and made sure she caught his gaze. "I want to kiss you."

She said nothing, just looked into his eyes. The passion she saw simmering made everything inside her vibrate with desire.

He smiled. "I've barely touched you, and you're falling apart. That tells me you feel the same."

The sensual rasp to his voice made her breath come in short gasps. She could not have answered him if she wanted to. Her silence was the invitation Shane needed.

He eased his hand across her shoulder, over her waist, and curled his fingers around her backside.

His lips found hers, the kiss deeper and harder than any they shared before. Giving in to the sensation of the fiery path Shane's kisses blazed down her throat to the vee between her breasts, Carly let her head fall back. She could feel his hands open and close on her upper thighs.

"You are so beautiful," he whispered against her skin. "You were always the one. I have missed you so much."

And she believed him, believed the seriousness in his voice. In that moment, she also believed in the man. Not the darling of the tabloids, but the man she knew in Philadelphia, the man she never stopped loving. His touch turned gentle, but she felt the heat as though she stood next to an erupting volcano. When he grasped the edge of her T-shirt and slowly inched it upward, she closed her eyes. God help her, she wanted him.

"Tell me no, and I'll stop," he whispered into her ear.

Immobilized by her need, she took a deep breath and looked into his eyes. "Heaven help us, I don't want you to ever stop."

Tonight was not about the band, not about their history, about their future, or her fears. Tonight was about him. About her. About this moment, and this moment only. Banishing everything else from her mind, she focused on the sensations, the slide of heat and flesh, and the feel of his rising erection pressing against her thigh. She kissed his collarbone, breaking contact with his body only long enough for him to slip the T-shirt from her body.

He whispered her name and pulled her closer.

When his kisses trailed down her throat and across

the top of her breasts, her world tilted. Nothing mattered but Shane—his taste, his smell, the feel of his body beneath her fingers as her hands opened and closed against his back. She skimmed her hands underneath his shirt, her hands moving over the ribbed planes of his torso and the muscles of his sides and back. Her fingers continued to explore, and she heard him groan right before his hands clamped on her waist. His kiss intensified as he lifted her and began walking to the bed.

She wrapped her legs around him, and her panties gave way to skin. The scrape of her inner thighs across the rough material of his jeans excited her. She heard what sounded like a growl when he cupped her bottom to support her weight. Her hips moved in rhythmic want. Moisture gathered at the apex of her thighs where her body met the frustrating layer of his pants. She wanted more. She wanted it all.

As though in answer to her wishes, he lowered her onto the bed. Their gazes never broke contact as she freed herself from her panties. He stripped away his clothes and covered her nakedness with his own. All she could think, taste, and feel was Shane until a small part of her panicked. *What the hell are you doing? This is insane and irresponsible. You have no idea what you are getting yourself into.*

But the voice was soon silenced by the way his expert caresses coaxed her body to sing with pleasure. His kisses encouraged her to touch as he aligned his body with hers. She spread her knees and invited him into her body, knowing she was probably also inviting him back into her heart. She inhaled sharply as her flesh first clenched then softened to let him inside. He stilled, and she lifted her head to meet his gaze. Then he moved slowly and waited until she lifted her hips and arched against him.

Desire tightened, flooding her with pounding needs. She tangled her fingers in his hair as their bodies rose and fell. What began as gentle lovemaking soon moved into a frantic scramble, a straining union growing to only one possible ending. Explosion. Climax.

When the moment came, Carly cried out his name, not caring if anyone had come back to the house and heard her scream. Shane's movements continued as she released, pleasure pounding her.

He said her name as he followed her over the edge, shuddering with the force of his climax until he went limp and collapsed alongside her body.

She curled against his side.

He wrapped his arms around her and held her close.

"I've loved you since the first day we met," she whispered. "Through all the years we were apart and despite everything you told me, I can't stop how I feel." She cupped his cheek. "I don't know what tomorrow brings but whatever comes, we'll face it together."

His agreement came in his kiss and his need to love her again.

Chapter Ten

At the school the next evening, the noise inside the auditorium sounded like the roll of thunder. As the fans chanted the name of each band member in a litany of idolization, the decibel level approached the limit of human hearing tolerance. Each time the curtain moved, or a stagehand stepped onto the stage, the screaming and shouting of fans tripled in volume."Shaaaaaane!"

"Niles, we love you."

"Troy!"

"Peter!"

"We want the Rangers! We want the Rangers!"

Emily McKennan sliced back the stage curtain with her hand and peeked through the small slit she made. "Oh my," she said. "Not one seat left, is there?"

Carly peered around her. The auditorium was packed. "The benefit will be a huge success, largely due to your efforts."

"Yours, too, dear. You've done a wonderful job organizing the ticket sales and handling the money." Emily closed the peephole she made and turned. A smile of satisfaction crossed her face. "How are you and that young man of yours getting along? I saw you walking arm in arm, talking with heads together, and smiling like a couple of teenagers on their first date."

Carly tilted her head to one side and tried to keep her smile. If only Emily knew how terribly complicated the relationship had suddenly become. "We have to fill in the details of some lost time, but I think we can find a way to make it work." Without warning strong hands clasped themselves around her waist and spun her. Shane's kiss smothered her cry of surprise.

"Oh my, I think you definitely will find a way." Emily's smile spread. She raised the fingertips of her right hand to her lips and covered her amusement.

"Hello, Mrs. McKennan." Shane placed a quick kiss on Emily's check. "How is my biggest fan this evening?" He winked and wrapped an arm around the older woman's shoulders.

When the hug released, Emily smoothed her hair. "Why if I didn't know better, I would think you're flirting."

He put one arm around Emily's shoulders, the other around Carly's waist. "I'm standing between two of the most beautiful women in Hillsborough, so why not flirt a little?"

Emily waved off the compliment. "If I were forty years younger, I'd listen all day."

Shane smiled. "I'm sure Mr. McKennan tells you how beautiful you are all the time."

"He'd better," Emily said. "And now I'll leave you two alone so you can tell Carly." She winked and walked away.

"The media is right," Carly said. "Shane Fox is loved by women everywhere." Out of the corner of her eye, she caught a glimpse of Bobby checking the special effects connections stage left. "Did you find out why your brother didn't come back to the estate last night?"

Frowning, Shane glanced at Bobby. "Not yet. He's

been busy with the setup. I'll ask him later."

"Is the bike back?"

"Yeah. Niles put the Harley in the garage, but Bobby never came home."

Carly's brow furrowed. "Don't you find that rather odd?"

What sounded like a nervous chuckle escaped Shane. "I've always found my brother rather odd."

Voices rose from behind them. "Hey, break it up. We haven't had any time to talk to Carly since you've been monopolizing her time!"

Troy and Peter strode to them. Peter looped his hands around Carly's waist and pulled her close before kissing her cheek. "Good to see you. Would have told you last night"—he looked at Shane and winked—"but you were a tad busy." He released the affectionate hug. "Well, I, for one, am glad to see you two together." He tossed his head toward Shane. "Shane's been a bear at times since the split."

"A very angry bear," Troy agreed, twirling his drumsticks in the air.

Carly felt the warmth of a blush climb her neck. "Well, it's not quite as simple as being together."

"But we have started working on our relationship." Shane lowered his head, his lips hovering over Carly's. "A very pleasant beginning."

"Before you two plan a nice domestic future together, the show must go on." Peter headed for center stage.

Niles strode over. "So, this is the lady who's been stealin' our lead's attention." A grin curved his lips. He nodded to Shane. "How'd you ever let her go?"

"Big mistake on my part," Shane confessed.

Stage left, a technician adjusted his headset and held up his hand. "Five minutes!"

"That's our cue, guys," Troy said. "Later, Carly."

Shane looped his guitar over his shoulder. "Right after the show, I'll make sure Bobby didn't get into any trouble last night. Then how about you and I celebrate?"

"Do you think we have something to celebrate?" she asked with a smile. Her thoughts drifted to their night together.

"Hell yeah we do, girl!" Shane's gaze engaged a promise of what would come.

"Then let's celebrate."

"It's a date. Meet me backstage."

****

As Shane walked to his spot on the stage, he finally felt as though he had a clear plan for the future. First, he'd deal with his brother. If Bobby had another battle on his hands, this time the fight would be his. He'd paid a high price for helping Bobby in the past. Tonight belonged to Carly. A long time ago, he bought her an engagement ring. He made sure he had the ring when the band started the trip home. The diamond was small and the setting simple, but the love tucked inside was pure. If Carly wanted something bigger, brighter, or more glistening, he would buy another. Hell, he'd get her the Hope Diamond if that's what she wanted. All he wanted was an engagement ring on her finger with the promise of a gold band to match when she was ready.

The curtain opened, and the intro video played on the screen behind the band. As Shane's face appeared on the huge monitor, the crowd went wild. He began the opening number, and the spotlights highlighted the band members one by one until the last one illuminated Shane in bright white. He looked out at the audience, and for the first time in years, his smile felt real.

****

For a few minutes from stage left, Carly watched the band play before leaving to organize the receipts. The lively music and Shane's distinct voice kept her company as she counted the ticket money in the back room and prepared the night's take for deposit. She reached for the after-hours deposit bag but stopped when a feeling she was not alone rippled up her spine. She looked up.

Bobby stood in the doorway, with his arms crossed over his chest. "Big purse?"

"Nothing near what you are probably used to seeing for a Rangers' performance, but a sizable amount for the Center." She tucked a bundle of bills into the bank bag.

"Yeah, scratch for the guys. I give away more money in just the comps."

"I imagine you do." She gave him a sidelong glance. She wanted him gone. "Shouldn't you be backstage in case something goes wrong?"

"Not in a small venue like this." Bobby took two steps into the room. "Freebies suck. Managers, theater owners, promoters, record execs, and their friends all want something for nothing. They all want to sit in front, but brother dear insists the front rows belong to the real fans. Can you imagine?"

Carly nodded. "Yes, I can." She stuffed the last of the ticket money into the bank drop bag and zipped it closed. She made sure she caught his gaze. "You didn't come back to the estate last night."

"I had business."

She saw his expression harden. "Shane was worried about you."

Bobby snickered. "I bet he was."

Carly stood and walked closer. "Bobby, your brother cares about you. Why can't you see that?"

"I see a lot of things." He raised his hand. "Look, if this is another lecture on family, you can stop now."

"I'm not lecturing, but if something is bothering you, tell your brother." She put her hand on his arm. "You know he will help you."

Bobby shrugged away her touch and sneered. "Yeah, right. Like always."

The look on his face clearly told her to back off. "I guess you'll be staying on in New Jersey for a while."

"I suppose I'll have to get used to the mind-numbing boredom." Bobby rolled his eyes. "I hope my brother gets over whatever fixation he has these days."

"Hillsborough is not the happening place you are used to, but it's home and not boring to those of us who live here."

Bobby shrugged. "Whatever."

Carly opened her mouth to respond, but Shane's voice rang out in a familiar song, drawing her like the first day they met. She felt a slow smile creep across her face as she remembered the emotion he had put into making sure she knew he meant every word. She peered around Bobby. "I'd like to watch the show for a bit before I take the gate receipts to the bank night drop."

"Sure. I'll see ya after." He lifted his hand in a dismissing gesture.

As he did, Carly noticed cuts and bruises on the back of his wrist. "What happened?" She motioned to his hand.

Bobby recoiled and covered the marks. "A couple of the instruments fell when I was setting up backstage."

"Some of the cuts look rather deep." She reached for his hand.

He shoved his hand into the pocket of his jeans. "Nothing more than scratches. I tried to catch one of the guitars and missed."

"Still, you can get a nasty infection. Maybe a doctor should look at that cut." She saw his eyes flare, and the intensity surprised her. She stepped back.

"I can take care of myself."

"I didn't mean to…" Bobby left before she could finish. His actions baffled her. The man had everything he could ever want including a brother who loved him. She wondered if he would ever be happy. Burying building uncertainty, she walked to the right side of the stage but stayed well out of sight of the audience.

Shane was near the chorus of the song.

When Carly came into his sight line, she caught his gaze. A sensuous spark passed between them as Shane sang through his smile, seemingly singing the song only for her. His gaze never left her face, and she felt his feelings release in the words.

Shane's voice surrounded her with emotions that wove themselves deep into her soul. She wanted to stay and listen, but she had a promise to keep. She sent an air kiss his way before returning to the back room. After gathering her belongings and the night drop bag, she walked out of the school to her car. Once the money was safely in the bank, her commitment to the Center would be over for the evening and her commitment to

Shane could begin.

****

Parked covertly across the street from the school's parking lot, Erno Scodari's gaze followed every move Carly made. "Remember her, Tino. Remember the car, her routine, where she goes, and with whom she speaks. You will become her shadow until all is settled."

Tino glanced at back seat through the rear view mirror. "But, boss, I don't understand. Who is the woman?"

"A wrinkle," Scodari replied, narrowing his eyes and creasing his brow in thought. "A small wrinkle in an otherwise perfect blueprint. One, I'm afraid, we may have to iron out before too long."

****

When Carly returned to the high school after making the night drop, the concert was over.

Wooden barriers lined the edge of the parking lot to help control the swell of people waiting for the Rangers. Screaming fans pressed against the barricade ignoring the police officers traversing in front of them.

Carly parked in the lot of the park across the street, walked to the school's rear entrance, and ran into almost as many fans waiting. She bounced off excited concertgoers as she made her way to the door. Members of the security team recognized her and let her inside. After passing through more security, she walked backstage. The first band member she saw was Troy. "Have you seen Shane?"

Troy tossed his head. "He was by the equipment van talking to Bobby. Must still be there."

"Thanks." She headed off toward the loading dock. When she got there, Bobby was helping to dismantle the equipment and directing the gear out the service door and into the truck blazoned with the Rangers logo. He didn't look too upset. Maybe the talk with Shane had gone well. She scanned the area. "Where's Shane?"

Bobby didn't look up. "Left about five minutes ago."

"He's gone?" She frowned. "We were supposed to meet here after the concert."

Bobby cut his gaze to her for a moment then continued breaking down the equipment. "His plans changed."

Because she knew the look, that none-of-your-business smirk, she stood over him. "Cut the crap, and tell me where he went. You know. I can feel it."

Bobby finished packing a guitar and glared. "His ultra-fanatic lady friend called during the concert. She said they needed to talk. I gave him the message after the last set, and he rushed out of here."

Carly dropped her lashes to hide the hurt in her eyes, an all-too-familiar sense of emptiness returning to her heart. "He's meeting her?"

"I guess." Bobby shrugged.

A jolt of heartache reverberated right through her. "Did Shane say anything else?"

"Nope. Ask Troy. Maybe he knows more."

"Troy said Shane was with you."

Bobby tossed his head. "Obviously, he's not."

Carly flinched and took out her cell phone.

"Don't bother," Bobby said. "I have his phone. Mine ran out of power, and I needed to make a call."

"How am I supposed to get in touch with him then?"

Bobby shot her a smug smile. "Guess you're not."

Carly ignored the cutting remark. "Did he say when he would be back?"

"No, but he was mad, mighty mad. Never saw him that angry."

"Did something happen?"

"Listen, I'm not Shane's babysitter. My job is to make sure the gear is packed up and out of here, so see ya." Offering her a distracted nod, he walked away.

His tone challenged. Hurt, angry, concerned and puzzled all at the same time, Carly could not move, her mind and body equally numb. Only one thing could have lured away Shane. The results of the paternity test must have come in. Another round of painful thoughts assailed her, and she feared the worst.

How ironic. After confessing her feelings and deciding to accept what destiny had in store for them, she suddenly felt trapped. Cold certainty hit her like a hard slap to the face. The time had arrived discover if the choice she made to give back her heart to Shane was the right one.

Chapter Eleven

Carly spent the rest of the night home on the sofa, waiting for Shane while trapped in a terror-filled nightmare laden with threats, accusations, and betrayal in which Shane and Danni were the stars. She felt empty, cold as though life inside her had been extinguished forever. In twenty-four hours, she had gone from the high of hope to the depth of despair. She shivered and pulled an afghan up to her neck. She didn't know if she would ever feel warm again.

Nothing appeared to fit into the gigantic paradox Shane had laid at her feet. Somewhere was the one piece of the puzzle, the one link, tying everything together—Shane, Danni, Bobby, the man in the limousine, the accident, the lost time. Like the proverbial round pegs in square holes, she could not make the events of the last few days fit and make sense. She sat and hung her head in her hands. *This cannot be happening. I can't lose him again.* She couldn't stay home and do nothing. She had to find him. She passed the front door on her way upstairs to shower just as someone knocked. "Shane," she whispered, more in hope than in anything else. Instead, she opened the door to a police officer and a detective holding out his badge. Heart began to race. *Something's wrong.*

"Miss Mitchell?" the detective asked.

"Yes. Can I help you?"

"I'm Detective Carter, and this is Officer Johnson." The uniformed officer nodded.

"We understand you were one of the last people to see Shane Fox last night," Carter said.

One of the last people? Icy fingers wrapped themselves around her heart and seeped into every pore of her body. A heavy feeling of panic settled into her stomach. "Is everything all right? Is Shane all right?"

"We don't know," Carter answered.

Eyes wide and heart pounding, she gripped the door, questions surfacing. "Where is he? What's happened? Is he hurt?"

Carter did not answer. Motioning past her, he asked, "May we come in for a minute?"

Carly opened the door wider. Her throat closed as she motioned for the two men to follow her. Visions of a twisted motorcycle and Shane's broken body face down on the road flashed before her eyes. A chilled silence surrounded her. "Please, sit." She gestured to the sofa, her voice shaky.

Carter shook his head as the uniformed officer walked the room. "We'd rather not. Let me get right to the point. Is Mr. Fox here?"

"He's alive?" Carly's heart leapt.

"I assume so." Detective Carter shot her an accusing stare. "Is he here?"

"No. I haven't seen him since before the show began. Why?"

"We need to talk to him."

"About what?" Carly asked. The icy feeling inside turned into an arctic blast.

Carter's face tightened. "Is he here, Ms. Mitchell?"

She straightened her shoulders and lifted her chin.

"I already told you. No."

"Ms. Mitchell, do I have your permission to search your house?"

Carter's tone was textbook calm. "Search my house?" She hardly recognized her own voice. She watched him shifted his gaze and knew he was inspecting the room. "No."

The detective wrote something in the notebook he held and slid it inside his coat pocket. "I can wait for the search warrant. A uniform has taken one to a judge for review. Shouldn't take long. I'll be outside." He gave her an impersonal nod and turned.

Carly grabbed his arm. "Wait." She fought to control the swelling panic. "Please, tell me what this is all about." She looked from the detective to the officer, but their stoic expressions told her nothing.

"You don't know?"

"No." Uncertainty made her voice raspy.

Detective Carter pulled out his notepad and sifted through the pages. "At approximately 6:00 a.m. today, the desk sergeant received a call from a Charlotte Kilmer, owner of a rooming house on Fifth Street." He looked up and centered his gaze on Carly's face before continuing to read. "Ms. Kilmer became concerned when one of her tenants did not answer the door. After knocking a few more times, Ms. Kilmer used her master key to let herself in the apartment. She reported that the place was in shambles and lying on the floor next to the sofa was Danielle Baker. Dead."

In shock, Carly dropped into a chair. Her hand flew to her mouth. Tiny black dots danced before her eyes and, if not for sheer determination, she would have collapsed. Bobby said Shane was going to see Danni, and now Danni was dead. She had to take several deep breaths until she could speak. "And you think Shane is somehow involved?" She could barely hear her voice over the white noise that filled her head from the rapid beating of her heart.

Carter's face did not betray any emotion. "How well did Mr. Fox know Ms. Baker?"

Carly took several deep breaths. "He said they were friends. Why?"

"We have reason to believe Mr. Fox might have been the last person to see Miss Baker alive."

"Are you sure?" Carly felt her stomach drop and fought to keep any reaction from her face.

Carter nodded. "When the coroner examined the victim, he found a slip of paper under her body."

Warning spasms shot through Carly. "A note?" Her voice was barely audible.

Carter shook his head. "The paper, Miss Mitchell, was the results of a paternity test. Mr. Fox and Miss Baker were a little more than friends. They were parents."

****

Carly hardly remembered dressing, let alone riding to police headquarters in the back of the cruiser. She didn't know how long she had been in the holding room sitting across from Detective Carter answering questions, but she realized several hours had gone by. Her stomach growled with hunger. "Listen," she said, angry at the hard line of lengthy questioning but trying to maintain calm, "I've told you everything I know at least twelve times." She balled her hands into fists. "I came here to help, but all I've gotten from you are questions and innuendo. Either charge me with something, or let me go."

Carter looked up from the papers spread across the table that separated them. "I'll be right back." With a glance at her, he left.

Frustration forced tears to gather in the corners of Carly's eyes. She agreed to go to headquarters and answer some questions, but in doing so, she became part of the homicide investigation. She knew criminal analysis took time, especially in small towns not equipped to handle something as explosive as a murder. She was more than exhausted from answering question upon question, denying charges carefully placed as facts, and going over the events of the past week until she thought her head would explode.

She rose and paced. She should have stopped the questioning hours ago. Drained both mentally and physically, she did not want talk to anyone anymore. All she wanted was to get out of the station and find Shane before the police did. He was the only one with the answers she needed to hear.

Carter returned and sat across from her. He took a small notebook from his inside coat pocket. "Just a few more questions."

Carly let out a long, exasperated breath of air and dropped into the hard wooden chair across the table from him. "If it will get me out of here, then fine."

"You said you were meeting Mr. Fox after the concert, but when you got back to the school, he had already left."

"That's right."

"He didn't say where he was going?"

"I told you, I hadn't seen him since the concert began."

"Well then, during the times you did see him, did he ever become violent for any reason?"

"No." Carly's mouth went dry with the lie. Knowing Carter was a seasoned veteran, she fought to control the expression on her face as the shoving scene she witnessed between Danni and Shane replayed in her mind.

"Did you know Miss Baker?"

"We met by accident one day."

"Did you know she was the mother of Shane Fox's child?"

"No," she quickly answered and then just as quickly she lifted her chin and added, "I don't believe Shane is the child's father."

The detective raised his eyebrows. "That isn't what the DNA test said. The test is accurate to 99.999 percent."

"Tests can sometimes be wrong," she countered. "Or mishandled. Mislabeled. Anything."

Carter smirked. "And you know this because?"

Heat rose with the blush forming on her face and neck. "Everyone makes mistakes."

He shook his head. "I don't think in this case."

She flattened her hands on the tabletop and leaned forward. "And you know this because?"

One side of Carter's mouth pulled upward. "Are you stalling until Mr. Fox has enough time to get away? I can charge you with aiding and abetting, Miss Mitchell."

Her anger finally broke. "Don't you point your badge at me." Her nostrils flared."Unless things have changed, the law says innocent until proven guilty, and that's exactly how I see the situation even if you don't."

She met his accusing gaze without flinching.

He pressed his mouth into a straight line. "We're not at liberty to discuss any evidence we do have at this time."

As disciplined as she was trying to remain, Carly's nervousness slipped back to grip her. She didn't know for sure what evidence the police had and hearing the results of the paternity test from Carter made doubt bubble inside her. She hoped she could control the emotional turmoil and not let her fear show on her face or slip into her voice. "I will believe the test results when Shane tells me." She was pleased her tone sounded neutral.

"Then you do expect to hear from Fox." He made another entry in his notebook.

"No, I don't expect anything."

Carter closed his notebook and slid it onto the table. "But you might."

She did not make eye contact. "And I might not." After a few seconds of silence, she looked at him. "Are we finished? Can I go?" Standing to signal she felt the question-and-answer session was over, she squared her shoulders and crossed her arms.

The interrogation door opened, and a uniformed officer entered. "Art, the Captain wants to see you as soon as you're done."

Carter rose from his chair. "I think Miss Mitchell and I have discussed just about everything we need to for now." He focused his gaze on Carly's face. "You can go now, Miss Mitchell, but if you do hear from Fox, be sure to let us know."

"Thank you." Carly was afraid to say anything else. She didn't want to waste time with more questions. She needed to get out of the police station and find Shane. Just as she got to the door, she spotted Carter step in front of her,

"Another thing, Miss Mitchell, don't leave town."

Carly made sure she captured his gaze. "I wouldn't dream of it." She gave Carter one last hard look and strode from the room. In the hallway, she leaned against the wall to gather her migrant thoughts. The interrogation room door was ajar, and she could hear the discussion inside.

"Well, what do you think?" The officer who last entered asked.

Carly heard the scraping sound of a chair sliding across the tile floor, and then a thud like a briefcase hitting the metal table. She took a step closer.

"The house was clean and, after hearing Mitchell's statement, I think she's telling the truth. She hasn't seen him. But we'll put a tail on her anyway," Carter said.

"What about Fox? Do you think he did it?"

The conversation hit her like icy air. Despite her refusal, the police searched her home while she was at the station. Furious, but being careful not to make a sound, Carly inched closer. She was anxious to hear what the detective might say next.

"Yeah," Carter said. "I think he did it. Perfect motive. Old love rekindled, so the jilted mistress counters with a love child. Fox has no choice but to get rid of the problem." He snapped his fingers. "No doubt in my mind he did it all right." He slammed shut his briefcase. "And I'm just the guy to nail the son of a bitch."

Having heard enough, Carly hurried away. Once outside the police station, she inhaled deeply to clear her head as she half-walked, half-ran to the parking lot. Then she remembered. A police officer had driven her to the station. She would have to walk. She hoped the trip home on foot would help her sort out truth from supposition, but by the time she arrived home, she had to admit the deck was certainly stacked against Shane. The evidence clearly showed he had both motive and opportunity. She strode to the back door of her house and stopped when the enormity of what occurred in the last twenty-four hours wound itself around her. Her heartbeat rose, and her breath came in short gasps as panic rose. She turned and scanned the backyard.

Where are you, Shane?

Was he hiding in a local motel, or had he run? She folded her arms across her chest and looked at the ground. His blatant absence made him seem guilty. That was what the police thought. The media would conclude the same now that Danni's murder was probably the lead story on every major television network and social media page.

She was alone, but so was Shane. She dropped her head into her hands. Tears filled her palms. She may be the only person left who didn't think Shane was murder suspect number one, and proving his innocence might very well be up to her alone.

Chapter Twelve

Carly pushed open her back door and stepped inside. She got as far as the kitchen table before a hand caught her around the waist and another wrapped across her mouth. Basic survival instincts made her struggle against the hold. Instead of tightening, the hold released.

"Don't scream."

Shane. Relief flooded her, and she flung herself into his arms. "I've been frantic with worry. The police were here."

"They still are." He took her hand and led her to the living room. Carefully staying to the right of the front window, he pulled aside the curtain just enough to see out. "There." With the toss of his head, he motioned to a nondescript dark blue car parked a little way down the street. "Unmarked police car got here a few minutes ago. Looks like you'll have company for a while." He moved his hand, and the curtain fluttered almost unnoticeably back into place. With a forefinger across his lips, he walked back to the kitchen.

Wordlessly, Carly followed and sat on one of the wooden chairs. She looked at him. He had the scraggy look of an unfinished statue, disheveled and fragmented. As he raked his fingers through his unruly hair, she could see a furrowed brow with worry and distinct lines of fatigue etched beneath heavy lidded eyes.

He moved slowly to a kitchen chair and placed both hands on the backrest before hunching over and letting out a deep sigh. "I should have stayed away, but I had to see you."

Carly tipped back her head and stared at the ceiling as she struggled to hold her conflicting emotions in check. "The police think you had something to do with Danni's death. The theory is you wanted her out of the way so she couldn't go to the media with the story about your love child." She kept her gaze locked with his.

Shane's muscles tensed. "What do you think?"

"I need to hear the truth from you." Carly wrung her hands in her lap while she waited for Shane's reply.

He dropped into the chair facing her. "The truth?" Dejection layered his voice. "Because of what happened last night, a future together may be impossible. A life we can share may only be a dream. That's my truth." The muscle along his jaw tensed. He shook his head slowly. "I really messed up this time."

Raw hurt glittered in Shane's eyes. Carly felt her stomach churn. "Did you kill her, Shane?" She forced out the words, the ache inside her feeling like a knife to her heart.

Shane bolted to his feet. "No. She was already dead when I got to the rooming house."

Carly searched his expression, hoping to see a sign affirming he was telling the truth, but she saw only exhaustion. She held his gaze but said nothing.

Shane's brows drew down as he sat. "You don't believe me."

Her body tensed. She was not sure that she did.

"Bobby said Danni called and asked you to meet her, and you did." She looked away and then quickly back. "You want me to believe in the twenty minutes or so you drove from the high school to the rooming house someone killed her and left before you arrived?" She shook her head. "Danni wasn't in town long enough to make that kind of enemy."

"We weren't meeting at the rooming house," Shane countered. A grimace pulled his lips together in a tight line.

She frowned. "Bobby didn't mention that."

"He probably didn't want you to get involved. He knows how Danni can get."

A cold feeling settled into Carly's stomach. "You and I were supposed to meet after the concert. Why didn't you wait and tell me?"

He reached for her hand. "Sometimes, Danni has a rough time staying rational. I'm used to her bipolar behavior, and she can be a handful when confronted. I didn't want her to lash out at you. That's why I went alone."

"I can take care of myself." Her pulse pounded in her ears as she tried to read Shane's face. Was he telling her the truth or another story? Troubled, she blurted, "From the beginning, Shane. Tell me what happened."

Shane's lips thinned, and he stared at the tabletop for a moment. Then his gaze captured hers. "Danni said we had to talk and what she had to tell me could not wait."

Carly saw a wave of worry wash across Shane's face. "Bobby told you that."

Shane nodded. "I assumed the paternity results had come, and Danni was distraught because I wasn't the

161

father of her child."

For a split second, Carly's vision blurred, and white noise grew inside her head. She took several deep breaths before she spoke. "We agreed to find out together. You must have thought a chance existed." She saw a look of anguish fill Shane's eyes.

He pinched his lips tight and shook his head. "You don't know her like I do, Carly. She has done things in the past to hurt people."

"All the more reason to not go alone."

"I should have sensed something was wrong." He leaned back in the chair and rubbed the back of one hand across his eyes. "I was supposed to meet Danni at the old Bridgepoint Farm in Montgomery. At first, I didn't like the idea. I thought she might be setting some kind of trap."

Her brow furrowed. "To do what?"

"I don't know. Cry rape afterward, or perhaps bring an uncle or a big brother to force me into admitting something that wasn't true. Who knows?" He shook his head. "Danni didn't deal always with reality well."

"But you left to meet her anyway." In his eyes, Carly could see regret. Determined to let him finish, she pressed her lips into a thin line.

"I thought she might want to avoid a public discussion because of the test results. I was actually hoping this would be the last time I ever saw her. I thought once we had this talk, we both could get on with our lives."

Her heart stumbled over mixed emotions. "You were sure the test results proved her claim wrong."

Shane nodded. "And because she wanted to meet

me outside of town, I was also sure she was upset and embarrassed." He rose from the chair and paced. "When I got to the farm, I parked the bike outside the barn then went inside. I didn't see Danni. I looked around, but the place seemed deserted. I waited for about an hour before deciding she must have changed her mind. I hopped on the bike and rode to the rooming house."

"What time?"

"Close to two a.m. by then. I remember seeing the door on the bottom floor open a little when I walked the stairs to Danni's room. The door to Danni's apartment was ajar. I knocked, and it swung open." His eyes widened. "The place was a mess, like someone had gone through it with a bulldozer. Then out of the corner of my eye, I saw her lying on the floor. I called out her name, but when I touched her hand all I felt was cold. I checked for a pulse, but she was dead." He groaned. "I know I should have stayed and called the police, but I thought about the accident and was afraid whomever killed Danni might be going after you. I reached for my phone and remembered Bobby had it. So I ran down the stairs and jumped on the bike, intent on getting to you."

She frowned. "But you didn't come back to the school." She stared and in his eyes, she could almost see the gears in his mind turning.

He nodded. "I rode a few blocks, and guilt kicked in. I had to go back."

Carly saw pain ripple across his face. "I stopped the bike a few blocks from the rooming house, because I could see flashing police lights. I guess the landlady got curious about the noise and commotion, went upstairs, saw Danni, and called the police right after I left. I ditched the bike and walked in the shadows until I got close enough to hear an officer taking her statement. She reported hearing shouting coming from the apartment earlier, suggested that I came back to finish the argument, and ended up killing Danni."

Her heart racing, Carly met his gaze. She swallowed hard to clear the lump in her throat. "You have to turn yourself in and clear your name."

Shane placed the heels of his hands on his temples. "Not yet. I have no alibi. No one saw me at the farm. Unless I can find who killed Danni, I am suspect number one. If I'm in jail, I can't prove I'm innocent."

She saw the way his eyes darkened. Her shoulders dropped. "Shane, you're a public figure. You can't hide."

"I have to try." He took her hand. "Once the tabloids get this story, I'll be convicted before I ever get to trial. This is a high-profile murder, sure to make a top ten countdown recap on some cable station special."

"Worse," Carly said in a low voice. "The results of the paternity test were found near Danni's body." Nerves fluttered in her chest as she waited for his reaction.

Shane paled. "Do you know the results?" A muscle ticked at the corner of Shane's jaw.

"The test confirmed you are the father of her child. The police are now calling her death a crime of passion and a love triangle murder." She saw Shane flinch and his eyes go dark. Shock? Fear? She didn't know for certain what caused the change.

He ran his hand through his hair. "Something has to be wrong with the test."

"DNA doesn't lie, Shane." She bristled.

"Hillsborough might not be a big city, but I am pretty sure the labs around here are competent." The pain in his eyes deepened.

His body slumped. Shane frowned. "I'm telling you the truth." He grabbed her shoulders. "I drank a lot the night Danni climbed into my bed, so I'm pretty sure the only thing I did do was sleep next to her. Despite what the tabloids say about me, I'm not a heartless prick. If for one moment I thought Nicky was my son, I would take care of him."

Heart racing, she shrugged free of his grasp. "I don't know who you are anymore, but I know I can't help you if you only tell me snippets of the past."

"Okay." He pulled over a chair and sat. He opened his mouth then stopped and let out a long breath. "I only wanted to shield you from the garbage and games people play in my world. TV, the media, and trash magazines all thrive on dirt. Good news doesn't help the ratings or sell copies of magazines and newspapers. I thought the test results would finally free me of Danni. Afterward, I planned on telling you every detail."

She heard the tone of his voice drop and lifted her chin. "Your plan didn't quite work out. Lies always get in the way."

He stared over her shoulder. "In my world, lies are second nature. You learn to ignore them." He recaptured her gaze. "But you haven't played the fame game, so I couldn't expect you to understand and accept my reality."

"Fathering a child is no game, Shane, and stop protecting me from what is real. Only deception can hurt me." She took a deep, shaky breath and held it, finding agreement among the pain in his eyes.

Shane let out a long breath. "Right after the Rangers' fifth album went triple platinum, the record company threw us the biggest party in rock history. The title song on the album was "Melody For A Memory," a song originally recorded by Hall and Oates. Do you know the song?"

Carly nodded. "Your remix of Melody was the most downloaded song on all the music sites on the web and stayed on top for nearly four months." The words to that song were beautiful, haunting, and very emotional, so reminiscent of her love for Shane. For a solid year after the song released, she could not bear to hear even the opening bars.

He took her hand and traced a heart in her palm. "I sang Melody for you." His voice broke. "I never told anyone in the group, but they all knew. The release party only made the memories worse. I grabbed whatever drink passed on a waiter's tray to get you out of my head. Either none of the drinks was potent enough, or the memories of us were stronger. To make matters worse, everyone in the damn room made it their mission to introduce me to one girl or another. Then Danni was there. She was on my heels all night, doing everything she could to get me upstairs and into bed."

Pulse pounding, Carly pulled free her hand. "She apparently succeeded." Anger built—anger at her young, naïve self for falling so hard for Shane, anger at Shane for spending ten years wandering through life without thinking of the consequences, and anger for allowing herself to think none of that mattered now. "Just tell me you didn't sleep with her."

"Sleep, yes. Have sex, no!" Shane drew his hand

into a tight fist until the knuckles turned white. He took a long shuddering breath and held her gaze.

She became acutely aware of her beating heart. Foreboding filled her. This was the moment she had been dreading since her world exploded the night of the concert. "Tell me what happened that night."

"I'm no romance movie hero, Carly. I'm human. I was lonely and stupid," Shane said.

His voice was rough with emotion, and the pain on his face made her realize just how divergent their lives had become since Philadelphia. He was right. She could not imagine what being in the public eye twenty-four/seven and three-sixty-five could be like. Maybe in giving his all to reach his dream, he paid for stardom with his freedom and the right to determine his own future. After taking a deep breath, she reached for his hand. "Go on."

His fingers tightened around hers. "I drank too much that night, so much that Bobby had to help me upstairs and into bed. I was alone then. I'm sure. The last face I saw before I passed out was Bobby's. But in the morning, Danni was in bed with me, smiling, naked, her arms laced around my chest. She said we made love all night."

Everything inside Carly went cold. "Did you?" Her voice trailed off to a hoarse whisper. "I need to know."

He tried to smile but failed. "Truth is, after all the liquor I put away, I don't think I could have."

Carly fought to focus on the possibility he could be right and not on the picture her mind conjured of Danni and Shane in each other's arms. She sucked in a breath. "I suppose that's feasible." Something else lingered in his eyes, something dark yet remorseful. He hadn't told her the whole truth. "Did you sleep around a lot while we were apart?"

Frowning, he looked away and then quickly back."In the beginning, when I realized any relationship with you was over, I tried to forget you. I dated plenty of beautiful women but even with them, I thought about you. I went through the motions of bringing arm candy to award shows, models to trendy restaurants, and willing groupies to after-parties, but I could never give myself totally to any woman. I always knew the only woman I would ever love was you." He reached for her, stopping short of touching.

Eyes closed, Carly rose and sucked in a deep breath. What seemed like an eternity later, she opened her eyes. Shane's hand still beckoned. She stepped forward and accepted.

****

Slowly, he stood. He could hardly believe she would stand by him. He closed his eyes and pulled her into his arms. He could feel her tremble and waited until she stilled before moving back and putting his fingertips under her chin. Gently, he tilted her face upward. Slowly, he lowered his head, hoping she would not resist when his lips took hers in a soft caress. He broke the kiss and looked into her eyes. She was staring the way a frightened animal looked at a predator about to pounce. The look in her eyes pulled deep inside, and his throat tightened. He feared he had lost her again, maybe this time for good. The question rose…would she tell him to leave? He had to let her decide. "I've loved you forever, Carly, and I'll love you for the rest of my life and beyond—no matter what you decide and no matter what happens after I walk out the door." He pressed his lips together and waited for her reaction. Tears formed in her eyes, and when a soft sob escaped her throat, he had his answer.

He kissed her, and confirmation came in her returning kiss. He lifted his mouth and buried his face against her neck. The hopelessness he felt released. He could now accept his fate. If no one else believed he was innocent, he knew Carly did.

Chapter Thirteen

Shane released Carly and placed his palms on the table.

She could see his forearms quiver as if supporting a great weight. Concern jolted through her. She grabbed his arm. "Are you all right?"

He straightened and ran his fingers along the bridge of his nose. "I'm fine."

He didn't sound fine. He sounded exhausted and depressed. She saw sadness in his eyes that deepened with each passing moment.

"That may have been a goodbye kiss." He pulled her close and rested his chin on the top of her head. "Now is as good a time as any to turn myself in."

The musky scent of his skin, a heady mixture of man and desire, was almost her undoing. She could not afford to let her own longing distract her. She closed her eyes to clear her head and thought back to nonstop questions and carefully placed innuendo so much a part of the interrogation she'd undergone. "You're too tired to think straight when the questioning starts at the police station. Before you do anything, you need to rest." She took his hand and walked to the hall staircase.

Shane stopped at the bottom of the stairs. "I can't stay here." He walked back to the kitchen.

She couldn't let him leave. She wasn't ready to

face the possibility she would never see him again except through thick glass in the visitors' section of a jail. "No one knows you're here. I know every law enforcement agency in the area is looking for you, but if we don't give the police watching the house a reason to come inside, you could get at least a few hours of sleep."

He took her hand and watched as his thumb traced circles on her skin. He looked up and met her gaze. "You understand if the police do come inside and search, you'll be considered an accomplice," he said through a small, tight-lipped grimace.

"Let me worry about that. No one's coming in without a search warrant." She steered him toward the staircase. "Go upstairs while I scrounge around for some clean clothes. I'm sure Ann's boyfriend left something."

Shane put his hand on the railing and turned. "This isn't the way things were supposed to turn out." He reached for her, and she folded herself into his arms. "I make the worst decisions when doing what is best for you." He sighed. "I should have asked you to come with me when I left Philly."

She sucked in a breath. "I would have followed you anywhere. Love. Sex. Lust. Whatever you wanted, I would have given you and never looked back."

His lips thinned. "That would have been a disaster."

His face was devoid of brightness. She had never seen his eyes so dark. "For whom?"

"For us both.

Memories she'd buried by sheer willpower broke free. Biting her lower lip, she shook her head. "We'll never know." Her words echoed her longing.

"Those years, I lived them. Every day came with temptations and distortions." He shook his head. "My life may have seemed exciting, but there are times I'd rather not remember."

"I remember other times," she said softly.

His eyes darkened. "What could you possibly remember about me that doesn't end in pain?"

"This." Knowing this was probably the worst time to be thinking about his arms curling around her and the way she fit into the curves and planes of his body, she ascended one step and kissed him with every ounce of conviction she had. She fed off the flare of heat rising between them and swallowed the sound Shane made as she swept her tongue inside his mouth. Rather than listening to the inner voice warning her of the consequences, she grabbed onto his shoulders and hung on for the ride as he carried her up the stairs and set her down on the landing.

When his hands cupped her backside and urged her closer, a small sound of surrender escaped between kisses. With no thought of retreat, she pressed deeper into his body. She murmured his name, or maybe he said hers. She wasn't sure, and it didn't matter.

Wanting more, she moved her thigh against his erection. With a groan, he freed her bottom and grabbed her around the waist before lifting her and backing her against the wall outside her bedroom door. He aligned his hand palm to palm, and their fingers intertwined. Slowly, he raised her hands over her head, pressed against her, and kissed her as desperately as she kissed him.

Then suddenly he jerked away. His handhold

tightened painfully. He stared.

The defeated look in his eyes frightened her. "Shane, what's wrong?" She tugged on their clasped hands. "You're hurting me." She yanked harder but couldn't break the hold. When he suddenly released her, she stumbled back, arms windmilling.

Shane stood silent, staring past her.

Carly reached out. "Please. Tell me. What is it?"

Shaking his head, he started toward the front door. "I can't let you do this. Forget me, Carly. Make a life for yourself."

Her breath caught. She would not let him leave her again. She blocked his path. "Never again." She put her arm around his waist and led him back to the stairs. "You aren't making sense because you are exhausted. When you get a few hours of sleep, we will decide what to do together."

"This is too much of a risk," Shane protested. He reached for her hand then stopped.

Carly saw his frown deepen. She took his hand and held it firmly. "One I am willing to take. I can't let you talk to the police before you rest. I know how I was treated. In your state, you may be talked into signing a statement you don't mean." She swallowed hard at the thought. "You can't prove you are innocent if you're in jail."

He put his hand on the wall and leaned away as he walked. "Jail seems inevitable, Carly."

"But you aren't there now. We can still fight." She took his face between her palms and captured his gaze. "Together."

Shane nodded and walked at her side until he stretched out on her bed. "I didn't realize how tired I am until now." He settled into the pillow. "I'll just close my eyes for a few minutes. I won't sleep."

Carly sat beside him as he lost the battle. Lightly, she fingered a curl tumbling onto his forehead. "I'll do a little investigating while you rest. The police will follow me when I leave, so you should be safe here." She knew he hadn't heard a word. The slow, rhythmic rising and falling of his chest were proof he fell asleep almost as soon as the last words of protest left his lips.

Leaning over, she kissed his cheek. He shifted but did not awaken. "Sweet dreams. When I get back, perhaps this will be all over."

****

Carly sat in the family room of Emily McKennan's large home and declined an offer of coffee with a small wave. "I'm sorry I didn't call first." She inhaled the aroma of fresh baked cookies. She looked over Emily's shoulder to the utensil-filled island that separated the kitchen from the living area. "I've interrupted your baking."

"The Judge and I are leaving for a short vacation, and Edmond likes to snack." Emily smiled. "It seems like years since we have any extended time together."

Carly nodded. She bit down on her lower lip and wondered if she should even involve the Judge's wife.

Emily stared for a long moment and shook her head. "I think I know why you've come."

The events of the past few days boiled inside her—all the confessions and admissions and an innuendo or two tossed in to complicate things—and suddenly she could not keep her lower lip from trembling."I don't think Shane killed Danni Baker," she said, conviction in her voice. "I could really use your help proving his

174

innocence." She was taking a chance confiding in Emily, especially with Judge McKennan still active on the bench.

Emily leaned forward. "Isn't that better left to the authorities, dear?" She grasped Carly's hand. "The truth always comes out."

"I don't think the police believed much of what I told them, and they certainly won't believe Shane." Carly stared at her lap and clutched Emily's hand before looking up. "I may be the only hope he has right now."

Emily broke the contact and straightened. "Tell me how I can help."

"The night of the concert, was everything all right?" she asked in a rush. She forced herself to slow when she added, "Did you see or hear anything that seemed odd?"

Emily tapped a forefinger on her chin. "I had a hard time hearing anything. The noise was incredible."

"Did you see anyone who looked like he or she didn't belong?" Carly leaned forward. "Did anyone act suspicious or try to blend into the background?"

"Not that I remember." Emily shook her head.

Carly hoped disappointment didn't show on her face. "If you think of anything that could help, please call me."

"Of course. But Edmond and I are leaving in the morning." She walked to a roll-top desk in the dining room and took out a brochure. "Here's where we will be staying." She handed the flyer to Carly and folded her fingers around it. "Call me if you need to talk."

"Thank you." Carly nodded, eyes brimming with controlled tears.

Emily started for the door then suddenly stopped. "I hate to ask you at a time like this, but I would like one favor." She opened a drawer in the library table sitting along the wall in the hallway and held out a DVD and flash drive. "Can you hold on to these while the Judge and I are away?"

"What are these?" Carly dropped the disc and drive into her handbag.

"One of the theater students recorded the concert to help the Center raise additional funds from DVD sales. He also saved the event on that flash drive so copying the material would be easy." Frowning, Emily shook her head. "But under the current circumstances, the Abuse Center Board isn't sure about those plans. Hopefully, your young man's difficulty will clear, and the Center can go forward with selling the concert footage."

The last thing Carly wanted right now was the opportunity to see Shane's concert on demand. She opened her bag and reached inside. "Maybe you should keep the video."

Emily waved off the attempted return. "I have developed a nasty habit of misplacing things. Until the Board makes a final decision, I'd rather you keep the recordings. Would you mind, dear?"

"Of course not." Carly tucked the video back in her handbag. She put her hand on the doorknob and turned to Emily. "Shane didn't kill anyone, Mrs. McKennan. He's a good man."

Emily patted Carly's shoulder. "I said the same thing to Edmond this morning before he went out for his daily run."

Carly nodded and stepped onto the front porch as

the door closed behind her. Disappointment welled in her heart. She hadn't obtained any information she could use to help Shane, and she didn't know where else to look for some. As she walked to her car, she heard the front door open and turned toward the sound.

With a wave, Emily called her back. "I did remember something. I saw Robert with that poor girl at rehearsal. He was only with her for a few minutes, but perhaps he could be of more help to you than I."

"Bobby was with Danni? Are you sure?" Panic erupted inside her. Her whirling mind recalled every bit of her conversation with Bobby. Never once had he mentioned Danni being at the school.

Emily nodded. "Robert handled the fans trying to meet the band, and so many were backstage that day."

"Do you know what Danni wanted?"

"I never spoke to her. Robert took care of things."

Alarm welled in her chest. Why hadn't Bobby tried to help? "Did you see them together later? Maybe during the concert?"

"No. Just that one time."

A sudden idea niggled in Carly's mind, growing stronger and more insistent until she acknowledged it. "Mrs. McKennan, if you were serious about wanting to help, I know something you can do."

****

Carly drove to the Clinton Estate and turned the last curve of the long driveway just as she saw Bobby's car pull out of the four-car garage. She rolled down the window and waved. "Wait."

The sports car skidded to a halt.

"I need to talk to you about Shane."

"Yeah, everyone does these days." Bobby got out,

slammed the driver's door, and walked to Carly. "What is it? I'm in a hurry. Got some business to take care of."

"I hope that means you're headed to help Shane."

Bobby folded his arms over his chest. "Other business. Life goes on."

His caustic tone surprised her, but she had no time for arguments. "I need to ask you a few questions."

"Get in line," he shot back. A scowl crimped his mouth.

Carly saw her knuckles whiten as her grip on the steering wheel tightened. He would not brush her off like some annoying fan. She shot out of her car and faced him. "I'm serious, Bobby. Shane needs your help."

His brow furrowed. "You seen my brother?"

"Not since before the concert." Fear crept over her. He couldn't know she was lying.

"Me either. So looks like I can't help you." Shrugging, he turned away.

Carly grabbed Bobby's arm. "Did Shane say anything before he went to meet Danni at the rooming house?"

He shook his head. "Not that I remember. Why?"

She hoped her face didn't betray she knew he was lying. "Shane didn't kill Danni," she said calmly, though her heart pounded like it would explode from her chest at any second.

Bobby shrugged. "That's for the police to decide, not us."

Carly slammed a hand on the roof of her car. "Sounds as though you're abandoning your brother."

Bobby's features rippled. "Look." He raised his hand and counted. "One, he had the time, two, he had the motive, and three, he had the opportunity." His eyes narrowed, and he shifted from one foot to the other. "To me, that adds up to maybe he did it. Anything else?"

Bobby's lack of concern threw Carly out of tempo. She swallowed hard to calm the anger she knew would be in her voice. "Mrs. McKennan said she saw you with Danni Baker during rehearsal the day before the concert. You didn't mention that."

"Why should I?"He folded his arms across his chest.

A hard ball of anger gelled in Carly's stomach. "Just how well did you know Danni Baker?"

"As well as any road manager knows pesky fans, okay?"

His clipped voice mirrored the irritation she could see on his face.

"Listen"—he waved toward his car—"I gotta go. I'm late for a meeting. You need answers…check with the police." Without waiting, he got into the car and sped off.

In disbelief, Carly watched until she could no longer see the car's taillights. For someone who had depended on Shane so much in the past, Bobby didn't care very much about the future.

She vowed to dig deeper into the events leading up to Danni's murder. As she put her car in reverse and backed out of the driveway, she saw a black boxy sedan slow as it passed the estate entrance before speeding up and continuing west. The car wasn't the same one that delivered the warning message. Only one other possibility existed—an unmarked police car. She would have an escort on the way home.

****

In the morgue located in the basement of the Somerset Medical Center, a white uniformed attendant pulled back the sheet and revealed Danni's lifeless, white face.

"Is this her?" a police detective asked.

"Yes. That is my Danniella." Scodari's chilly tone matched the cop's unemotional one.

"I am sorry about your daughter. We're doing everything we can to find out who did this."

The officer's word sounded rehearsed, as though he had said them a thousand times. "Yes, we are all sorry." He fought the urge to destroy the room and everything in it. Instead, he reached out a shaky hand and smoothed Danni's hair. "When can I take my daughter home?"

"After the autopsy."

The attendant replaced the sheet over Danni's face and slid the drawer back into the cubicle.

"I want to be alone with her for a few minutes."

The officer nodded, and he and the attendant left the room.

He reached out, his hand visibly shaking. His fingers closed around the handle of the cold metal drawer and, for a moment, he froze. *She shouldn't be in such a bitter place. My sweet daughter should have had much more time in life*. If she had let him, he would have given her anything she wanted, even the man he despised. Slowly, he pulled open the compartment and uncovered his daughter's face. He cupped her pale cheek, the lack of warmth jolting him. "Soon, we shall be going home, my cherub. You never took anything once your mother and I divorced, not even my name. You refused my help during your short life. I will give you something you cannot refuse now. I will give you justice. Once you are at rest next to your mother, I promise you, my angel, my justice will not be swift nor painless in its conclusion."

****

When she arrived home, Carly went straight to her bedroom and was relieved to see Shane still sleeping. He looked so peaceful and untroubled. For a moment, she could almost believe the murder was part of someone else's nightmare. But a cold shiver ran through her as she remembered the bitter exchange between Shane and Danni in the back of the school auditorium. Could Shane have become so angry he lost control and killed Danni in a turn of uncontrolled rage? Did she even have the right to hide him as the prime suspect in the murder?

She looked at his peaceful expression as he slept and wondered about the man who'd walked back into her life. Was he the gentle, sensitive person who captured her heart many years before, or was he a cold-blooded killer who could charm with a smile and expect the world to believe him?

Weary of the argument, she pulled together her drifting thoughts. The only way to know the truth was to see this situation through. Perhaps if Mrs. McKennan persuaded her husband to help, more of the puzzle would fall into place. However, one dreadful fact remained steadfast and strong. If she discovered Shane was Danni's killer, she would turn him in and walk away forever. Closing her eyes, she whispered a silent prayer for help. A few hours ago, the future belonged to them once more. Now, the allegations of murder balanced their fate upon a shaky past. Her fingertips outlined his face with its light shadow of an emerging beard.

Shane reached up and covered her hand with his. His eyes fluttered open, and he smiled. "Hi."

"Hi, yourself." Her bottom lip trembled. She couldn't let him know of her turmoil. Instead, she ran her forefinger across his chin. "You need a shave."

He moved the back of his hand over his chin. "You're right. What time is it?"

"Nearly seven."

Shane bolted upward and stared at the time on the digital alarm clock on the bedside table. His eyes widened. "I slept for almost eight hours." He reached for his shirt. "I wanted to be gone by now. Why did you let me sleep?"

She took the shirt from his hand and laid it at the foot of the bed. "Because you needed the rest." She sat on the edge of the bed near him. Despite the gravity of the predicament, as she looked into his eyes, she felt the familiar ache of want stir.

Shane put his hand on Carly's arm and began a slow massage. "God, you're beautiful. When I opened my eyes and saw you, I felt as though we were back in the loft in Philly after a long night at one of the clubs and an even longer night of loving you. Do you remember, Carly?"

She closed her eyes and swallowed a sigh. She never forgot. Being young, carefree and in his arms had been her slice of heaven. She could only nod. Of course, she remembered. Though she tried, she found forgetting those nights of love and passion impossible.

He wrapped his arms around her and pulled her down beside him. "I was wrong to involve you in this mess," he whispered through the kisses. "Having you close helps, but I have to turn myself in."

With a trembling hand, she cupped his cheek. "I'm afraid."

He pressed his lips into a thin line."So am I."

She searched his face before returning to capture his gaze. "I'll go with you."

Shane shook his head. "No. You'd be a suspect." He sat up and swung his legs over the edge of the bed. "I'll go out the front door and tell the police you convinced me to give up."

Carly rose to her knees and covered his mouth with a kiss that cut off anything more he might say. "I want to go back to Philadelphia when life was so much simpler," she said between kisses. "Let's just run away."

"No one can give us back all the years we lost." He tucked a strand of hair behind her ear and kissed it in place. "Besides, we'd never get far enough away."

As she sat next to him, she held his gaze. "We have to find a way to prove you didn't kill her. What can we do?"

Frowning, he shook his head. "I don't know." He pulled her into his arms and held her. "If I can't prove I'm innocent, I guess we'll see each other on visiting days."

He hugged her as though his life depended on the contact. His warmth enveloped her. Would this be one of the last times she would feel the warmth of his body? Would her only contact in the future be her hand mirroring his in a thick pane of cold bulletproof glass separating them forever? She put her forefinger across his lips. "You are innocent and somehow, we'll find a way to prove it." She looked into his eyes for emphasis. "Together."

He took her hand and kissed her palm. "Together."

She stood and walked to the bedroom door. "You shower and shave, and I'll see what's in the fridge. After you recharge, we'll put our heads together and come up with a plan. Stay away from the windows, and I'll do the same. We don't want our friends outside to know two people are inside."

Shane winked and closed the bathroom door.

In another minute, she heard the water running. On the way to the kitchen, she fought the urge to rip off her clothes and join Shane. If this was the last chance they had to be together for a while, she was torn between using the little time left to plan Shane's defense and making love until the world turned red with their fire. After serious deliberating, good sense prevailed, and she opted to throw ham onto rye bread on a plate instead of throwing herself into Shane arms in a tiled shower stall.

Shane was out of the shower and dressed in his leather jeans when she returned upstairs. He sat on the bed. Shane reached for the sandwich as though accepting a Grammy.

"When was the last you had something to eat?" Carly watched half of the sandwich disappear in three bites.

"Before the concert."

A spot of mayonnaise on Shane's chin became much too inviting and, as she reached to wipe it away, he leaned forward and kissed her. "Dessert," he said before kissing her again.

Carly cradled his face between her hands. His eyes

were ringed with tension lines, and he looked defeated. "I know this is hard, but justice is supposed to always win. If you're innocent, you have nothing to worry about."

"If, Carly?" Shane eased from her arms and stood. "I can't face what is waiting outside if I think you have the slightest doubt." He turned away, and his shoulders drooped.

She put her arms around his waist and ran her hands up his chest. Leaning her head against his back, she struggled to find the right words. "I do believe you are innocent, and I'll be by your side every step of the way until the real killer is found."

Shane spun, his arms surrounding her. His gaze searched her face. "This may be the last time we can be together for a very long time. The night we had at the house in Clinton was magic. We were close, so very close to having everything back, and now, in a matter of a just few days, we are just as close to losing everything."

She closed her eyes and tightened her embrace. "We'll get through this. I promise we will." She laid her cheek on his chest and heard his heart pounding. She should not make any more promises, yet she did. "I swear we will find Danni's killer."

Shane cupped her head and pulled her closer. "I need you, Carly."

His breath breezed against the side of her neck where he pressed his bowed head."Your love and your faith in me will help me find the courage to walk out the front door and turn myself in to the men in the unmarked car."

Carly could feel the tension inside Shane's body

ready to burst like a tightly coiled spring. The harsh, uneven rhythm of his breathing now mirrored hers. As gently as she could, she levered him away. "Part of me wants you to run and not stop until you are in a country where no one can find you."

"I ran once." He brushed the hair from her face. "It solved nothing." He pulled her back into his arms. "We both know my chances aren't good. The evidence against me appears overwhelming." Their lips were only inches apart. "I know how dark this world can be. When the media gets this story, the push-back won't be pretty."

Tears welled in Carly's eyes, and she turned her head to keep him from seeing them. She had to be strong because when Shane was taken into custody, her life would never be same. By the time he got in front of a judge, she might be the only one left who believed he was innocent. She pulled back and looked into his eyes. Pain and longing swirled in equal mix, and she knew she wanted more time with him before she could let him walk out the front door into uncertainty. "I love you so very much, Shane," she whispered. She rose on her toes and pressed her mouth to his. "If this day is all we have for a while, help me make a memory I could never forget."

Shane showered kisses along her mouth and jaw line as he spoke. "Do you want to make love to a suspected killer, instead of waiting until the world knows I am an innocent man?"

"I want to make love to Shane Fox. The man I loved in Philadelphia, and the man I love now." She cupped his cheek. "Just for a little while, I want to forget what is waiting outside."

****

With a groan, he swept her into his arms and gently eased her onto the bed. He lay next to her and brushed the hair from her face while kissing the tears from her eyes.

She did not resist when he unbuttoned her blouse and traced the line of her lace bra with his forefinger.

"Look at me, Carly," he whispered, moving his fingertip moved across one cup to tease the tip of her breast. "I love to look into your eyes when we make love." He slipped his fingers inside her bra and caressed her hardening nipple.

Then his mouth took a tortuous path down her neck as he licked, nipped, and circled the hollow of her throat. Kisses dropped between her breasts, and she threaded her fingers in his soft hair.

With a roll of his shoulders, he growled his pleasure.

He tasted her as though it was the first time, pressing light kisses along the rising slope of her breasts. He felt her hips arch as her need rose only to subside when his teasing kisses slid away from her nipple. When a moan escaped her, he smiled against her skin and cupped one breast before giving it a long lick with his tongue before drawing the nipple into his mouth. He felt her begin to convulse, but he held her still. When his mouth moved to her other breast, he used his fingers on the first.

Her fingers dug into his shoulders then slid down to his biceps. His body screamed for completion, for a joining, but he held back, enjoying the fire in his belly that grew with each stroke he made. His hand reached between her legs cupping her. She arched, and the feel of wetness on his palm became intoxicating. When she moved against him, he murmured her name as though she was a wildcat he needed to soothe. He stroked and petted her, Because he knew her secrets, his fingers found all the places he remembered would give her pleasure. He paused only long enough to remove his clothes, and she groaned when he no longer touched her.

Both naked now, he kissed her jaw, her neck, the hollow behind her ear while her mouth trapped his tongue, stroking and sucking, holding him fast as she lifted her hips, telling him she was ready. With a groan of anticipation, he entered her. Nothing felt so good or fit so perfectly. He inhaled at the sheer pleasure of filling her so completely. He smiled against her lips and moved until he found the rhythm she liked. She arched and followed the rhythm. As his thrusting deepened, he murmured his pleasure as his thrusting deepened, slowed, quickened and circled, hitting every familiar place inside her. He felt her stiffen, then wait, then rise and fall, almost begging him to give her what she wanted. Stiff-armed, he stopped and caught her heavy-lidded gaze. Despite the years apart, nothing had changed. He lowered himself only long enough to press a kiss on her lips and then began a rhythm he knew would bring them to heaven on earth.

****

She gasped for air and begged him to stay with her as her hips rose and fell in a furious tempo. Together, they climbed toward climax with a furious rhythm. Her fingers dug into his back, and he urged her to even greater heights until her orgasm exploded with the scream of his name. As though in synchrony with her wishes, he orchestrated more, one after another until she screamed again in final release. His end followed hers, rocking her with more power than she thought possible. Their problems fell away, and her eyes closed in exhaustion. She smiled as she drifted off listening to the music of love played like a symphony by her beating heart.

Chapter Fourteen

Carly heard Shane cry out her name and ran into the bedroom. She clasped a hand onto his cheek. His skin was cold and moist, and sweat glittered in tiny beads in his face. In his eyes, she could see fear. "What's wrong?"

Shane sat up, closed his eyes, and leaned back onto the pillow. "I reached for you, but you were gone. For a split second, I thought last night had just been a dream." He opened a cradle between his arms into which Carly willing sank.

"I'm not going anywhere." She laid her head on his chest.

Shane stroked her hair. "Think of all the wasted years. We could be starting on our third daughter by now, instead of facing the uncertainty of not knowing if we'll ever be together again once I walk out the front door."

"Third daughter?" Carly raised her eyebrows. "No sons?"

He scooted upright.

Carly rose with him and leaned against his shoulder.

"I want to be surrounded by three little girls with auburn hair and big, perfect eyes just like their mother." He kissed the tip of her nose.

Carly smiled and mentally counted the days since

her last cycle. The timing wasn't right. Another child needed them more right now.

"An hour, Carly. That's all I'm asking." His hand trailed to her breast. "One more memory. Please."

She closed her eyes and toyed with the pleasant suggestion, and leaned forward to kiss him just as the telephone on her nightstand rang.

"Let the call go to voice mail," Shane mumbled between light kisses.

The idea was tempting, but she moved back. "When I was interviewed, I gave Detective Carter the number to the land line. This may be him. No doubt in the morning report, my babysitters outside told him I'm home. If I don't answer, someone might drop by to investigate." She picked up the call, her brows drawing down as she listened. In between nods, she spoke in one-word answers.

Shane moved away and grabbed his clothes."The police?"

Concern shown in his eyes. She wished she could assure him everything would be fine, but she was no closer to information that could help than she had been a few hours earlier. "No, Emily McKennan." Nervously, Carly smoothed the sheets. "I asked for her help."

"She agreed?"

Carly nodded. "I asked if she could get a copy of the autopsy results."

His eyebrows rose. "Did she?"

"Mrs. McKennan just told me the Medical Examiner noted that Danni Baker was killed by a blow to the back of her head. He puts her time of death anywhere from about 10:00 p.m. and 2:00 a.m., meaning Danni was possibly killed before the concert was over. That could be why she didn't answer the telephone when you called her." Carly saw hope in Shane's eyes.

"If she fell and hit her head, maybe her death wasn't murder after all but an accident. If that can be proved, I could possibly be exonerated."

"A chance." She took a deep breath, hoping he would have faith in her. "But another option exists."

Shane's lips drew down. "Someone went to a whole lot of trouble to murder her just to pin it on me?"

Carly nodded. She searched his face and struggled with what to say. She believed that was the case and needed him to believe it also. "No other explanation existed."

Shane paced. "So, then in order to clear myself, I have to convince the police Danni died while I was on stage, and someone is framing me?" He shook his head. "Even if that is true, I have no alibi for the time after the concert. The evidence of paternity makes me look damn guilty."

"You sound like you're giving up." The possibility he would echoed through her.

A muscle tightened along Shane's jaw line. "What I sound is frustrated." He shook his head slowly. "The trash rags probably already have Danni's murder and my connection to her as the lead story on the web. Want to guess the headline?"

Carly tried to smile but failed.

He raised a hand, spread his fingers, and slowly moved his hand from left to right.

"Deadly Secrets
Rock Star Kills the Mother of his Love Child"

Dread seared though her veins. He sounded as though announcing the future. "Somehow we'll find a way to prove your innocence." She reached for Shane and drew him close as the final minutes of their time together ticked off. "The truth always comes out." She saw acceptance in his eyes when he pulled back and held her at arm's length."Enough stalling. Let me do what I have to do before I change my mind."

The pressure of building tears stung Carly's eyes. "We will get through this. I won't lose you again," she whispered as they moved along the stairs.

The slam of the kitchen door accompanied by footsteps caused Carly to put her hand on Shane's chest. "Get upstairs," she whispered.

Shane's brows furrowed. "It's probably the police, and since I'm turning myself in, this is as good a time as any."

Carly shook her head. "If the police thought you were here, the house would be surrounded, and we'd be talking to someone with a bullhorn in his hand. Let me check the kitchen."

He grabbed her arm when she turned. "I'm not sure that's a good idea."

"It's the only idea we have." She waited until Shane retreated to the bedroom before walking slowly down the stairs. She rounded the corner and stopped dead in her tracks. Her heart surged to her throat.

Erno Scodari stood in front of the kitchen table, his hands folded in front of him.

She turned to run and get outside to alert the police but skidded to a halt when his henchman stepped in front of her. The gun in his hand made her turn and walk into the kitchen. The urge to warn Shane roared through her, but the sight of the weapon pointed her way kept her quiet.

When they came face to face, Scodari smiled. "Ah, Miss Mitchell. You are even more beautiful in person than you are in your photographs." He tugged at the fingers of his gloves before removing them.

Scodari's associate reached around Carly and took the gloves from his outstretched hand.

Scodari slid out a chair from under the table and motioned to Carly. "Please. Join me."

"How did you get past the police?" Carly asked as she sat.

Scodari smiled. "I have my ways."

"I don't believe we've formally met." Fear and anger knotted inside her. "You're Erno Scodari."

"You are correct." He bowed from the waist and swept one hand in the air. "And this is Tino, my assistant."

"Yeah," Tino clasped his hands in front of him.

He stood in the center of the room like a sinister barrier. Carly had no opportunity to get away. "Why are you here?" Her voice sounded shakier than she would have liked. "Get out, or I'll call for help!" She reached for her cell phone resting on the charger.

With the silver edge of his cane, Scodari knocked it from the counter. "Just asking your friends to come in would be simpler. Although, I think that would be most foolish because, my dear, Tino would have to shoot them."

The truth in his eyes was a hard, cold read, but she forced her fears at bay. If Scodari knew Shane was here, he probably would have killed her already.

He walked to the living room. "Tino, bring her."

Tino grabbed Carly by the arm and dragged her to the sofa where Scodari motioned for her to sit.

She swallowed a heart-thump as she sat. "What do you want?" Keeping one eye on Tino, she prayed he didn't go upstairs.

"Who do I want?" Scodari asked."I want Shane Fox. I plan to kill him."

Carly bolted to her feet. "No!"

Scodari nodded to Tino, who pulled out his gun and adjusted his aim from Carly's heart to her head. "Along with anyone who gets in my way."

****

When Shane heard Scodari's voice, his first instinct was to get to Carly, but a quick, deadly thought formed. Scodari wanted revenge, and if Shane surrendered, Scodari might be crazy enough to start shooting. If he began firing, Carly could be hit before the police crashed through the front door. He couldn't risk charging downstairs to reach her side. He had to find another way.

****

Carly felt as though she couldn't breathe. "Shane isn't here." Her gaze stayed on the gun as she tried to keep her voice composed. "Just leave. I promise I won't call the police."

The landline telephone rang.

She flinched and reached for the receiver.

Scodari's cane got there first. "Let the machine answer."

After the fourth ring, Carly recognized the voice as a bank co-worker who asked Carly to return the call as soon as she could.

Scodari removed the cane. "Problem solved. To get

back to my intentions, Mr. Fox and I have a matter to settle." His eyes narrowed, and his expression grew even colder.

Carly's stomach clenched, and she fought the fear rising in her throat. "Why do you want Shane?"

"I think you know." Scodari paced, slapping the end of his silver-tipped cane into the palm of one hand. "However, I will allow this poor attempt at acting nonetheless. I do not care about you. You are incidental." A sneer curled his lips. "Shane Fox killed my daughter, and I intend to kill him."

"Danni was your daughter?" His words hit Carly like a slap from the grave. She held his gaze and kept her expression neutral, but the chaos turning inside threatened to spill out at any moment.

Scardari's lips twisted. "Yes. My daughter." A tired sadness settled onto his face. "After my wife discovered the nature of my business, she left me. We ultimately divorced. She took back her maiden name, moved to a small Midwest town, and refused to let me see Danniella." He lifted his chin. "For my daughter's sake, I allowed this, but I watched over her and loved her as much as I could from a distance."

An eerie parody of pride and anger swirled in his eyes. She thought back to the bond she had with her own father. Though not a perfect relationship, she knew he loved her. "I'm sorry," Carly said in a voice barely above a whisper.

Scodari turned his back. "I am sorry about many things, but mostly, I regret the day she met Fox. I should have protected her from men like him." He spat out the words. "First, the man gave her a child, then denied the act and left her to raise the boy alone. When she threatened to force his hand, he killed her." He suddenly smiled. "But I can still give my daughter what she so desperately wanted. I can unite them in death."

Carly's brain jammed, and she sucked in a short breath when the phone rang again. She saw rage build in Scodari's eyes. Her stomach clenched when the phone rang again. She looked down and refrained from answering the call. "I told you, Shane isn't here," she said over the ringing.

Scodari grabbed her hair and forced back her head just as the phone quieted. "I am losing patience, Miss Mitchell. Don't do anything that might add you to the covenant I must keep." He glanced from her face for only a second. "Tino, search the place."

"And if I find Fox, do I kill him?"

Scodari tugged on the cuff of his jacket and shook his head. "That pleasure will be mine."

Tino nodded.

With every ounce of restraint she possessed, Carly resisted the urge to charge Scodari. Her mind ran through scenarios Shane could use to escape. *Shane, please don't be a hero. I can take care of myself.* After this was over, maybe others would call him a coward for not intervening, but she just wanted him to live.

Neither Scodari nor Carly said anything more until Tino returned. "No one upstairs, boss, but someone was. One unmade bed and dinner for two on a tray."

Scodari grabbed Carly by the throat.

Her eyes widened as she clawed at his hands, struggling to free herself. Her pulse raced. Was she going to die?

Scodari tightened his grip for a few seconds.

Carly gasped before he relaxed his hold just

enough for her to breathe.

"Where is he?" He squeezed her throat again and then released. "And for your sake, I suggest you begin telling the truth!"

The phone rang again.

Scodari's expression twisted in a sneer.

"I use the land line for bank business," Carly whispered through struggling breaths. She dug her fingers at his hold underneath his hand. "If I don't answer, my manager may stop by."

Smirking, Scodari removed his hand from her throat.

Gasping, she fell to her knees.

He dragged her up by her hair and gestured to the phone. "Answer it, but no tricks. Make whoever is calling think all is well."

Carly's head throbbed, and her eyes watered. Somehow, she had to let the caller know something was wrong. With trembling hands, she picked up the receiver. "Hello." Her voice was surprisingly calm.

"Carly, are you all right?"

She recognized Shane's voice. Relief made her knees weak, and she leaned onto the table for support. "I am. Where are you calling from?"

"Where I am is not important right now. Give the phone to Scodari."

Carly could hear panic in his tone. "No," she whispered, keeping her voice even.

"I know what I'm doing."

The white noise of fear buzzed her ears. "I can't."

"You have to."

Mixed feelings surged as she shifted her gaze to Scodari. "It's Shane. He wants to talk to you."

Scodari took the phone and stepped back.

The move created enough space for Carly to reach the lamp on the table. She held it over her head with both hands. "If you two aren't out of here by the time I count to three, this lamp is going through the window. I'm sure the noise will get the attention of the police in the car outside. You might shoot me, but you won't get very far, and Shane will be safe." Seeing Scodari took a step toward her, she raised the lamp higher. "I mean it. I would love to see the police come running, guns drawn, ready for war." Narrowing her gaze, she lifted her chin and gestured to the back door. "Get out!"

"You would risk everything for a man who fathered a child by another woman?" Scodari sneered and stood still.

He was baiting her. "I would risk everything for the man I love," she affirmed.

Scodari cut his gaze first to Tino and then back to Carly. "This foolish act of courage may be the last thing you do."

Her determination and heartbeat rose in unison. "Then so be it." She leaned back and prepared to throw the lamp.

Scodari put down the phone and raised his hands.

Carly heard Shane's voice on the other of the line end, shouting her name. "Everything's okay, Shane. Just hang on."

Scodari brushed at the front of his coat while Tino stood motionless, the gun on his hand pointing at the floor. "For a time, our business is concluded, Miss Mitchell," Scodari said. "But I warned you, and you ignored my generosity. The next time we meet, I promise, you will not be as fortunate as today." He looked to the telephone. "Tell Mr. Fox he has no place where he can hide. Not even prison." He gestured toward the kitchen. "Tino, we must go. We are not welcome here."

Tino holstered his gun and disappeared into the kitchen.

Scodari stopped at the back door and tapped his cane to his forehead. "I will not forget what you have done here, Miss Mitchell."

Until she heard the back door close, Carly didn't move. Trembling, she replaced the lamp on the table and picked up the phone. "Shane, where are you?"

"Carly. Baby. Are you all right?" Shane's voice broke.

Her hand shook. "I'm fine. Please tell me where you are."

"Just listen, Carly, I don't have much time. When I heard Scodari's threats, I had to give him a reason to leave before he hurt you. I left the same way I got in—I used the tree outside the bathroom window."

"Come back," Carly begged, her grip tightening.

"I can't. Scodari coming to your house changes everything. Now I can't give myself up, Carly. I can't prove my innocence if I'm dead. Scodari can get to me no matter where I am. You heard him. Not even prison will be safe."

"Danni was his daughter, Shane." A pain like a fist closing clamped around her heart. "Did you know?" She heard his sharp intake of breath.

"No. I didn't know much about Danni. She never talked about herself. I assumed she was just some rich kid out for a few kicks. However, I do know Scodari. He doesn't just threaten. I need to get as far away as I can until I figure out how to clear my name."

Building tears blurred her vision and choked her voice. "Don't run again. We can work out something."

"Carly, I'm not running. Scodari will focus on me. You'll be safe."

A chill ran through her. "No, I won't. He said he would not forget what I did today. Let me come with you. We can be safe together."

"Alone, you may have a chance. You don't know Scodari like I do. Revenge on me is what he wants most right now. He will stop at nothing until I'm dead."

His voice was softer now, almost a whisper. A sharp pain stabbed her heart. She could not change his mind.

"I'll call you as soon as I can."

Then, before Carly could protest, he hung up.

****

Shane leaned against the rough wood of the neighbor's pool house. He knew if he talked to Carly much longer, he would not have the willpower to leave her, and leaving her was the only thing he could do to keep her safe. He was well versed in the depth of Scodari's cruelty. If Danni was truly the man's daughter, Scodari would not rest until he had his revenge. With heavy sadness, he cautiously made his way away from Carly once more.

****

When the telephone line went dead, Carly pressed the receiver to her chest and imprisoned a sob. History was repeating itself. Yet again, the man she loved was being forced from her life. However, this time she was not letting someone else decide her future. Scodari would not win again.

Chapter Fifteen

The sun was setting, and although the unmarked car normally parked outside her home hadn't followed her, another was. Using the rearview mirror, Carly kept an eye on a white sedan she noticed behind her for the last three miles. The car mirrored her every move, turning where she turned and stopping when she stopped. So much for adventure and intrigue on a small town police force. Rookies, she surmised. They needed to watch a little more Investigative Discovery on cable TV. She checked her watch. Five minutes more. She turned down a side street, and her shadow stayed at a respectable distance. The timing had to be perfect or else her plan would fail.

As she approached the railroad tracks, she could see the freight train coming. She eased her foot onto the brake and stopped the car just as the crossing lights came on. When the rail gate began to lower, she looked in the rearview mirror.

The sedan rolled to a stop, and the driver took his hands off the steering wheel. He stretched while his partner turned and fumbled with something in the back seat.

This was her chance. Just as the train was about a hundred yards from the intersection, Carly slammed her foot onto the gas pedal and yanked the steering wheel to the left. The car jerked forward and sped toward the crossing.

At the same time, the locomotive's horn blared.

Carly's car started across the tracks.

Sparks flew from the train wheels as the engineer applied the brakes, missing Carly's car by only a few feet but successfully splitting her from the police babysitters.

Once on the other side of the crossing, Carly stopped the car and took a few long deep breaths to calm her thumping heart. She looked over her shoulder at the freight train.

The engineer had left the train's cab to ensure the train hugged the tracks despite the emergency stop. Carly had some time before the train started and cleared the intersection, but not a whole lot. Besides, the detectives in the unmarked car had probably already called in the incident. If she hurried, she could still have enough time to lose herself on side streets. She drove to the Clinton Estate and parked the car behind a clump of decorative shrubs outside the estate gates. A fallen tree near a section of wall looked like a living ladder, and she grabbed the large branches to climb. When even with the top of the privacy wall, she grabbed the top stone cap with both hands and lowered herself until she only had to drop a few feet. Shadows of overgrown landscaping hid her as she made her way to the house.

Bobby was home. She called him, and he said he was staying in for the rest of the day in case Shane tried to contact him. Unmistakable deception in his voice, she sensed he was lying. Maybe Bobby always banked on bloodline to charm and lie, but he was dealing with her now. Whatever information he knew would not stay hidden long.

Anger built as she walked toward the home. A small part of her panicked and shouted, "You have no plan or proof. Do you even know what you're doing?" All true, but she shoved aside the voice and kept walking. About ten feet from the house, she pressed deeper into the shadows when Bobby came out the front door. Anticipating she would have to watch Bobby from a distance, she brought along her digital camera with telephoto lens. She raised the camera and focused Bobby's face in the crosshairs of the lens. She clicked off a few shots, capturing a sequence she hoped would be useful.

He opened the trunk and tossed a wrapped parcel inside. He then looked over both shoulders and got in the car.

She waited until Bobby made the first of many winding turns to get to the gate and barreled straight through the landscaping, barely making it back to her car before the sports car came to a stop and waited until the ornate iron gate moved slowly out of the way. She ducked low in the driver's seat, watching and hoping he didn't notice her car.

But he never looked in her direction before continuing on and heading east.

She took a deep breath, gave him a minute's lead, and followed him. She stayed well behind Bobby but close enough to keep him in sight.

He drove on the interstate for about twenty minutes before he turned onto a side road.

She shut off her headlights and followed.

A few miles later, he made a right into the parking lot of an abandoned strip mall.

Keeping her gaze on the red taillights, she pulled to

the shoulder and watched the car turn left. When it disappeared behind the building, she drove past the mall and parked in the driveway of an abandoned house that once was a real estate agency.

Apprehension jabbed at her stomach as she made her way to the line of crumbling storefronts. What if Bobby saw her? What would he do? Nothing or no one was around for miles. Reality echoed through her. She had to continue. Shane's life counted on her. When she turned the corner of the last building, she saw Bobby rummaging through the trunk. In the dim light, she could see him lift a package and carry it toward a fenced-in area that appeared to have been a plant nursery and outdoor section of a large department.

After a quick look over his shoulder, he pulled the edge of the chain link fence free and slipped inside.

Carly squeezed behind a line of rusted outdoor shelving and zoomed the telephoto camera lens to maximum. Through the lens, she could clearly see Bobby toss the package into a small rusting dumpster.

After taking one more look around, he hurried to the fence, slid out, and got back into the car.

As soon as the car's taillights disappeared, Carly ran to the fence and wiggled her way through. As a warning voice screamed inside her head, she glanced over her shoulder. Maybe this was a drop spot, and Bobby planted the package for someone else to find. The icy silence of the empty mall gave way to imagined sounds and voices, prompting her to run to the dumpster.

With trembling fingers, she lifted the lid. The bundle had landed on a pile of concrete blocks. After throwing back the lid, she rose on tiptoes and retrieved the bundle. Half in anticipation, half in dread, she clawed at the package. Her stomach clenched tight. When she saw what was inside, her hands shook as she lifted a steel gray rifle from the brown paper and tape.

Her mind replayed the shooting on her way home from the park, realization hit her like a blow to her gut. She would not need a ballistics test to tell her the gun was most likely the same weapon that fired the bullets through her car's windshield. The shooter on the road was Bobby. No other reason explained him getting rid of the gun.

Her stomach clenched again, and a feeling of nausea swelled. Her suspicions were right on target. Bobby was involved.

****

Carly went straight home after taking six pictures of the weapon and carefully replacing the package inside the dumpster. Panic she'd never known welled inside. She had to talk to Shane before he called Bobby. He needed to know he would be safer in police custody than with his brother.

She glanced at the wall clock. Midnight. She picked up her cell phone and dialed. Maybe if she begged her father, he would open his vast sheaf of resources and help her. Anxiously, she swept the hair from her face with one hand while she waited for the call to connect. "Dad," she said breathlessly when she heard his voice. "I knew you would be awake. It's afternoon there." She prayed the waver in her voice was not as evident to him as it was to her.

A feeling worse than a fist to her stomach settled inside her as she closed her eyes and listened to her father. He wasted no time tearing into Shane. As she listened to his rant, she knew she would have to find another way to help Shane. She forced her voice to be calm. "No, Dad, I haven't let Shane destroy my life again. I just thought you might—" *Help me*. Despite the glimpse of regret she'd seen in her father's eyes before he left on his business trip, his contempt for Shane remained strong. "I thought you might like to know the concert was a huge success." Tears filled her eyes, but she refused to let the sadness show in her voice. "The Center can do a lot of good with the money." As she realized this instance could be the last time she ever spoke to her father, she closed her eyes and inhaled. If she could not prove Shane's innocence, she would spend the rest of her life on the run with him if that was the price she would have to pay to be together.

She knew her father would not see her sad smile. "Dad, I love you. Bye." When the call disconnected, she hugged the receiver to her chest. "I'm sorry, Dad," she whispered. "I know you will never understand." She pulled out the number Emily McKennan gave her and dialed.

"Hello?" Emily's sleepy voice said.

"It's Carly. I'm sorry to bother you, Mrs. McKennan."

"Is everything all right, dear? What time is it?"

"It's very late." She shook her head. What had she been thinking? "I didn't mean to interrupt your trip. I'll talk you to when you get back."

"Carly, are you sure nothing is wrong? You sound worried."

Carly hated to lie but had no choice. She could not turn the McKennans into accomplices. "Yes. Fine. I just felt a little anxious."

"Are you sure, dear?"

"Yes. Just nerves. I'll talk to you soon. Bye." Carly leaned back in the chair and sighed. She felt numb, too unfocused to do anything but wait. She pulled out the DVD Emily gave her and slid the disc into her portable player. As the concert began, she couldn't stop her mind whirling with impossible thoughts and outrageous scenarios when she heard Shane sing. She ejected the disc and slid it into the lamp table drawer to her right before stretching out on the couch and closing her eyes. Though she tried to get some rest, a maddening combination of facts and theories replayed in her mind. At four a.m., she showered and checked on her all-night baby-sitters in the unmarked car before finally falling asleep on the sofa.

Ann called at seven a.m. to say she was cutting her trip short to come back and do whatever she could to help. Despite Carly's protests, Ann was insistent about her decision and told Carly she would be home the next day.

Now wide awake, Carly opened the front curtain. The first thing she noticed was an empty street. The police car was gone. New fears twisted around her heart. Did the police have Shane? Why hadn't someone told her? She grabbed the TV remote and switched on the cable news station. Faces blurred as she frantically searched until she found a station showing Shane's picture.

"...and the search continues for Shane Fox, rock star and prime suspect in the murder of socialite Dannielle Baker. Unconfirmed reports say Miss Baker was the mother of his young son, Nickolas, also citing a possible love triangle as a motive for the slaying."

She flinched as the story and its sound bites portrayed Shane as a wild, depraved rock star followed by a picture of Danni and her son. She started to change the channel when the next story began.

"...and in an unrelated incident, police were called to the home of Judge and Mrs. Edmond McKennan around dawn this morning after a neighbor reported seeing a prowler on the grounds. Police responded and found their house ransacked. At present, detectives have no leads or suspects."

Carly listened as the secondary story continued. Could the stakeout have been diverted to help search for a suspect in the break-in at the McKennan home? This could be the chance Shane needed to come back for her. Alternate pounding on the door and buzzing of the doorbell lifted her attention from the TV. She yanked opened the front door.

Bobby. Shock forced the air from her lungs. Gasping, she slammed the door. Why was he here?

The banging began again. "Carly, open up."

Carly's heartbeat skyrocketed. "Go away. I'm tired."

The pounding became louder and more insistent. "Let me in, Carly."

She straight-armed the door. "I'm not dressed."

The hammering stopped, replaced by the sound of Bobby's body slamming against the wood. "I...don't...care." He spaced the words to coincide with the battering. "I'm...coming...in!"

His voice sounded both desperate and angry as he threw his body against her door. She toyed with calling the police but knew though they might scare Bobby away now. But he'd be back. She had no place to hide.

On the sixth thrust, the hinges gave way. He pushed her backward and stepped over the debris. "What the hell is wrong with you? I thought you wanted me to help you find Shane." He positioned himself between her and the outside. "You heard from him?"

Every instinct confirmed she was in trouble. She inched backward. "No, I was hoping you had."

Bobby's expression clouded as he grabbed her arm and walked into the living room. "I need to find him."

"So do I." She held her hands away from her body and kept her weight balanced on the balls of her feet, poised to fight or flee as necessary. *Stay calm. Be careful. Don't let Bobby know you're suspicious.* She stepped back. "What do you want?"

His gaze darted behind her and back. "Why didn't you let me in, Carly? Is he here?"

She saw desperation in his eyes. "I wanted to be alone."

Bobby hitched a thumb over his shoulder. "Sorry about the door. I'll fix it." He walked the room, picking up and replacing various articles on the bookcase. When he saw the portable DVD player, he stopped. "What did you watch?"

"An old movie." She pitched her voice low and soothing, even as a sense of danger pulsed along her nerve-endings like fire.

He hit the eject button. "Where's the disc?"

Her blood went cold. He knew the concert had been filmed and wanted the disc. Something was on it he did not want seen. She could not let him find the DVD. "Listen, I'm really tired. If you don't mind, I want to get some rest."

"Actually, I do mind."

She was close enough to see his expression darken. Her mind filled with thoughts of running. She'd decided not to go to the police with what she found. Her decision. Her failure.

Strong fingers clamped on her arm. "Where is the video of the concert?"

"No." She glanced at the side table drawer long enough for Bobby to notice.

Panic swelled in her throat when Bobby pulled open the drawer and snatched the disc before she could react."Old movie?"

She felt his fingers tighten around both the disc and her arm. "I watched one earlier."

"Have you watched this?"

She hoped he couldn't feel her shaking. "Bobby, this conversation is ridiculous. Why do you want the video from the concert when your brother is in trouble?"

With a jerk, he yanked her forward until their faces were only inches apart. "I asked you if you watched the recording."

She saw anger flash in his eyes, pushing the fear in her stomach up another notch. A low buzz began in her ears as the blood rushed through her veins. "Bobby, you're hurting me."

"Did you watch it?" he asked through clenched teeth.

Desperation exploded in her chest. Admitting anything would be a serious mistake. "No," she lied. "I fell asleep."

He snapped the DVD in half.

Her suspicions were now dead on. Bobby was

involved. She looked down at the broken halves. A sense of defeat settled inside her. "That was the only copy."

"Thank you for that information, but I can't take the chance you're telling the truth." He grabbed her again and leaned into her. "Are there more copies?"

She shook her head. "Is something on the video that could help Shane? If there is, we should give the video to the police."

Bobby grinned, his expression frightening. "Nothing's going to the police." He stomped on the broken DVD and ground the pieces into the rug.

Wide-eyed, Carly stared. "What's wrong with you?" Disillusionment flared along with disappointment and betrayal. "He's your brother. Help him."

Bobby grabbed her around the waist. "I can't take any chances. You're coming with me."

Carly grabbed his arm and twisted in a vain attempt to get free, but he was stronger and pulled her toward the back of the house. As she passed the dining room, she grabbed the back of a chair, hoping to knock it between them so Bobby would trip.

But he just laughed and stepped around the shattered wood.

The slight distraction did make him relax his grip just enough for her to wiggle free and run into the kitchen.

He vaulted over the kitchen chair she threw in his path and jumped toward her.

She sidestepped his lunge. "Bobby. Stop," she shouted, knocking another chair in front of him.

With a sneer, he picked up the chair and tossed it

across the room, the impact sending dozens of articles tumbling from shelves. "Don't make this any harder."

"Why are you doing this?" Carly circled the table, keeping a barrier between them.

Bobby pitched forward and grabbed her shirt. He reeled her across the table. "I'm over my head, Carly, and I can't fix it alone. You have to help me."

As he dragged her back to the living room, she clawed like a wildcat. "I won't leave Shane."

Bobby spun Carly and slapped her across her mouth "Damn it, don't fight. I hate when women fight me. It makes me mad. I don't want to hurt you, too."

The blow opened a cut on her bottom lip. Blood trickled a warm path down her chin. She searched his face and saw only anger bubbling inside his eyes. "Bobby, stop!"

He raised his hand to hit her again.

From behind him, a hand grabbed his wrist. "Robert, let her go. I need her."

Bobby froze. "Mr. Scodari."

Scodari released Bobby's wrist. With a flourish, he gestured to the sofa. "Please. Do sit."

Tino grabbed Carly's arm and steered her into a chair. "Sit, girlie, and zip it until the boss says otherwise."

Bobby stood silent.

The power Bobby previously displayed suddenly disappeared. Carly buried her fear with a deep breath and glared at Scodari. "What do you want?"

Tino raised his hand to silence her.

But Scodari hit Tinos's forearm with his cane, stopping him. He cupped Carly's face and stared at the reddened skin. "Does your cheek hurt much?" He ran his knuckles over her cheek.

Carly shrugged away his touch. "Why are you here?"

"I think we both know."

Heart pounding and palms sweaty, Carly lifted her chin. "Why don't you tell me anyway?"

Scodari nodded. "Very well." He sat across from her. "I have always watched my daughter from afar, making sure she was safe and secure. When she had a child, I tried to reconcile, but she refused me. But she was my heart and my blood, so I continued to watch from a distance, doing what I could when I could."

"I'm sorry she felt that way," Carly said.

Scodari waved off her apology. "No more than I." His back stiffened. "I may be a poor father, but I am a very good businessman. I have associates everywhere. Even at your bank. When Fox came back to this town, I watched. When he began spending more time with you, I called my contact and inquired about you. Then I waited."

Carly's mind reeled. She thought she knew her coworkers. Who betrayed her? "What does the bank have to do this?" she asked with a slight headshake.

Scodari patted her cheek and rose. He paced, tapping his cane on his thigh as he spoke. "Well acted, my dear." He spun to face her. "We'll play it your way. When the night drop bag was opened, a little problem became obvious."

"What kind of problem?"

He lifted his hands. "The bag was empty."

Carly's brow furrowed. "Impossible. I put the ticket receipts money there myself."

Scodari raised his eyebrows. "No money was

inside so the calls here began. No one at the bank wanted to call the authorities. The head teller thought maybe you took the money home and would come by the bank in the morning. So she decided not to report the missing money until she spoke to you." He smiled. "Fortunately, your reputation is stellar, giving me the time I needed to stop you."

"What are you talking about? Stop me from what?" She felt a pump of adrenaline course through her veins. Everything was coming together in horrible detail.

"Do not be coy, Miss Mitchell. I know you took the money. Obviously, you were planning to leave town with my daughter's murderer and use the money to finance your getaway." The corner of his mouth twitched. "Justice is sometimes extremely slow. But I am not."

To think she might be used as a lure chilled her. "I didn't take the money. I put the deposit bag in the night drop."

He tossed his hand in the air exposing his gold watch. "The money is not important to me. However, the connection is. I want Shane Fox, and Shane Fox wants you."

Carly's breath caught in her throat, and her heart beat wildly. "What will you do?"

"Nothing, my dear. You'll do it for me." Scodari's smile vanished, replaced by an expression of pure hatred.

Her fears confirmed, she took a deep breath. "I won't help you hurt Shane."

"You already are helping, my dear."

She squared her shoulders. "Leave, or I'll scream and keep screaming until the neighbors call the police."

Scodari laughed. "Oh, did I forget to tell you? I already called the authorities with some very important information. At one a.m. this morning, Shane Fox and a passenger were seen in a dark van driving north on Route 22 in Union. An hour later, the van was reported in New York City. At three a.m., in Connecticut. At five a.m., in Vermont. Later, in Maine."

She saw his lips form a small smile of satisfaction. He had thought of everything. Her hands shook and her mind raced. This could not be the end. She would not accept that.

Scodari took a step closer. "The authorities believe you and Fox are headed to Canada and have put up roadblocks along every interstate leading north, with every law enforcement agency from New Jersey to Maine participating. No one is coming here, and I will have the time I need to conclude my business."

Realizing she was totally alone made her throat go dry. "That's why the stakeout was pulled," she managed to say.

Scodari raised his cane to his forehead in a salute. "Precisely. I am counting on Mr. Fox to come to the same conclusion and return here to be sure you are safe."

Fear and anger knotted inside Carly. She felt like a caged animal at the mercy of its captor. She turned to Bobby.

He stared at the floor.

"Please. We can't let this happen to Shane."

Bobby stayed silent.

Scodari laughed. "Look at him. He won't help you, my dear. He can't even help himself."

His laugh sounded as though it came from the

depths of hell. "My roommate is returning today," Carly announced, the glimmer of hope moving her from the edge of panic. Scodari's expression stayed impassive, and he seemed unaffected by the news.

"For her sake, I hope she is detained at a road block. I would hate to have to hurt her. Besides, I have no plans to confront Mr. Fox here, among the neighbors. All I need is for him to call, and then we shall arrange to all meet at an appropriate place."

"He won't call." Carly shouted just as the phone rang.

Scodari smiled. He glanced at the phone. "Answer it," he demanded. "On speaker."

Her hands shook when she connected the call. "Hello?"

"He's there, isn't he?"

The blood rushed from her head when she heard Shane's voice. She looked at Scodari and saw him press his forefinger across his lips cautioning her not to speak.

"I am, Mr. Fox," Scodari confirmed.

"Carly, are you all right?"

"For now." Scodari's lips lifted in a sneer.

"Shane! Run!" Carly shrieked, hoping Shane could hear her.

When Scodari tossed his head in annoyance, Tino grabbed Carly around her waist and put his hand over her mouth before dragging her into the kitchen.

She tried to fight him but was easily overpowered.

"Carly!" Shane shouted. "If anything happens to her, I swear I'll kill you."

Scodari laughed. "I do not doubt you will try, but she is quite safe for the moment."

"Where is she?"

"Tino is entertaining her in the kitchen."

"If you hurt her."

"She is of no consequence to me. But you and I have business."

"What do you want?" Shane demanded.

"Meet me. Alone," Scodari said, his knuckles turning white.

"Where?" Shane asked.

"Somewhere quiet. You choose." Scodari punched the phone off speaker. "I'll find it," he replied. "Miss Mitchell will be released once our business is concluded." He paused then laughed. "That will be your hell. You will never know for sure."

In the kitchen, Carly's knees went weak, and she slumped against her captor. If Shane met Scodari, he was as good as dead.

"Tino, bring Miss Mitchell here," Scodari called.

On command, Tino dragged Carly into the living room and dropped her into a chair.

Scodari turned to Bobby. "Robert, help me convince Miss Mitchell she should stay here and remain calm." He reached into his coat pocket and pulled out a gun. He handed it to Bobby. "Be sure she does not make any trouble while I conclude my business with your brother."

Bobby took the weapon with trembling hands and aimed at Carly.

Bobby's expression was blank and robotic, but Carly could clearly see chaos in his eyes. She shifted, planning a way to move so the bullet wouldn't hit her heart if he fired.

Scodari placed the tip of his cane on Carly's

shoulder. "Cooperating would be in your best interests, Miss Mitchell." He ran the cane over her shoulder and down her arm. "And, Robert, if she gives you any trouble"—he raised the cane until the silver tip was even with Carly's heart before pushing it into her chest with firm pressure—"you know what to do." He took a step then turned. "Do not underestimate me, Miss Mitchell. I really do not need you. I can make Fox believe you are alive even if you are not."

"How?" Carly's mouth went bone dry, and her heart pounded in her chest.

"My dear, I think part of that question has already been answered." Scodari bent forward at the waist until his eyes were just inches from hers. "The rest is a surprise."

Chapter Sixteen

When the back door slammed shut, Bobby turned to the sound.

Carly didn't hesitate. She ran toward the front door, but only made it as far as the hallway.

Bobby grabbed her. "Goin' somewhere?"

Pulse racing, she yanked her arm free. "We have to go to the police. Scodari plans to kill Shane."

"It's not my fight."

"He's your brother." Her whirling mind moved between disbelief and outrage.

He shrugged, "Family is overrated."

She had to make Bobby listen. "He didn't kill Danni."

Bobby stared at the wall. "He could have."

Carly's brain jammed. The expression on Bobby's face made her heart beat so fast she thought she might black out. She took a few deliberate deep breaths to calm herself. "Do you honestly think he would kill Danni, kill anyone, after what he did for you?"

Bobby punched his chest with his forefinger. "He didn't do anything for me. He did it for himself. Nobody else."

"That's not true, Bobby." She pressed her lips together and held out her hand. "You and I can fix everything, but we first need to find Shane."

Bobby gestured to the door with his gun hand. "By

the time we find my brother, he will be dead, and Scodari will be long gone."

Carly's heartbeat rose, the rushing blood making her lightheaded. She blinked to stay focused. "We can try to stop Scodari."

He pointed the gun at her. "Don't be naïve. We both know the situation is beyond stopping."

Her breath came faster. She didn't want to think no solution existed. "Tell me why."

"Too many loose ends." He shook his head. "Someone will talk and then, like Danni, everyone has to die."

Carly's mind raced as questions formed into answers, and coincidences lined up in a theory more dreadful than believable. "Danni never called Shane, did she?"

Bobby cut his gaze to her but said nothing.

She rushed through a mental list of everything that happened, and realization sucker-punched her. "Danni didn't know this area. She could have never found Bridgepoint Farm at night."

Bobby's brows drew down. "You're just guessing."

Carly's hands balled into fists. As angry as she was, outwardly she had to remain calm if she had any hoping of getting the whole truth from Bobby. "If the plan was to confront Shane about paternity, wouldn't she want to do that in front of witnesses?"

"The woman was crazy. Who know what she was thinking?" He snickered. "Guess we'll never know."

"I think you do," Carly said. "Danni wasn't strong enough to pull off something like this by herself. She needed someone to plan her every move and guide her through each step, someone who knew his way around." Her gaze searched Bobby's face, but she found his expression unreadable. "You are behind everything," she said, her voice shaky. As Bobby walked toward her, she shrank backward until she felt the edge of a table press into her thighs.

"I had a plan. A good plan," Bobby said slowly. "If everyone did their part, the plan would have worked. But you and Shane screwed up everything. Now it's him or me."

Contempt filled his eyes. Carly felt dizzy, as though she fell without a parachute. "Tell me about the plan, Bobby," she whispered.

"I told her exactly what to do." A sneer crossed his lips. "She screwed it up, too."

Carly held herself still, forcing herself to breathe evenly. "Who, Bobby? Who did you tell?" She knew, but she wanted to hear Bobby say her name.

He grinned. "Danni." He combed his fingers through his dark hair and walked to the front window. Moving the drapes aside with one hand, he studied a near-empty street.

She could tell by Bobby's body language he was on the verge of panic. She leaned onto the table in the hall for strength and saw the voice recorder. With Bobby still staring out the front window, she turned on the recorder and slid some mail over top. If she could keep Bobby talking, maybe she could get his confession on tape. The risk was huge. Beneath the paper, the conversation might be fuzzy if understandable at all. She took a deep breath. "You took the concert money. You were the only person who could have."

He spun, narrowing his gaze. "Shut up."

Though she could see a dark warning in his eyes, Carly had no intention of backing down. "You must have slipped back to the music room in those few moments I watched Shane sing. You stuffed the bag with paper, assuming I would be too absorbed to re-check the deposit when I came back to the room. And you were right. I never did." Carly's heart hammered. Her gaze slipped to the gun pointed at her chest.

Bobby's hand shook. "Okay, yeah. I took the money. So what?"

"How did you get the money out of the building? A lot of people were milling around that night."

Bobby's gaze roamed the room. "I stashed it behind some of the scenery and went back for it later."

Her fears solidified, and she felt surrounded in darkness. "You showing up after someone shot at me was no coincidence." Sadness rose, nearly choking her. "You fired those shots." His silence confirmed his guilt. "Why?"

Bobby put a hand to the back of his neck. "Because she asked me to warn you off."

"She?" Carly repeated.

"Yeah, Danni Baker. She thought if you got scared enough maybe you leave Shane alone."

Carly's mind spun, and her eyes narrowed. Shane's homecoming all made sense now. "The trip back here was never about helping anyone but yourself. You told Shane about the benefit and suggested he volunteer to do the concert, didn't you?"

Bobby waved off the allegation. "You're guessing. You have no proof."

Carly needed to lead him and keep him talking. He had to tell her everything if she hoped to clear Shane.

"You wanted him back here for a reason."

"He wanted to come," Bobby insisted.

"To see me?"

Bobby looked away, and then looked back. "The last year or so, he wasn't the same. He needed to get you out of his system. I figured you'd send him packing, and things would go back to normal." Frowning, he shook the gun. "But you didn't cooperate."

As everything fell into place, Carly's mouth went dry. Disillusionment flared. Betrayal burned. Shane meant nothing to Bobby. He was simply a pawn. "And you made sure Danni would be here to pick up the pieces."

Bobby's eyes darkened. He laughed. His gun hand shook again, and he used his left hand to steady his aim. "Bright girl. I'll be long gone before anyone else figures out that part."

"I don't understand why you took the money. You don't need it. Unless...." her voice trailed off and her eyes widened. "Unless you needed some fast cash. For you to need money before you could get cash from a bank only one reason makes sense. You killed Danni Baker."

A smile curled his mouth, and he pointed. "Bingo, baby. You're a regular homicide hunter. Too bad no one else will know just how smart you are."

"If I connected the dots, eventually so will the police," she said, praying the voice recorder was picking up the conversation.

He thumbed back the trigger on the revolver before walking to Carly and placing the barrel alongside her left temple. "I should kill you, too."

At the touch of the cold, gray steel, Carly flinched. She struggled with the uncertainty of her fate but knew she needed to play the scene to its end. "But you won't."

Bobby pressed the gun harder. "Are you so sure?"

Though her stomach churned and her heart pounded, she fought to sound as calm as she possibly could. "I am."

Bobby laughed. "I'm not."

Carly reached out, "Shane loves you. Everything he did, he did for you."

"Will he still love me if I kill you, too?"

The words sounded forced, like a decision not yet made. Carly locked her gaze with Bobby's. Heart pounding and palms sweating, she reached up and grabbed the barrel of the gun. "You don't want to shoot me, Bobby. I can help." She saw his expression change from anger to a deadly blank stare. Each second passing in silence seemed like an hour. She inched the gun away from her temple. "If you do this, you'll hate yourself forever. Let me help you." She leaned forward and kissed him on the cheek. "I promise you won't be alone."

Bobby shattered. His breath expelled in a rush of air, and he dropped to his knees. He looked upward as he thumbed the hammer back into place. "It was an accident. You have to believe me. Danni wanted Shane, and Scodari wanted his daughter happy. I had a plan, and it would have worked, but you didn't play your part, Carly. You were supposed to play your part."

Carly battled the urge to run to safety, but she needed more on the recorder if she had any chance of clearing Shane. With a hand on his arm, she urged

Bobby to stand. "What should I have done, Bobby?" she prompted in a soft voice.

"You were supposed to tell Shane to marry Danni. You were supposed to fall back on your sense of honor and get Shane to do the right thing." His shoulders slumped, and he shook his head. "But you didn't, Carly. Why didn't you?"

Carly's gaze drifted to the gun and held out her hand. "Give me the gun, Bobby. We can't have another accident if we have any hope of helping Shane." When he handed her the weapon, she heaved it as far down the hall as she could and stood between him and the weapon in case he changed his mind. "I'm sorry, Bobby."

"You're sorry!" A frown set onto Bobby's face. "What do you have to be sorry about? You've done okay since I saw you last."

"You've been successful, too." Again, she touched his arm.

But he pulled back. "Successful? Me?" Mockery laced his voice. "My life? Yeah, it was really great. I always had to take a back seat to my brother. He was the big-shot celebrity. I was only the rock star's kid brother. Then Danni came along. She was so beautiful. I wanted her to notice me, but she wanted Shane." He poked a finger into his chest for emphasis then he grinned. "Well, I had her first. Right there, at the big party and in Shane's bed. After I made sure I liquored her up, I had her." He laughed.

Carly gasped. "Are you saying Nicky is your son?"

Bobby laughed. "Can you beat that? My kid."

"But the DNA test confirmed the paternity."

Bobby's smile faded. "I watched the technician

swab Shane's cheek. She was so wrapped up in my superstar brother that she didn't even see me swipe a kit. Didn't take much to switch the swabs after that. A little distraction because a rock-star was in the lab, a little sleight of hand, and the DNA test report is a 99.9999% match."

Nausea filled Carly's stomach. "You let Shane believe he slept with Danni and got her pregnant." She felt as though she couldn't breathe. "Why?"

"Because Danni wanted Shane, and Scodari wanted whatever Danni wanted." His shoulders slumped. "What was I gonna do? Tell Daddy I was the one who knocked up his daughter? He would have killed me."

She could see both fear and pain on Bobby's face.

"Besides, even if the kid looked more like me, who'd say anything? Anyone who looks at us can tell Shane and I are brothers. Our looks aren't exactly the same, but close enough. So I hatched this plan. She'd get Shane, and I'd stay alive. It would have worked if you hadn't screwed up everything by reconciling with Shane."

The fire was back in his eyes. Carly tried to control the shock racing through her. "How could you lie about something as important as a child?" She saw fear fill his eyes.

He ran a hand through his hair. "I told you, Scodari would have killed me. It's all survival, baby."

Every nerve Carly had went on full alert. "But now, you're willing to let him kill Shane."

Bobby grabbed his head with both hands. "Shut up!" he demanded. "I can't help him now." He looked at her. "Help me," he pleaded.

Torment lay bare in his eyes. She reached out and

touched his arm. "Danni's death was an accident."

Bobby's shoulders drooped, and he paced. "Yes. An accident."

Though she knew time was running out to save Shane, she needed this confession. "Tell me," she said quietly.

Bobby stopped pacing. His eyes softened as he remembered. "When Danni finally realized she'd never have all of Shane, she said she planned to tell him everything." He whirled and caught Carly by the upper arms. "Don't you see, I had to stop her. If Scodari ever found out what really happened, I'd be a dead man."

Carly saw madness wash over Bobby's face like a breaking wave. She swallowed with great difficulty and then found her voice. "I can help you."

Bobby acted as though he hadn't heard. "The Rangers were only into their first set when Danni called me. I knew I could get to the rooming house and back before the concert was over so I told her to stay put. But when I got there, she was getting ready to go to the school. I tried to talk her into sticking with the plan, but she said she couldn't live a lie any longer. We argued. When she started to leave, I grabbed her by the hair. She screamed and dug her nails into my hand. I got pissed and hit her. She shut up for a couple of minutes, but then started yelling again. She told me I'd be sorry for what I did and tried to get around me."

She saw a muscle tic at the corner of his jaw as though he was losing control.

"I grabbed her arm and punched her a few times as hard as I could. The last blow was to the side of her head, and she fell backward and didn't move."

Carly fought the dread rising in the pit of her

stomach. "So, you left her there and told Shane to meet her at the farm."

"I panicked."

Carly saw his features darken and his eyes shine with a mad-like acceptance.

"This was the end of the Rangers unless I could give Shane an alibi." He shook his head slowly. "But trying to help only made things worse."

Her mouth went bone dry, and her heart pounded as too many things started making sense. "You didn't know she had a copy of the test results, did you?"

"She told me when I got there."

"Your plan worked then."

Bobby snickered and looked at his hands. "When you saw the scratches, I knew others might, too. I figured I needed to skip town. The cash was right there and, with you so wrapped up in watching my brother sing, easy enough to swipe."

Everything finally made sense. "You were afraid the police would watch the concert DVD for potential evidence."

Bobby nodded. "They would as part of the investigation. A sharp detective would notice the scratches and ask questions."

"So, you broke into Judge McKennan's house to get the tape."

"I knew she had a copy after the show, but when I couldn't find it, I thought she might have given you the DVD." He shrugged. "I guess I shouldn't have taken the money." He snickered. "That was stupid."

Carly began to inch away. When the voice recorder was found, Bobby's confession would clear Shane, but in getting him to talk, she may have sealed her fate. He couldn't afford to let her go now. She began to bolt but wasn't fast enough.

Bobby grabbed her and wound his fingers in her hair. He spun her and frowned. "Now you know everything."

His expression was more frightening than his twisted smile moments earlier. Though terror slapped at her, Carly held herself still and forced herself to breathe evenly when she said, "What can I do to help you?"

"I don't know." Bobby released her and raked his fingers through his hair.

She saw panic grow in his eyes so reached out and touched his arm. "We can figure this out together."

He shrugged off her hand and paced again. "Shane would know what to do. He could always fix anything I did." He put his hands on the top of his head and kept walking.

Carly felt her pulse in her throat. She pressed herself against the wall. The fear she heard in his voice seemed on the verge of breaking free.

Bobby stopped moving. "But Shane's gone," he continued with a moan. "Nobody can fix this." He raised his hands and shook his head. "What am I going to do?"

Gathering her tattered courage, Carly captured his gaze. "I'm here. I'll help you."

"How?"

"By first helping Shane," she said firmly.

"It's too late. Even if we get to Shane before Scodari does, when Shane realizes what I did, he'll send me away for sure."

Her heart pounded so hard she wondered if he could hear it. "No, he won't. He will know how to fix this. You said so yourself. But we have to find him first."

"How do we do that?"

Fear was in his eyes now. "First, we call the police." She hoped her voice sounded confident and assuring. Everything opposite of what she was feeling.

"No!" Bobby's gaze sharpened and his voice became insistent. "No cops!"

"Okay," Carly agreed in a quiet voice. "Then we have to make sure we find Shane before Scodari does."

"Shane will hate me." Bobby muttered.

She could sense barely controlled panic radiating from every pore in Bobby's body. One wrong move and he would explode. "No, he will understand. I promise."

Bobby headed toward the front door. "I have to leave."

She grabbed his arm. "You need to help Shane." She shook Bobby hard. "We have to find him now!" Bobby looked as though someone struck him in the face.

A measured silence seemed to last forever before he finally said, "Okay, what do you want me to do?"

The sudden determination in his voice stunned her. Just moments before they had been on opposite ends of a deadly gun, now they seemed allies, trying to save Shane from an even deadlier foe. "Do you have any idea where Shane might go to meet Scodari?"

Bobby's eyes narrowed. "To that farm. When we were kids, Shane and I used the barn as a secret hiding place."

"Then let's go," Carly said. Excitement and urgency replaced the fear in her heart. "We need to get there before Scodari does."

Chapter Seventeen

Ann Tyler fidgeted. She shifted from one foot to the other while she waited for the police officer to finish checking her ID. She folded her arms across her chest and watched rubber-necking drivers on the interstate slow as they passed her to see what was happening. *Damn.* She was still thirty miles from home, and the patrol officer was taking forever. She should have been there for Carly, instead of hopping around Midwest meetings, vying to be the next vice president of the company.

The media was really playing up this case. Murder, robbery, dodging the law. None of what was being reported made any sense. Carly would not have taken the benefit money, nor would she ever help a killer escape no matter how much she loved him. Then there was the phone call.

The wire services reported Carly and Shane's car on Route 22 in Union, New Jersey at seven a.m. *Impossible.* She'd been on the phone with Carly at seven. If Carly and Shane were on the run, what were they doing back at the house?

"Sorry to take so long, miss." The patrol officer handed back her identification. "I called the detective assigned to the case, and he is very interested in your story."

"It isn't a story. I called Carly this morning. She

was home." Ann tucked her driver's license inside her purse and released the driver from the limousine service taking her home. She eased into the back seat of the patrol car. "Are we going to the station?"

"No. Detective Carter will meet us at your place."

Ann pumped her fist. "Now we're getting somewhere. Put on the disco lights and kick this thing in the tail." She settled into the seat. "Let's see what one of these babies can do."

****

Bobby's sports car bounced and bottomed out as he sped across the overgrown field near the Bridgepoint barn. He shut off the engine and slapped the steering wheel. "If we go any farther, we'll rip out the trannie. We'll have to walk the rest of the way."

Carly was out of the passenger seat before he finished speaking. "Which way?"

He pointed in the direction of the river. "The barn is behind those trees."

She broke to a run. "Are you sure this is the place?"

"As kids, we always hid out there whenever we got into trouble. If the barn hasn't burned down or fallen down, he'll be there."

As Bobby kept pace beside her, all she could really do was pray he was right.

****

The patrol car made the trip from Union to Hillsborough in record time. Ann flew into the house and saw police everywhere. She stepped around an officer lifting a fingerprint from an upturned table and nearly tripped over a fallen lamp. Near an overturned chair, broken glass from a light bulb glittered in the sun coming through the front window. What stood out in all its lethal calm was the gun laying in the middle of the floor. She watched a member of the evidence team slip a wooden rod through the finger loop near the trigger and slide the gun into an evidence bag. She grabbed the nearest officer. "Is Carly here?"

"No, but she was. Looks as though her company got a little rough."

Detective Carter looked up from making notes in a black book. "You must be Miss Tyler."

Still taking in the scene, Ann nodded.

"Now, tell me about the phone call, Miss Tyler," Carter prompted.

"As I told the officer at the road block, Carly could not have been in any of the places she was reported seen with Shane. I called her at seven this morning, and she told me she was here all night." She shook her hear. "Carly isn't one of the X-men mutants. She can't be in two places at the same time."

"I see." Carter wrote a few more notes in his book and then motioned to the couch. "Please sit, Miss Tyler." He sat on the coffee table and faced her.

Ann's gaze darted between Carter and the team of officers still searching the house. "Is Carly a suspect in the murder?"

Carter shrugged. "Not officially, but I don't know."

"What do you know?" Ann asked. Every instinct warned Carly was in serious trouble.

"Not a lot I can tell you right now."

"I heard the news say Carly took money from the benefit." Ann waved her hands in front of her face. "No way. She would never do that."

Carter raised an eyebrow and nodded. "Actually,

we don't think she did."

Ann's stomach twisted. "Now I am really lost."

"If Miss Mitchell took the money to help Fox, they would have had plenty of time to put as much distance between them and Hillsborough as they could before the cash would be missed. Plus, the erratic sightings don't make sense." He paused and caught her gaze. "We think someone else had a hand in the robbery."

She grinned. "I told you! This whole thing is a mistake." But her joy quickly faded as she watched three uniformed men enter through the front door and go directly to the second floor. She looked at Carter and felt he was holding something back. "You know more. What else?"

With a toss of his head, Carter directed another man with evidence bags to the kitchen before flipping through the pages in his notepad. "As a matter of routine, we ran the numbers on the phone records as soon as we got them. One was an overseas call to Southeast Asia."

"She probably tried to call her dad. He told us he was going overseas on a business trip."

Carter added the information to his notes. "We're still attempting to reach the person on the other end of the call. One person we did reach was Emily McKennan. According to the phone records, the call was placed to her at three a.m. Mrs. McKennan is ready to swear in court Miss Mitchell was on the line. Your call is logged at three minutes after seven in the morning from the hotel in Chicago." He looked up from the paper and shrugged. "The getaway looks like a set-up to get the unmarked away from the house."

Ann folded her arms across her chest. "And it

worked."

"We didn't have a choice at the time. We had to go on the facts we had." Carter turned away to answer a question shouted from the kitchen. "Sorry. Anyway, that's all we know so far."

She leaned forward. "Do you have a theory on who might have gone to all this trouble to set up Carly and Shane?"

Carter shook his head. "We don't get cases like this here, so we have to start slowly and explore all possibilities. That takes time. But I can tell you, whoever did this was someone a whole lot bigger than this department normally comes in contact with. Someone who apparently wanted to get to Fox before we did. We have some leads, but I'm not at liberty to confirm anything just yet."

She saw his expression tighten. "You think Shane and Carly are in real danger, don't you?"

Carter sighed. "Looks that way."

****

When Carly circled a large cluster of trees, her knees started to buckle, and she grabbed onto Bobby to keep from falling. The barn was there but so was Scodari's limousine. "Shane is in there. We've got to help him." She poised to run and head for the barn.

Bobby lunged and grabbed her right arm. He swung her behind the trees so they wouldn't be seen from the open barn door. "Don't be a fool. We can't help him now."

The blood rushed from her face, making her light-headed, but she refused to accept what Bobby meant. "If Scodari is in there, then Shane is still alive."

"Maybe, maybe not."

Carly forced herself to be calm. "I can't stay here. I have to do something." Her voice was firm.

Bobby's shoulders dropped. "Okay, relax. But do what? I'm in no mood to run smack dab into one of Scodari's retaliations."

She glared a warning and grabbed the front of his shirt with both hands. "You'll do whatever is necessary. You got Shane into this, and you will help me get him out. You owe him, Bobby. It's time to repay the debt."

Bobby brushed away her hands. "Look, all I'm saying is we have to be careful." He looked over her shoulder. "And quiet. First, we have to scope out the situation, and then we can decide what to do. Agreed?"

"Agreed," Carly said, caution heavy in her tone. What choice did she really have anyway?

****

Back at the house in Hillsborough, Ann drummed her fingers on her thigh. "So, what are you waiting for?" She put her hands on her hips and tossed her head. "I know I'm not your boss or anything, and I know you have policies and procedures to follow, but I know Carly wouldn't so any of the things reported in the news. I'm not just her roommate. I'm her best friend." She felt her stomach clench. "No. Better than that. I'm the closest thing she has to a sister. We've wasted a lot of time dotting I's and crossing T's. We need to find Carly. I told you she was innocent, and I'll bet my last dollar Shane is, too."

"Calm down." Carter scratched the back of his neck with the pencil's eraser. "Exactly where do you expect me to start looking for Miss Mitchell?"

"You're the cop. You're supposed to have all the answers. So, stop asking questions and just go do what you do best." Ann pointed to the door as though she really expected him to follow her directions.

Carter gave her a sidelong glance. "She could be anywhere and with anyone. Finding her won't be easy."

Ann grimaced. She had to agree. She swung her head to one side in exasperation just as one of the officers signaled to Carter.

"Sir, found something." The officer pointed. "Looks like a voice recorder."

Ann's heartbeat rose, and she jumped to her feet. "I wonder." She ignored the detective's puzzled stare and walked toward the officer, reaching for the recorder he held.

"Don't touch it," Carter said.

She waved off Carter's warning and picked up the recorder. "Carly was a bit retro. Didn't trust the uber-digital stuff. She liked to use voice-activated recorders to make notes. Normally, she never goes anywhere without this dinosaur—my words, not hers. Yet, here it is. I think she wanted someone to find this."

"Let's find out if you are right," Carter replied.

Ann hit Rewind and then Play. "Atta girl," she said they heard Carly's voice.

The conversation that followed stunned everyone in the room to silence.

"Damn." Carter rushed to the nearest police cruiser and grabbed the radio from its cradle. "Pull all roadblocks and get everyone back here as fast as they can. We know who killed Danni Baker, and it wasn't Shane Fox."

****

Carly and Bobby saw Scodari and Tino emerge from the barn.

"Get down!" Bobby whispered. He shoved Carly behind a low clump of hedges and covered her with his body.

From their low position, they watched Tino pull the weather-faded barn doors closed.

"Think he'll get loose?" Tino asked, picking up a large plank and muscling it into the slots on both doors.

Scodari glanced over his shoulder at the barn. "Not in his condition. He'll keep until we return with the girl."

Tino nodded and waited until Scodari got in the back seat of the limo before dusting off his clothes and sliding behind the wheel. In another second, the drone of the car engine disturbed the life in nearby trees as both the car and birds left the area.

Carly's heart pounded a frenzied rhythm inside her chest. "Shane's hurt," she whispered in a voice clearly on the verge of hysteria.

"And probably out cold or they wouldn't leave him," Bobby added.

She gasped. "We need to get him out of here." She ran to the barn doors and clawed at the wooden brace. "Help me with this!"

After muscling the heavy plank from its resting place, Bobby pushed open the doors.

The sudden explosion of light into the barn rested solely on Shane. He sat on the dirt floor, his hands securely tied to the center roof support. His head bowed to the left with his chin resting on his chest and his body slumped. He didn't move.

From the doorway, he didn't appear to be breathing. Carly ran to him. When she touched his face with trembling hands, his head rolled to the right, and he moaned. He was alive. Relief brought tears to Carly's eyes. "Wake up. Please wake up!" She tapped his cheek to bring him around.

Bobby untied Shane's hands and laid him onto the floor. "How bad is he hurt?"

"I can't tell for sure," Carly replied, relieved he still breathed. A deep gash sliced his forehead and would require a few stitches. Shane's face was badly bruised, and a small trickle of blood ran from his mouth, but a strong but rapid pulse beat against her fingers at the side of his neck confirmed he was still alive. She ran her hands along his body and could not feel any obvious broken bones. She held out her hand. "Give me your shirt."

"Why?" Bobby asked, taking off the shirt even before he finished speaking.

Carly ripped the shirt into strips. "The wound on his forehead needs to be cleaned." She held up half of the torn shirt. "Take this to the river and soak it."

Bobby nodded and dashed from the barn.

Carly gently patted Shane's face. Her vision clouded with forming tears. "Everything will be all right now, baby." She cradled his head. "You're getting out of here." She looked at Bobby. "We all are."

Shane didn't respond.

She dabbed at his cuts and let out a long breath of relief when he opened his eyes.

"Get out of here," he said. "Scodari went back to the house to get you. When he finds out you're gone, he'll come right back here."

Tears welled in her eyes when she heard his pain-filled voice. "I'm not going anywhere without you," she replied without hesitation. The shallow breath Shane took painted fresh agony on his face.

Shane looked beyond Carly and saw his brother. "Bobby, get Carly out of here!"

"Not without you." Bobby dropped the tattered shirt and looped Shane's arm around his neck. Bobby lifted him.

Shane's pain-filled cry filled the barn. He slumped against his brother.

Each time Shane groaned in response to Bobby adjusting his position, Carly felt like a fist squeezed her heart. She could do nothing to ease his pain. Right now, the important thing was getting as far away from the barn as they could. She looped an arm around his back to support him. "Can you walk?"

Shane nodded.

Bobby leaned the full weight of Shane's body against his hip while Carly draped Shane's free arm around her shoulders.

"You ready?" Bobby asked.

****

"Let's do it." Shane steadied himself against his brother. Nothing prepared him for the knife-like pain galloping through every part of his body when he tried to move. His knees buckled, and he pitched forward, nearly taking all three to ground.

"This is no good. He'll never walk out this way." Bobby shook his head. He eased Shane onto a stack of hay bales and turned to Carly. "You stay here with him. I'll get the car closer even if I end up putting some dents in the undercarriage in the process."

Shane leaned back his head against a molding hay bale and waited for a fresh wave of agony to pass. He didn't need a doctor to tell him some serious damage had been done. Tino did his job well—ruthless, precise, and with such perfection that Carly could not be aware just how thorough the beating had been. "Carly, please, get out of here," Shane whispered through vision-blurring agony. The pain pounded more frequently now, but he had to ignore it and keep any hint of how badly he felt from showing on his face. The only thing he cared about right now was her safety.

"Not on your life." Carly knelt and took his hand. "I'm not leaving without you."

Chapter Eighteen

Carly relaxed. Bobby would be back soon. The nightmare was almost over. Once Shane was safely at the hospital, they would be fine. All of them. Even Bobby. "Look where we are." She wiped a fresh drop of blood from the corner of Shane's mouth with her fingertip. "All because we couldn't stop loving each other."

Shane licked his lips. He pushed back against the hay bale and winced. "Star-crossed lovers always have to deal with adversity before they live happily ever after."

She smiled. "Do you think we will, too?"

"I do," he mumbled. "Deep in my heart, I always did." He looked into her eyes. "If you'll have me."

She gently kissed his bruised mouth. "I will."

"Don't answer so quickly. I'm no prize." He laughed, the act turning into a cough. "One day I'm on top of the world, the next I'm hiding from the police behind shrubs."

"Try to lie still," Carly begged. "Bobby will back soon."

"I'm okay." With shaky effort, he raised his bloodied hand and touched her cheek. "I love you, Carly. If you love me, you have to go. Scodari won't stop until either I'm dead or we both are."

She stroked his matted hair. "You shouldn't have

come back for me." Her composure fragmented, and hot tears slipped down her cheeks. "Look what I've done to you."

His hand dropped. "You haven't done anything. I put you in danger."

She heard the desperate edge in his voice. "We can argue the point later." Carly tried to sound convincing, but the nervous crinkle she felt would not go away. She touched his arm. "You're freezing."

"I'm okay, but I need you to tell you something before it's too late."

"Save your strength. Whatever you have to say can wait."

"No, it can't." Shane shifted, his face twisting as he moved. He inhaled and held the breath. "I was too emotional at the time, but thinking back now, I realized Danni could not have known about the Bridgepoint Farm. This place was abandoned and left to rot after the land was devalued because of the reroute of the interstate bypass. Someone had to tell her about the place. If we could find out her contact, the information could help clear me."

"I know." Carly hesitated, brushing off the urge to tell him about Bobby. "But we can't worry about that right now. You need medical attention. We don't know just how seriously you've been hurt."

Shane nodded but said nothing.

Carly moved closer and cradled his head. "You know," she said, stroking his cheek, "I was really angry when I saw you in the hall at the school. I knew we would have a showdown, and I could do nothing to prevent it. I thought about leaving, but then said, the hell with running, the hell with him. I planned to walk up the aisle, look into your eyes, and walk out the door without saying a word. If I could do that, I'd finally be over you."

Shane flinched. "How could either of us know that day was only the beginning of a deadly game we probably can never win? Scodari has an unbeatable hand. You don't deserve this."

"He won't win, Shane." Carly drew in a deep breath and commanded herself not to tremble. "If I have to, I'll fight him myself."

"When did you turn into such a wildcat?"

"About the same time you came back into my life."

Shane tried to laugh, but his lips clamped tight and his head dropped.

"Where's the pain?" Carly asked, anxiety tightening her chest.

"Everywhere." He pressed a hand against his stomach and looked up. "You need to go. I want you miles away from here by the time Scodari comes back."

"I'm not leaving." Carly wiped more blood from the corner of Shane's mouth and adjusted her expression not to show fear. Shane's condition had to be worsening. He shouldn't be bleeding so heavily from the small cut on his lip. She ran her hands down his chest, feeling nothing broken. When she touched his abdomen, he cried out.

His eyes watered, and the muscles in his face constricted.

"Probably just a muscle strain."

"Scodari is psychotic." He winced and inhaled as deeply as he could. "Grief and rage have blinded him to any type of rational behavior. He won't stop until I'm dead. When Bobby gets back, just go. Leave me here. I will only slow you down. I'll handle Scodari and his goon until you can alert the police."

Carly shook her head. "Scodari wants revenge, and I think we both know what his ultimate plan may be. He wants me dead, too. Why else would he have gone back for me? He's won't be satisfied until he has destroyed us."

As he sat up, Shane grimaced. "I can face anything if I know you're safe." He leaned back against a rotting wooden stall.

"Safe? For how long? Passing years haven't protected us. Do you think anyone can ever be safe from a man like Scodari?" She gathered her fading strength and tossed her shoulders. "Besides, I refuse to think a higher power would have put us back together just to watch us die in this dingy, decaying barn."

Shane laced his fingers around hers. "If this was a paperback novel, the cavalry would burst in right about now and save us."

She smiled. "I'm afraid I don't hear the pounding of hoof beats." She wiped a trailing tear from her cheek with the back of her hand. "So, I guess it's just you and me."

"And Bobby," Shane reminded in a low, throaty voice.

"Yes, and Bobby." She was afraid she sounded uncertain. She may have been wrong to trust Bobby. She prayed he would come back. "We will all leave together."

Shane smiled sadly. "Even if we do manage to wiggle out of this trap, there's still the matter of murder charges."

Carly shook her head. "You won't be charged with

murder."

Shane's gaze searched her face. "Did the police find Danni's killer?"

Carly had to fight her own personal battle of restraint not to reveal too much. How could she tell Shane Bobby was responsible for everything happening to them? How could she tell him that his brother fathered Danni's child and ultimately killed her? She couldn't. Bobby would have to tell Shane. She hoped Bobby's confession was clear on the voice recorder, and she knew Ann would eventually find it. The only variable left was whether she and Shane would be alive or dead when his name was cleared. Outside the barn, a car engine died.

Carly held her breath.

"Let's get the hell out of here." Bobby walked to Shane. He draped his brother's arm around his neck and lifted him.

When he did, Shane cried out with the pain.

"You okay?" Bobby asked.

Shane nodded. "Let's go."

Bobby shouldered his brother's weight and half-dragged, half-carried him toward the door. "Hang on, bro. We're almost home free."

Carly grabbed Shane around the waist. When he looked at her, she noticed a fresh line of blood coming from his mouth. "Hurry, Bobby. He's bleeding internally. We have to get him to the hospital."

Bobby looked at Shane's pale face and then at Carly. "Maybe we should carry him."

Shane gritted his teeth. "No. Just keep going."

They were nearly to Bobby's car just outside the barn door when they heard another car approaching.

She didn't have to see it to know Scodari was returning for Shane. "We've got to make a run for it." Carly dragged Shane in a desperate attempt to get to Bobby's car.

Bobby sighed. "It's useless. We have nowhere to run. We gambled, and we lost."

Carly saw the surrender in his eyes and knew he was right.

Chapter Nineteen

Trapped. The word spread through Carly mind like a plague as all three were forced back inside the barn.

Bobby lugged Shane to a pile of hay bales and lowered him to the floor. He knelt next to Shane to support him.

Two sets of approaching footsteps signaled to Carly the valiant attempt to save Shane had failed. Slumping, she looked up, saw Tino draw a gun from his belt, and point the barrel at Shane.

"Should I off him now, boss?" Tino asked.

Carly cradled Shane, shielding him with her body. An icy chill washed over her, and she resisted the urge to look at Tino. He would not see the fear in her eyes.

When Bobby tried to do the same, Tino grabbed him by the back of his shirt and threw him to the side. "Sit there and shut up," Tino ordered.

Scodari yanked Carly away from Shane. "You can't save him."

Using the hay bales, Shane pulled himself up. He swayed and held onto a roof support pole. "Scodari, you son of a bitch, let her go."

Carly strained against Scodari's grip. "Take me and leave him alone."

Scodari's dark gaze impaled her. "Very noble, Miss Mitchell." His grip tightened. "But it won't be quite that easy." He slid his stare from her face to

Shane's. "For either of you."

"Can't you see he's hurt?" Carly still fought a brave battle to get to Shane's side.

Scodari smirked. "See he's hurt, Miss Mitchell? I demanded it be so." He cupped her chin. "Such a pretty face. Perhaps I'll tell Tino not to damage it very much."

Gaze not leaving the barrel of Tino's gun pointed at his heart, Shane clamped one arm against his stomach and took two steps forward."Let Carly go."

Scodari grabbed Carly even more tightly and dragged her closer. He held her around the waist and pulled a small pearl-handled revolver from his jacket pocket. "How touching." He angled his head. "Exactly what are you willing to do for this woman? Beg for her life? Die, perhaps?" He cocked the trigger of the small weapon and placed the barrel against Carly's temple. "Or maybe she is willing to die for you."

****

Shane reached out. "Don't!" He watched Scodari drag Carly away from his outstretched hand. He tried to step closer, but the effort came with mind-splitting agony and confirmed his injury was more than just a few broken ribs. The terror he saw in Carly's eyes made the pain easy to ignore. Adrenaline pumped through his body, dulling the throbbing for the moment. Slowly, he took another step but reeled and grasped a roof support to steady himself.

Bobby lunged toward Shane.

But Scodari waggled a warning with his gun. "Ah, ah, ah, Robert. You stand there like a good boy."

Scodari nodded to Tino. "I believe you know what to do."

Carly looked at Shane. "Don't hurt him," she

screamed, twisting in Scodari's arms as Tino slowly made his way to Shane.

"Hush now," Sccodari whispered into Carly's cheek. "Do not interrupt again." He brushed a damp lock of hair from her eyes with the barrel of his gun and kissed her cheek. "I want you to witness what happens to men who hurt my family."

Tino flexed his fingers before balling his right hand into a fist. Then reaching back, he took aim at Shane's face.

Despite the pain, Shane moved to the left, barely dodging Tino's fist.

"Tino," Scodari called. "Do not play with your prey. Finish him."

Shane saw rage fill Tino's face and watched him prepare to strike. He was too weak to avoid the next hit. Once Tino finished him, what would happen to Carly? Somehow, he had to save her. But how? Maybe if he let Tino do his worst, Scodari would be satisfied and let Carly go. He prayed his death would be revenge enough. He stared at Tino and mentally prepared for the punishment to come.

Tino stood, arm cocked, ready to deliver a blow. "Boss. This ain't gonna be no fun if he's gonna stand there like a punching bag. Lemme pump him fulla lead instead, and let's get outta here."

Scodari's gaze tilted upward. "I have a better idea. One sure to entertain us both."

"What are we gonna do?" Tino asked.

"We play a little game that will decide who dies first." Scodari pointed the gun at Bobby. "The brother who decided not to honor a bargain?" He moved his aim to Shane. "The brother who robbed my Danniella of life?" He jammed the barrel of his gun into Carly's cheek. "Or the women who deprived my daughter of the man she loved?"

"Take me," Shane shouted. "Carly has nothing to do with you or me, Scodari." He staggered backward. "Let her go."

"No," Carly screamed, twisting against Scodari's grasp. "I won't leave without you."

Scodari shook his head. "So many choices. A new game, Tino."

Tino stepped back.

Scodari smiled. "What would you do for this woman, Mr. Fox?"

Shane saw Carly wince as Scodari stroked her face with the tip of the gun. "Anything, I'd do anything for her."

Scodari's lips curled into a sneer, and he pushed the gun deeper into Carly's cheek. "She is beautiful. A bullet would put quite a large hole her face."

Carly gasped for air. Her eyes rolled back, and her knees buckled. She clutched at the arm around her waist and pulled herself up.

In contrast, Scodari's demeanor was a lethal calm. "You'll do anything for her?" he asked. "I wonder."

Shane staggered forward. "Name it!" he demanded.

Scodari moved the gun away from Carly's face only long enough to signal to Shane before returning the revolver to Carly's cheek. "Get on your knees." His mouth twisted. "And beg me to spare her." He cocked the gun. "Plead with me for her life, as my Danniella pleaded with you for your love."

A chill hung on the edge of his words. Shane slipped to the ground, supporting his weight on all fours until the pain subsided and his vision cleared. He lifted his head, locking is gaze with Scodari's as he slowly rose to his knees.

Scodari shoved Carly forward. He pulled her with him as he circled Shane. "Beg for her life before I grow weary of this game and end it." He cocked the trigger.

Carly closed her eyes.

"Don't shoot," Bobby shouted. He stepped forward. "Shane is innocent."

Tino shook his head, and a slow smile crossed his face. He slammed the barrel of his gun against the side of Bobby's head.

Bobby stumbled backward, and a trickle of blood ran down his cheek.

"Sit down and be still," Tino commanded. With one hand, he forced Bobby to the ground. "The boss is talkin'."

In the center of the barn, Shane inhaled sharply and blinked hard to keep the room in focus. If Scodari wanted him to beg, he would beg with every ounce of life he had left in his body. If these moments were his last, at least he could spend them saving Carly and his brother. He raised his face and met Scodari's cold stare. "Do whatever you want with me, but let Carly and my brother go." The words came slowly in a voice filled with barely checked anger and shaded pain.

Scodari laughed at the offer and shook his head. "Now, you try to up the stakes?" His gaze held Shane's while he stroked Carly's hair with the gun. "For two lives, you must beg twice as hard."

Shane straightened his battered body as best he could and pressed his palms together as though in prayer. Every nerve in his body screamed for release, and he suspected he could not stay conscious much longer. He prayed whatever time he did have left would be long enough. "I beg you. I'm the only one you really want. Let Carly and my brother go." He could barely concentrate as the barn softly muted into grays and blacks, the edges blurring as a loud ringing began in his ears.

Scodari looked from Shane to Carly, and then back to Shane. "Very nice, but not good enough!" He spat out the last phrase from between clenched teeth and pointed his gun at Shane, relaxing his hold on Carly just for a second.

When he did, she spun and grabbed his wrist with both hands, forcing his arm up just as the gun fired. The bullet discharged into the roof.

Cursing, he grabbed her throat.

Carly clawed at the hand around her neck with both hands. Her eyes widened as his grip tightened.

Shane made one desperate attempt to get to Carly, but Scodari easily angled away his body, and Shane fell to the ground. He looked up. "Don't hurt her."

Scodari merely laughed as he watched Shane's struggle to stand.

"Stay down," Bobby shouted. He jumped up, dove by Tino, and grabbed Scodari's gun hand, surprising Scodari enough to release his hold on Carly. The two men fell to the floor in a breakneck attempt to control the gun.

Tino spread his legs wide for balance and aimed his weapon at the pair rolling on the dirt floor.

Shane could see Tino's gun hand moving back and forth, as he struggled to get a clear shot.

Using the commotion as cover, Carly ran to Shane.

She dropped to her knees, eased Shane to sitting, and cradled his head in her arms.

Scodari gained the upper hand and rolled Bobby to his back on the barn floor. "You will regret this, Robert," he said with a sneer. He balled his hand into a fist and struck Bobby on his chin.

Bobby pushed upward and turned the advantage. "I already do. I regret the pact I made with you. I regret what I did to my brother and Carly. I regret it all. It's over. You have your revenge. Just look at us. We're beaten."

"This will never be over until I am certain the life of the man who took my Danniella from this earth joins her." Despite Bobby's efforts, he summoned the strength to angle his arm and point the gun at Shane.

"Bobby," Carly screamed, folding her body over Shane's.

"No!" Bobby grabbed Scodari's wrist with both hands and moved the gun upward and away from his brother.

Tino surged forward.

Carly threw her body in front of him.

He stumbled over her, losing his balance and hitting his head on a support pole, opening a large cut on his forehead. He fell to the ground unconscious.

Scodari and Bobby continued to fight. "You want me, not Shane," Bobby said through clenched teeth. His forearm shook as he held Scodari's hand and kept the gun pointed at the roof. "Nicky is my son."

"Your child?" Scodari stopped struggling.

Bobby nodded. "My son."

Both men stood, Bobby still gripping Scodari's arm. "Danni's death was an accident," Bobby said.

"The night she died, we argued about Nicky, and she pushed me. I got mad and pushed her back. She fell and hit her head on the coffee table."

Scodari's eyes widened, and a muscle along the side of his jaw line twitched. "You! You killed my Danniella?"

"I didn't mean to hurt her." Bobby licked his lips.

Scodari's face contorted into a mask of pure evil. He cursed and threw himself at Bobby. "Then you will die first!" Scodari folded his arm, locking the weapon between his body and Bobby's.

Carly looked over her shoulder to a broken length of wood. She eased away from Shane and laced her fingers around the board.

Shane was too weak to stop her as he saw her gaze lock on Scodari. Just as she started toward him, a muffled shot rang out. The fighting stopped, and both men lay still on the ground.

"Bobby!" Carly screamed. She dropped the plank and started toward the fallen men.

Out of the corner of his eye, Shane saw Tino rise and wipe the blood from his eyes.

The bodyguard picked up the plank Carly dropped and started toward her.

"Carly!" he shouted in warning.

She turned, and her eyes widened. She leaned away as Tino swung the board and caught her shoulder. Her eyes rolled up, and she fell backward.

Shane's gaze locked on Carly as he tried to crawl to her.

"Your turn," Tino said.

As the large man approached, Shane patted the dirt floor, hoping to find something to use to defend himself. He found nothing.

Tino raised the board to shoulder level. "I'll do you first, and then I'll take care of your girlfriend."

Shane rolled to his side and lifted his hand. "Not if I can help it," he whispered between clenched teeth.

Tino laughed and began to swing the board.

Shane heard his abrupt intake of breath and saw his eyes widen.

Tino's body paused, suspended in air as his hand lowered. Tino falling was the last thing Shane saw before his vision blurred and then faded to black.

Chapter Twenty

Carly opened her eyes. Light stabbed at her eyes, but she could see two people rise from chairs and rush forward. Her father's face came into focus first then Ann's. She looked back and forth between them, confused, before speaking. "Dad? Ann? Where am I?"

Noel Mitchell stoked his daughter's hair. "You're in a private room at the hospital. You're safe."

She wrinkled her brow then her eyes widened as one by one thoughts of her ordeal swirled in her mind. The fight. The blood. The gun. Her heart pounded. "Shane? Where's Shane?" Her voice bordered on hysteria. She tried to sit, but pain stabbed.

Noel pushed her back with soft pressure on her shoulder. "He's here, too." He put a hand on her cheek. "Detective Carter filled me in. Thank God, you're okay."

"You were in Hong Kong." Her head ached, and she tried to form thoughts that made sense.

"I was until your call." He reached for her hands. "Your call troubled me. A few well-placed calls later, and I was on a plane heading home." He looked away and then back. "I need to tell you something."

"Whatever you have to say, it can wait," Carly whispered.

"No, it can't. I've waited too long already, and," his voice cracked, "I promised your mother I would make this right."

"Dad, I—"

"Please." He cut her off with a wave of his hand. Listen to me. I feel as though I had a part in this, but please believe me, everything I did, I did for you. Misguided, perhaps, but I thought I was doing the right thing." He ran his fingers along the sides of his nose and blew out a long breath. "Honey, I did something a long time ago. I'm not very proud of what I did, and even more ashamed of keeping a secret, but, now, you need to know."

Carly put her hands on his forearms and felt his muscles tense. "You don't have to say anything. I found the check."

Noel looked into his daughter's eyes. "When?" Noel's voice broke.

"It doesn't matter." She bit her lower lip to keep from trembling, but the tears spilled any way from seeing the pain and the guilt etched on her father's face. "I forgave you a long time ago."

He swallowed. "Then I must ask for your forgiveness a second time." He inhaled and held her gaze. "Shane never took any money. He sent back the check. I signed his name and had my accountant cash the check." He ran a forefinger under his eyes. "And I made sure the check was somewhere you would find it."

Carly closed her eyes, and a single teardrop ran down her cheek. She thought she accepted his betrayal a long time ago, but the sadness that settled in her chest proved otherwise.

"I know you said you forgave me, but you didn't know the extent to which I went to keep you and Shane apart. Now, you do." He bowed his head and sighed. "I'll leave now." He turned and walked to the door.

"Dad, wait," Carly called, stopping him. "I nearly lost Shane because I didn't fight for what I wanted. I won't lose you for the same reason."

Noel turned slowly. "What do you want, Carly? Tell me, and it's yours." He stood silent, eyes closed, holding his breath.

She smiled. "I want my father in my life."

Noel walked to Carly and held her hand. "I should have trusted you and let you live your life your life." He straightened. "If you ever need to talk, about anything, from now on, I'll listen. I promise."

As a sense of urgency overtook her, she nodded. "I love you, Dad, but right now, I need to find out about Shane."

"I understand." With a smile, he walked to the door. "I'll see what I can do."

The new direction her relationship with her father was taking was a relief, but she had someone else on her mind. She turned to Ann. "I have to find out about Shane. I know he was rushed into surgery as soon as he got here, but nothing more." Urgency colored her voice. She swung her legs over the edge of the bed and stood. When her feet hit the ground, a rush of colors danced in front of her eyes.

Ann steadied her. "Are you sure this is a good idea?"

"I know it isn't," Carly said, brushing away the helping hands.

"I assumed that," Ann replied, stepping aside. "After what you've been through, I wouldn't dream of stopping you."

Once she got out into the hall, Carly grabbed onto the arm of a doctor in surgical scrubs passing by her room. "Do you know anything about the condition of Shane Fox?" The panic she felt turned into a deadly fear churning her stomach.

"He's in ER 3," the doctor answered.

A rush of optimism flooded her. "He's still alive then." Her words sounded like a prayer. She licked her dry lips. "Will he be all right?" she said, searching the doctor's face for confirmation.

The doctor glanced at her hospital gown before his gaze moved to her face. "You're a patient?"

Carly suspected she would not get much from the doctor, and her mind spun with a thousand answers she could use to try. "Shane and I were brought here together." She held the doctor's gaze. "No one has told me anything. I just need to know how he is."

The doctor hesitated then said. "The surgical team is doing everything possible."

"You were in there? Can you tell me how much longer he will be in surgery?" Fear replaced the relief she felt moments before. Nausea surged into her throat, and she found focusing hard.

"No, I'm a first-year intern and not on the surgical team, but I know the doctors working on him are some of the best," the doctor assured, touching her arm. "I can't tell you much only that he's in good hands. Someone will let you know when he's out of surgery."

Carly swayed and leaned onto the wall to steady herself.

The doctor grabbed her. "I think you had better get back to bed." He steered her back to her room.

Once in bed, Carly put her hand on his arm. "What

about Bobby Fox? Is he okay?"

"ER 4," he told her.

Carly's mind moved from total panic to cautious optimism. She closed her eyes and did one more thing she hoped would keep him alive. She prayed.

****

"Doctor, I'm getting gallops and rales. We're in trouble here. Blood pressure 60 over 10."

"I can't close yet. I need a few more minutes to tie off some pesky bleeders."

"We don't have a few minutes. You have to close now! We can go back in when he's stronger."

"With all the damage in the chest, he won't last the night if we can't stop this damn bleeding." The doctor's head snapped around as the data-based-video readout machine began a series of wide erratic sweeps with irregular audio blips. "Shit! He's fibrillating! Give me the paddles!"

At full charge, the doctor applied the paddles to the bare chest as everyone stood back.

The electric current raced through the still body, the man's back arching and then falling onto the operating table. The monitor recorded the corresponding surge but then fell to a flat line once again.

The doctor tried again. Again, nothing. "Lidocaine!"

"On!"

"Stand back!"

Another shock. Another failure.

"Bicarb!"

"On board!"

"Stand back!"

Another jolt to the heart failed to produce normal rhythm. The fight continued relentlessly, but the erratic beeping signaled an uncooperative heart. Soon, the beeps turned to a long, steady whistle.

"Flat line!"

The operating surgeon began compressions. "Come on, come on, stay with me!"

However, the monitor line refused to move.

"No response, beginning direct massage!"

Reaching into the chest cavity from the open abdomen, the surgeon palpated the heart with his right hand. "Heart syringe! Stat!"

A nurse slapped the long syringe into his waiting hand.

He stopped compressions and plunged the needle into the heart.

"One minute thirty since flat line," an attending nurse called out.

"Keep forcing air, and get the internal paddles ready again!"

"Two minutes!" the nurse said, keeping pace.

The surgeon pressed small silver paddles onto the static heart. "Clear!"

The body jumped and arched as the electricity surged to shock the heart back to life.

"Three minutes, doctor."

"Again!" he screamed. "More bicarb!" Each attempt at resuscitation failed.

Feverishly and without hesitation, the trauma team kept working. They watched the monitors carefully for any sign their efforts would be rewarded, but only the rush of forced air from the ventilation tube and the high-pitched steady tone of the heart monitor sounded.

Finally, after about fifty minutes, the surgeon's gloved hand reached up and removed his surgical mask. "He's gone."

"Shall I call it?" a second doctor asked.

The surgeon nodded.

"Time of death 9:00 p.m."

One by one, members of the team filed past the operating table and out of the room. The last nurse to leave stopped at the side of the operating table. "Maybe the team in the other room will have better luck," she whispered right before covering the young man's face with the hospital sheet.

****

"Excuse me," Detective Carter said to the doctor examining Carly. "I'd like a word with Miss Mitchell, if she feels up to talking." He held out his badge.

"Five minutes," the attending doctor warned. "She needs rest." He patted Carly's arm. "I'll find out something for you."

"Want me to leave?" Ann asked.

Carly shook her head. "Stay."

Carter walked closer to the bed. "Pretty clever of you to find a way to get a confession on a voice recorder, Miss Mitchell."

She nodded. "I watch both *Investigation Discovery* and *Ghost Hunters* and picked up all sorts of how-to information." She wiped a tear from her cheek. "What about Scodari and his thug? Are they in custody?"

"We caught them at the state line. They will be guests at the county jail for now." He thumbed through his notebook. "The prosecutor has the recorder, so I think those two will be staying in New Jersey for a very long time."

"And what about Bobby?" Carly bit down on her bottom lip, stopping only when she felt the pain.

"Mind if I sit?" When Carly nodded, Carter slid a well-worn metal chair close to the bed and sat. "His situation depends on a whole lot of things but mostly your statement and what Shane Fox can tell us."

Carly's eyes widened. Hope rushed through her body. "He's awake?"

Carter shrugged. "I was told he's still in surgery."

Closing her eyes, she prayed. She pressed her hands to her burning eyes. He had to live. He couldn't leave her again. She needed him. Bobby needed him.

Ann patted Carly's shoulder. "Can't this questioning wait? This is a really difficult time for her right now."

"No, I'm afraid it can't," Carter replied. "The first forty-eight hours are the most critical time in a murder case. We like to talk to involved parties while the information is fresh."

"I'm okay." Carly looked at Ann and nodded. "I want to tell him."

Carter took his notebook from his inside coat pocket.

Carly began talking. From the first moment she suspected things weren't right, to Bobby's strange actions, the video tape, the confrontation at her house, the climatic incident barn, she told him everything she knew including how Bobby saved their lives.

Carter closed the notebook and stood. "You know I have to check most of this." He winked. "Joe Kenda would."

At the reference to one of her favorite crime shows, she smiled.

"We'll probably need to talk again," Carter said before leaving the room.

Immediately, Carly's thoughts switched back to Shane. She sat upright. "Help me escape," she said to Ann. "I need to find out about Shane and Bobby."

****

Carly caught up with a doctor in the surgical waiting room. "Doctor, I'm Carly Mitchell. I need to know if you have any information on Shane and Bobby Fox."

The doctor took one look at her and motioned for her to sit. "I wasn't on the operating team."

The double doors leading to the surgical suite swung open, and an exhausted-looking O.R. nurse walked out.

"Wait here," the doctor said, patting Carly's hand.

Her heart beat a furious rhythm as she watched the two professionals. More than once both looked her way. When the doctor did turn to walk toward her, his expression remained somber.

Tears welled in Carly's eyes, and her shoulders slumped. The doctor did not say anything. His face told her although two men had fought for their lives in the surgical suites, one, if not both, had lost the battle.

****

When Carly was finally allowed into Shane's room, she took a step backward in shock. His skin looked deathly pale, and he lay still with tubes and wires running from his body to monitors recording the vital signs of a very battered body. She held his hand and whispered his name. Her heart skipped a beat when, for a split second, she thought she felt his fingers tighten around hers. "I can't stay, Shane. You need rest.

But I'll be in the next room until you wake up." She kissed his swollen lips and ran her hand across his cheek. "Don't keep me waiting long." She couldn't be sure, but she thought he smiled.

****

Shane wanted to open his eyes. He could hear noises surrounding him but felt as though he were floating. Slowly, he began to remember. His heartbeat raced. *Carly*. She had been with him. Where was she now? By sheer force of will, he opened his eyes.

Above him, a dark form outlined by a bright light was asking questions. "Do you know your name?"

Of course, he knew his name, but for some reason, he couldn't speak.

"Can you move your legs?"

He tried and thought his toes wiggled but could not be sure.

"Where is the pain?"

Everywhere. Why did he hurt so much? What happened?

The dark shadow hovering above called his name. "Shane. Shane. Open your eyes."

He tried to answer, but no words formed. He barely had time to wonder why he couldn't speak before his head lolled to the left, and he succumbed to sleep.

****

The medication should have kept Shane sedated for at least a week so he could rest and heal. But by the third day, he fought the drugs to stay awake, along with the doctors and nurses who administered them.

That is when Carly smiled again. Shane would be all right.

"I can barely keep my eyes open," he said in a

hoarse voice.

She kissed his cheek. "You need to rest."

"No," he protested, "I need to think. Tell the nurse no more of whatever she is sticking in the IV."

"You gave us quite the scare for a while," Carly whispered. "But the doctor's say you'll be all right. You'll have to take it easy for a while, though."

Shane pried open his eyelids. "Are you hurt?" Relief flooded him when she shook her head. "Where's Bobby? Is he okay?" He saw her gaze drop. "Where's Bobby?" he repeated, the concern he saw on her face helping him stay awake. When she didn't immediately answer, he knew something was terribly wrong. "Is he all right?"

"I'm sorry, Shane. Bobby's dead."

Shane's sharp intake of breath filled the room. He felt as though someone had plunged a knife into his heart. Rejecting what he heard, he shook his head. "That can't be true. Why would you lie to me, Carly?"

Carly leaned over the bedrail. She took his hand in hers. "I'm not lying, Shane. Bobby's gone. He sacrificed himself for us. That's the only reason we are alive."

Shane's gaze searched her face, and when it settled on her eyes, he knew the truth. He closed his eyes and cried.

Chapter Twenty-One

"What are you doing off the couch?" Carly shouted when she came in from the garden at the estate carrying a basket of flowers.

Shane turned. He held a silver-framed picture of Bobby and himself, taken at an after-party held at the Space Needle in Seattle, Washington following the Rangers' last tour. "We did a show at the harbor before coming here."

"Shane, don't." Carly set the basket near the doorway. "He did love you." She put her arms around him, hoping her comfort would soothe the ache in his heart.

"I know." Shane sighed and set the picture on the piano. Running his hand over the highly polished ebony finish, he smiled. "Waiting for this piano to be delivered was the last thing Bobby did before he died."

"No, Shane. You're wrong." She connected with his gaze. "The last thing he did was save us both."

"I never knew Bobby had so much anger bottled inside."

"How could you?"

Shane shook his head. "Maybe I ignored the signs. I wanted to be the consummate big brother. I guess I never let him grow up." He smoothed a finger along her cheek. "Is Bobby's death my fault? Could I have done something differently?"

Carly ran a loving hand over his cheek. "You were not responsible for the choices Bobby made. He did what he thought he had to do, and in the end, he proved he was a good man."

"You're a very forgiving woman, Carly, considering all he did to you."

"And to you. Bobby paid his debt with the ultimate interest. I think we should remember the good in Bobby and forget the bad."

Shane nodded and covered her hand with his. "I got a call from Danni's mother. She is petitioning the court for full custody of Nickolas, and I agree. Nicky should be with her. She lost her daughter; she can't lose her grandson, too."

"I'm sure she'll let you see him." She reached up and cupped his face. "You're his uncle and the only one who can tell him about his father."

Shane smiled. "And I've instructed my attorney to put all of Bobby's assets into a trust fund for Nicky. He will never have to worry about his future." He pulled Carly into the cradle of his arms. "Now that one future is secure, what about ours? Any suggestions for a guy with half a spleen, a few broken ribs, and a belly looking more like a road map than a six-pack?" He chuckled. "I won't be going shirtless much."

She was happy to hear him laugh. "I would say he definitely needs someone to keep an eye on him."

"And who might that someone be?"

"You're looking at her, and you will be for a long time to come!"

****

Judge Edmond McKennan married Carly and Shane in the English gardens of the Clinton Estate.

Noel Mitchell accompanied his daughter down the aisle. Ann Tyler and Troy Stone stood as witnesses to the outdoor ceremony carefully planned and meticulously hidden from public scrutiny.

That evening, after the small group of guests left, Carly and Shane looked out over the terrace off the master bedroom suite and watched the sun set in a spectacular cascade of color.

"Mrs. Fox, I believe we are home at last."

"We are," she agreed.

Shane's hands slipped from her back to her side and then lower to caress the soft arch of her thigh. "I always thought a sunset was the most beautiful thing in the world. But then I looked in your eyes when we exchanged vows today, and the love I saw eclipsed anything in heaven or on earth."

"Is this real?"

"Very real." Shane held up her left hand, lightly fingering the golden band he placed on her finger.

Carly sighed and rested her head on his chest. "I'm glad."

"So am I. I think we need to take care of a small detail too long ignored."

Her brow wrinkled. "What?"

"Our first daughter."

She offered no resistance when Shane scooped her into his arms and carried her to the bed. As he spread kisses across her face and down her throat, a brief thought crossed his mind before he became lost in the sound of her pleasure. Their story would inspire a great hit song.

A word about the author...

Kathye Quick, an award winning, internationally selling author based in New Jersey, began writing in high school for her school newspaper. After taking a short break to have a family, during which time she became a voracious romance reader, she decided to write in the genre she loved.

Now, many books later, some of the characters she imagined are still trapped in her imagination, waiting for their stories to be told.

In additional to her contemporary series, she writes urban fantasy (as P.K. Eden, with writing partner, Patt Mahailoff), romantic comedy, medieval romance, and has contracted nonfiction.

For a list of her books, please visit her website at www.kathrynquick.com or follow her on Facebook.

~~

Other Titles by this author
and available at The Wild Rose Press, Inc.
BACHELOR.COM
(Book 1 in the *Bachelors Three* series)

Thank you for purchasing
this publication of The Wild Rose Press, Inc.

If you enjoyed the story, we would appreciate your
letting others know by leaving a review.

For other wonderful stories,
please visit our on-line bookstore at
www.thewildrosepress.com.

For questions or more information
contact us at
info@thewildrosepress.com.

The Wild Rose Press, Inc.
www.thewildrosepress.com

Stay current with The Wild Rose Press, Inc.

Like us on Facebook

https://www.facebook.com/TheWildRosePress

And Follow us on Twitter
https://twitter.com/WildRosePress

www.ingramcontent.com/pod-product-compliance
Lightning Source LLC
Chambersburg PA
CBHW060527260626
47161CB00003B/797